FORGET me not

AUTHORS NOTE

Forget Me Not may not be suitable for some readers due to: loss of a spouse (off page), loss of a child (off page), loss of a sibling. This is a simplified list to avoid to many spoilers. For a full list of content warnings, please check here:

authoralexandriasharpe.square.site/content-warnings

FORGET
me not

ALEXANDRIA SHARPE

Book Cover by Kier Smelcer, @foxlore_art on IG

Duplex (inner cover) art by @mefoghall on IG

Chapter headers & page breaks by Morgan Speer at Book Nook Blooms, @booknookblooms on IG

Proofreader: Sarah Emmer, @emmer_edits on IG

ISBNs: 979-8-9986566-0-6 (paperback), 979-8-9986566-1-3 (hardcover)

PRONUNCIATION GUIDE

Syve .... sigh-ve, rhymes with five
Bastien .... BASH-tin, like Sebatian -se
Aimi .... literally just Amy
Cyrus .... SIGH-rus
Delanira .... dell-ah-NEAR-ah
Soriah .... so-RYE-ah
Erhard .... AIR-hard
Desiderio .... DEH-sea-dare-EE-oh
Oisín .... oh-SHEEN

B, thank you for pushing me to, "DO THE THING!" This book would not have been finished without you. I love you!

Time does not heal all wounds, but it does make them easier to bear.

SYVE

FLUFFY, WHITE FLAKES FELL atop the nearby headstones, casting an ethereal glow around her as she peered up into the stony face of an angel. Peace. It was a symbol meant to bring peace to visitors, but peace was the last thing Syve felt.

Darkness engulfed the statue, much like a dust cloth being pulled over a piece of furniture in an empty home. The waning moon had disappeared behind the midnight clouds, and she closed her eyes for a moment before turning to take the thirteen steps from the marble's skirted base to the cold, packed earth where her heart now lay six feet below.

Twelve. Her hot breath sent spirals of steam to dance before her in the crisp December air.

Eight. Soft snow crunched beneath her delicate hooves, enunciating each step.

Two.

One.

As the moon reemerged into the night sky, a pillar of light appeared, faintly illuminating the stone before her. With her heart aching, she curled her body down onto the frozen ground to lean against the granite. Blearily, her eyes traced the lettering carved deep into the stone. Then, tipping her head back, she unleashed a mournful cry to the heavens.

At twenty-nine years old, Syve was no stranger to nightmares. She had suffered from night terrors as a small girl, but they paled in comparison to the images that recently began to plague her every night.

It had been a little over a week, the same dream playing out in her mind—it would start with her turning down the street to find her loft shrouded in blue and red lights and would end with her plodding across the cemetery to lay across her young son's grave. A constant reminder of her sweet little boy and the family she lost far too soon. Every morning, she woke with her heart in pieces, all too aware of the silence that now accompanied her empty home.

Whoever said time heals all wounds, was a liar.

A somber cello prelude pulled Syve from her reverie, her arm stretched across her husband's empty side of the bed. Perhaps one day she would stop reaching for him when she woke, bereft with grief over the loss of their son, just to be reminded he too had been lost on that same, God-forsaken night.

Forcing her feet to the floor, she silenced the alarm and looked over to the crib pushed against the opposite wall—little blankets and tiny clothes still draped over its edge.

Maybe, one day, she would be strong enough to pack them away.

Tearing her eyes from the soft linens, she padded across the hall to the bathroom, squinting as the fluorescent lights flickered to life. Syve stared at the woman in the large mirror above the vanity. Once, bright hazel eyes peeked through thick lashes and high cheekbones. Now, all that remained were dull, unseeing eyes set in sunken sockets, rimmed with dark skin from months of sleepless nights. Her auburn hair was a tangled mess on top of her head, with more than half having fallen loose from the messy bun she had gone to sleep with, leaving staticky strands sticking out this way and that. Grimacing, she fought to free the scrunchie, tossing it toward the sink and not bothering to correct it when it landed short on the tile and slid beneath the counter.

Instead, she reached into the shower to turn the water on as hot as she knew she could without risk of blistering her skin. One last glance at the clock above the door assured her she had just enough time to attempt to burn off her sorrow before she would need to go downstairs and pretend to work—not that a heat rash ever made the urge to crawl out of her miserable, surviving skin any less.

Thirty minutes later, chased out by the water going cold, Syve found herself standing in the middle of her closet, one side full of men's flannel, the other housing her chaotic mix of thrifted and homemade clothes. Her eyes lingered on the former—another task for a stronger day.

With a sigh, she retreated back, leaving the door to her tomb of memories open. She reached into the basket at the foot of the bed and pulled out a wrinkled forest green long-sleeve shirt and a pair of jeans. Even though she owned enough clothes to go a month or more without ever having to wash a load of laundry, she had resorted to living out of a basket and wearing the same few outfits every week.

The tile under her was cold as she ambled across the small house into the dark kitchen, guided by the chirping of the old coffee pot and the heady aroma emanating from it—it would likely require at least the entire carafe for her to get through the day. The cabinet door squeaked open as she dug out her favorite mug, one which required two hands to hold and read—'Sewing all day, but first coffee'—written in big, bold script twisted around it. She yawned and poured a full cup, forgoing cream because that took more effort than she had to give, then left the kitchen.

That morning, she truly did have an order to fill—Dorothea needed her cooking apron repaired again. The sweet old lady had just turned eighty-three, but that did not stop her from spending every waking minute in her kitchen. At least once a month, she brought the apron in with a broken strap or a hole in one of the pockets. Syve asked her once, years ago, if she would rather have a replacement. Dorothea had refused, saying it was a gift from her husband for their 50th anniversary. At the time Syve had not understood why that had made a simple smock so special, but now...

Stepping around Erhard's boots, which lay dust-covered in the middle of the floor where he had last left them, Syve slipped into her own, not bothering with the laces. She made her way down the narrow stairs from her loft to the large, open room below that made up her storefront. According to her phone, she still had fifteen minutes before she needed to turn on any lights and unlock the door, so she dragged her feet over to the front counter, woke her tablet, and checked for any new work requests.

Being a seamstress was not what she had dreamt of doing when she was a child, but after years of fixing her own things and those of literally everyone around her, it just made sense to make a career of it. First it was just hemming and patching holes, but eventually she ended up doing more difficult repairs and even creating a few things of her own. Next thing she knew, she was not only enjoying it, but dreaming about what she could make next.

Two years into her bachelor's degree, she met a handsome German exchange student at a house party. They locked eyes from opposing sides of a beer pong table and never looked away. The energy between the two of them was palpable. One date became two, then three, which then became a ring while they both wore graduation gowns.

After permanently relocating to the states for her, Erhard put his double major to work. He secured a job in Montana working as a cartographer, mapping the National Parks, and started his own photography business on the side. When the newlyweds found a loft tucked above a little storefront in the quiet town of Timberfall, Erhard convinced Syve to use her business degree to open her own seamstress shop. Within three years, Sew It Seams was more than just keeping itself afloat; Gehring Photography was listed and known as the ninth-best photography business in the state; and 'E.G.' was listed in the fine print on the back of every atlas you could pick up at the travel center.

Now, at seven years old, Sew It Seams was barely being held aloft by a life insurance payout—and Gehring Photography? All that remained of it was a few news clippings, a dusty crate of neglected cameras in the closet, and the framed prints surrounding her now.

Out of habit, Syve ran her fingers over the inked ring on her left hand while she surveyed her shop. Each wall of her little shop was painted a different color: mint green, periwin-kle, robin's egg blue, and a soft salmon. Adorning all four walls were nine of Erhard's favorite photos—blown up and framed, hung all around with price tags dangling from the bottom in hopes that someone who wandered in would be interested in buying—not that she could bring herself to let them go now, regardless.

A sharp knock tore Syve from her thoughts, pulling her attention to a man at the front door.

"Morning, Doll!" the man called, his voice muffled through the glass. "Mind getting the door?" He punctuated his question by holding up a drink carrier with one hand and a paper bag in the other.

"Gunther," Syve grumbled to herself, dragging her hand down her face. Gunther was her late husband's cousin, and after Erhard had passed, it was like he had taken it upon himself to step in and keep an eye on her—family duty, or whatever. At least, that's what he called it when he offered her half of his bed—an offer she swiftly rejected every month when he asked.

Shoving the glass with her shoulder to engage the old latch, Syve unlocked the door and swung it open. She made a mental note to add the wonky door to the steadily growing list of things that needed to be fixed—once she found some-one handy who came with their own tools.

"Shit, it's cold in here! You got that heater off again?!" Gunther groaned, faking a shiver as he ducked his way through the door. Erhard, at six foot five, had been the only person in town who could look Gunther straight in the eye. After half-heartedly stomping the snow off his boots, he made his way over to the counter to set down his loot. "I know you probably made coffee upstairs," he added, gesturing to the back of the shop before pulling a cup from the carrier. "But I know you can't say no to a cup from Aim's."

Syve forced a smile as she took the cup from him, and watched as he ruffled the snow from his short blonde hair, hair the same cut and color as his cousin's used to be. She did not bother to answer any of his questions, knowing they were all rhetorical. She also did not bother to correct him for the thousandth time that Aimi hated that nickname, as he clearly never listened anyway. Even though he was dancing on a fine line of being annoying with his constant presence, she could not argue that he was right about the heavenly bean-water.

"Listen, Hardy would have my *hide* if he knew I was letting you freeze yours off in here," Gunther scolded for the thousandth time as he fumbled with the thermostat. "I don't know how many times I gotta tell you that sixty-eight degrees is too damn cold for winter. Jesus, Syve, it's December!" Syve rolled her eyes behind his back as he cranked the heat up to his usual seventy-five. She would just wait ten minutes after he left, to make sure he wasn't coming back, and then shut it off again. Fighting with him was not a hill she had the energy to die on.

"Gunther, you know I appreciate the coffee and—" she tipped her cup pointedly at the bag on the counter. "Donuts?" She paused long enough for him to wink a green eye back in response. "You really don't have to keep stopping in to check on me."

"It's my job to check on you, and I'll continue to do so until one of us gets to meet that damn husband of yours again," he growled, turning toward the door. "Now, heat stays up. And Syve," he said over his shoulder, "you look like shit. Get some more sleep, yeah?" The door slammed shut behind him as he trudged off into the snow.

"Fucker," Syve muttered into her cup before taking a long pull of her latte, moaning as she swallowed. No one on this planet could make a cup of coffee like Aimi, and Syve also knew that the only reason her drink was exactly how she liked it was because of her best friend. Setting the drink on the counter, she pulled out her phone and opened the messages.

Syve:

This tastes EXTRA caffeinated.

Aimi:

You bet your ass

You're welcome

Syve:

How many shots are in this?

Aimi:

Yes

Like I said, you're welcome

Tell me you were going to handle Gunther's grumpy ass with anything less than a straight fucking espresso, and I'll call you a liar.

75 degrees?

Syve:

75 degrees.

Aimi:

EW. Tell me all about it tonight?

You're not backing out of girl's night

I already told Cam to ignore any messages from you

So don't even think of trying to cancel

Again

Syve:

OMG I canceled ONE TIME and it was for WORK!

Aimi:

Excuses

Syve:

I'm not canceling.

Aimi:

You're right, because we're showing up regardless

See you at 6 <3

Syve huffed in amusement, setting her phone down to open the bag on the counter, noting once again, only raspberry jelly donuts inside. There were only so many times she could remind the man that she was, in fact, allergic to raspberries. She shook her head, shoving the bag to the side. At least she could give them to Cam to take home to her kids so they would not go to waste.

BASTIEN

EVERYONE IS FAMILIAR WITH the theory that twins have a special connection, one which transcends human understanding—twin telepathy, they call it. Bastien and Desiderio were a prime example of said connection, and the entire Yerovi family would be willing to agree.

There were multiple different occasions over the years in which the two men acted as one. Such as when they turned twelve and gifted each other the same video game, or when they were seventeen and had gotten in trouble at school—even though they were separated immediately for questioning, they had both told the exact same lie as a cover story.

This particular day had been no different. Bas had woken up just *knowing* Dez was coming home. He had hit the floor running and ripped open the door just in time to see his brother turning his gaudy Jeep into the drive.

"Dez!" Bas called out, jogging across the concrete barefoot and in nothing but shorts.

"Hey, Brother," Dez returned, stepping down out of his seat and reaching out to pull Bas in for a hug.

"Not that I'm complaining or anything, but uh... What the hell are you doing here?"

"I had some PTO to burn and instead of going to Cancun or some shit like a normal person, I decided to drive my happy ass all the way back here to this tiny little shit-hole town to see your ugly face." He barked a laugh, smiling as he took a playful hit to the shoulder. "Nice scruff, by the way," Dez teased, scratching Bastien's lightly stubbled chin.

"Alright, smart ass," Bas huffed, knocking his brother's hand aside. "Let's go wake Del and when she leaves for school—"

"We run?"

"We run."

An hour later, after their mother screamed, cried and threw her slipper at Dez, and they had seen their little sister off to school, the twins were jumping down the back steps, tearing off their shirts—leaving them wherever they landed in the yard.

They both leapt as they hit the tree line, shifting with ease from years of practice, before they hit the ground and shook out their fur. Bas stretched, sniffing the air and baring his teeth in a wolfish smile as the wind blew through his silver fur. A huff drew his attention down to his brother. Dez was prancing from paw to paw, his obsidian fur like a black hole, not glistening or reflecting any light at all. His copper eyes twinkled with mischief as he spun and bolted into the woods. It took only a split second before Bas was tearing through the brush after him.

Timberfall was nestled between Custer Gallatin National Forest and Yellowstone, just north of the Wyoming border. Bastien had been ecstatic when they found this little house tucked up against the trees, it was perfect for a family of shifters—protected lands with plenty of wildlife to provide cover, in case they were seen. Spotting a wolf outside a National Park was a lot easier to explain than say, Central Park. There were not many places left for them to live that they could hide in plain sight.

Dez had gotten lucky when he was accepted into Wesleyan University. While the red wolf population in North Carolina was devastatingly low, and his black wolf did not perfectly blend in, it was still easier to explain when a trail camera, or rather lucky photographer, managed to capture a photo.

Fifteen minutes later, the two spilled out of the trees, slowing to a stop on the southern edge of a small, oblong mountain lake. The trip had taken them three times as long as it would have if they'd run a straight line. Naturally, the brothers had taken turns tackling each other and wrestling playfully along the way. Aside from the occasional ripples caused by the wind or fish feeding, the water was calm, reflecting the clouds above perfectly—a window to a mirrored world. Small enough that Bas could see the entire surrounding shore, the lake could not have been more than two football fields across and was completely surrounded by tall, thin lodgepole pine trees.

An acrid smell blew in on the breeze, reminiscent of the old, cheap cigars their father used to smoke. Bas flinched, the hairs on the back of his neck rising and a sense of foreboding that he could not quite explain overtook him as he began to frantically scan the woods. He could see Dez out of the corner of his eye; he had moved further from the trees, obviously contemplating getting in the water. During his third pass of the trees around them, he noticed it—the quick glint of the sun off of...metal? Glass? Squinting, he searched for the source. His blood ran cold as his eyes landed on the shape of a man moving ever so slightly just inside the tree line.

A scope. The glint had come from the scope of a rifle the man had shouldered. Bas turned his head, following the line of the barrel, until his eyes met his brother's.

Time froze.

Dez cocked his head to the side, completely oblivious to the impending threat, and then thunder cracked through the clearing.

But it was not thunder.

Dez howled in pain as his body dropped, his rear leg bloody and twisting at an unnatural angle. Bas dove toward his twin, whining as he slipped his nose under Dez' shoulder in an attempt to push him up. A second shot rang out, dirt flying up only a foot away from where the two wolves were, the bullet having gone just over their backs. Dez snapped at Bastien's legs, growling while tossing his head toward the trees. The message was clear.

Go.

Run.

Bastien bared his teeth in return, ignoring the order and trying again to shove his shoulder under Dez' neck for support. They only needed to make it ten yards to the trees to have cover—if he could buy his brother time to shift, he could carry him home. Shifting injured was nearly impossible and incredibly risky, but their options were limited and getting more so by the second, they had to try.

Dez bit into Bastien's neck, using the hold to toss him aside before snarling, blood dripping from his teeth.

A third shot.

Dez' jaw slackened, his body slumped forward and one long exhale left his chest.

Bastien jolted upright with a yell, tears streaming down his face, chest heaving with ragged breaths as he reached a hand up to the rough scar across his collarbone. A permanent reminder of the nightmare he lived and the only physical connection that remained between him and his twin.

The wind tore at his body, and in that moment, he was more thankful than usual for the thick fur keeping him warm. He could hardly see more than twenty yards ahead, forced instead to rely on his nose and memory as a guide through the trees. Running in a snowstorm was something Bastien normally avoided—if only because stripping to shift in the blistering wind threatened to freeze his balls off.

It had been a while since he'd woken in a cold sweat, tormented by memories. The only thing that seemed to numb the pain was running until his legs gave out, or reading. So, here he was, barreling through the frigid woods toward his secret hideaway.

The snowfall began to lighten, revealing the silhouettes of tombstones and marking his destination. Tucked in the back corner of the graveyard was a small mausoleum—that was where he was headed. For as long as Bastien had been skulking around, there had been no signs that anyone still visited its occupants. So, after the third time he found himself standing in the empty tomb on his quest for silence, he came up with a plan. He started by stopping in during the day to stash clothes—ensuring his next midnight visit would not consist of him hanging around stark naked—and a book.

After a few months, he had pants, snacks, a few books and matches for the oil lamps that were hung from the ceiling—all tucked into a plastic tote that he kept under the stone bench. Figuring out those lamps had a finite amount of oil had been an adventure all on its own. The lamps had burnt out once when he had only a few pages left, forcing him to leave the main character face-to-face with a dragon. The next morning, before going to work, he added to his little hoard: a battery operated lantern and a small reading light.

A mournful cry shattered the silence, sending every hair along Bastien's spine standing on end. Still barely out of the trees, he crouched into a low, defensive stance and crept along the shadows, searching for the source of the heart-breaking wail. A large marble angel stood sentinel amid the dead, her sightless eyes staring straight through to the core as he crept closer, using her flowing, stone robes to conceal his canine body. He peered past the harp held down at the statue's side, startling when his eyes locked on a figure not even five yards away. Blinking rapidly, unsure if what he saw was real or some sleep-deprived hallucination, he continued to gaze at the scene before him.

Her song of sorrow was the only reason Bastien had not completely overlooked her. With a coat as gray as the old concrete sidewalk running through town and her body pressed tightly to the headstone, the doe was practically invisible. He remained, a voyeur incapable of stepping away, as the minutes wore on. The doe continued to lean against the granite until her wailing eventually wound down to soft whimpers.

Then, without warning, she simply stood and gently stepped his way. Bastien froze, panicking, trying to determine where he could possibly move to remain unseen. Later he would need to unpack this interaction, why he felt so compelled to stay with her. Why the thought of her seeing him—of her being frightened by his presence—made his chest ache. With mere seconds to spare, he managed to snap out of his petrified stupor and slink backward, effectively keeping the divine shield between himself and the mysterious deer.

She strode past him as if in a trance; not taking her eyes off the front gate until she was on the outside, and even then only turning her gaze to the buildings across the street. Bastien continued to watch as she mindlessly bound across the road toward the alley. He turned his head to check that he was now alone and when he looked back, she was gone.

With careful steps around the eternal beds of strangers, Bastien approached the doe's stone.

Noah
June 3rd 2016 - December 5th 2017
Sleep sweet, until again we meet.

SYVE

Staccato thumping from her sewing machine echoed off the walls as Syve finished off Dorothea's apron, neatly trimming the edges before folding it and setting it aside. Normally she'd have her customers pick up their orders when they were complete, but Syve had a soft spot for the old widow and planned to take it to her in the morning. Of course, the chance to indulge in some variety of freshly baked goods may have played a part in that decision.

"Syve! SYVE!" Aimi was running down the sidewalk, barely managing to stay upright while sliding through the snow as she reached the front door. "SYVEEE!" she hollered again, the bell jingling violently as she burst inside. Clad in her red, knee-length, puffer parka and black knee-high snow boots, she looked like she belonged in Antarctica.

"We literally talked on the phone twenty minutes ago, what the hell?" Syve shook her head at her friend and watched as she began the de-mummification process of removing her winter gear.

"I know! I know, but—" She paused to unwrap her scarf, unceremoniously throwing it in the corner with her already discarded coat and gloves. "When I was locking up—" another pause, as she hopped on one foot to pry off her boots, "I looked at the bulletin, the one by the door! You know—" snow pants went next, "the one you told me would be stupid to have because it would just gather bullshit?"

Syve rolled her eyes and nodded for her to continue. "Yes, yes, bulletin. Is there a point to this—"

Aimi cut her off. "Obviously, there's a fucking point, woman!" With a flourish, Aimi ripped a crumpled piece of paper out of her oversized shoulder bag and slapped it onto the counter. "Look!"

Syve looked down at the paper, read the header and then snatched it up to keep reading. It was an ad for a state grant, specifically for women owned small businesses with less than ten employees.

"Is this legit?" Syve asked as she flipped the paper over and back, looking for a big "SIKE" to be written across the page. After the accident, Syve had gone close to six months without even so much as unlocking her front door once. The state of Montana had cut a check—one that took a month to cash after Aimi had dragged her to the bank drive-thru. Thanks to that money, the bills were being paid—usually with egregious late fees attached and only when the cloud of grief would dissipate long enough to tease her with a breath of clarity, but it wouldn't last forever. She was starting to dance the line of financial ruin.

Eight women across the entire state would be chosen to receive a sum of money to invest into their business—a sum hefty enough to, say, dig a small business out of debt and completely fund its rebirth and expansion with a few zeros to spare. All she would have to do was present a business plan—outlining how she would use the grant money to make more money. Syve would need to prove she was worth the investment, and show the board what she could do if they backed her. Securing the grant would change *everything*, both for Sew It Seams and for *her*.

"I know you've put the brand on hold." One last pause as she pulled her hat off her head, leaving her long, sleek, split-dyed hair in a static, black and blonde mess. "And I don't blame you for doing it. But if you got this—if you had this money—you could really finish what you started and get your clothes out there."

It was true. The grant would be more than enough to cover the production costs and personal expenses until she could start earning from the clothing line itself. Not to mention, the publicity would be great for marketing—which would in turn be great for sales.

One year ago, three weeks before Christmas, Syve had been struck by the idea to produce her own clothing line. She was annoyed that the only clothes you could find any more were trendy, impractical pieces—less comfortable than they were useful. After a three-hour brain-storming session at her kitchen table with her husband and her best friend, Syve had shaped her idea into a realistic dream. An entire line of Men's, Women's and Children's clothing that was casual, yet practical. Pants with pockets that could actually hold things, shirts long enough to cover your ass when you bent over, reinforced knees for the kids, and *everything* would be machine washable. That was just the tip of the iceberg. She had an entire notebook full of notes and sketches.

A few days later, Syve and Aimi braved the weather and made the eighty-mile drive north to Bozeman to raid the fabric store. But when they returned, Syve's entire world had ended.

She had left her home to the tune of laughter and came back to the sound of sirens. Every penny she owned had gone toward repairing the loft and funeral expenses. Any cent left after that didn't matter anymore.

The day after the funeral, she had tossed her notebook into the closet under the stairs and put herself on autopi- lot. Her dreams went untouched as her life changed forever—frozen in time. It never even crossed her mind to finish the project.

"Do you still have the plans?" Aimi probed.

"They're...in the closet..." Syve sat down on the loveseat by the window. "Do you think I should? I mean, the main reason I was doing this was for *them*..." She placed her head in her hands and sighed.

"I think they would want you to try." Aimi smiled, then clapped loudly. "Right, you need to drink on this! Now let's lock this shit up so we can go get drunk like we're still twenty-one. Cam will be here any minute—"

Syve cut her off. "Cameron is likely already upstairs, since she uses the loft entrance like a normal visitor." She gave her best friend a pointed look as she reached for the broom.

"Ha! Girl. You know I'm *anything* but normal." Aimi laughed, skipping away when Syve swung the broom at her.

Once the floor had been swept, counters wiped, trash taken out, and the door firmly locked, they migrated to the loft. As Syve had guessed, Cameron was already there, with various bowls overflowing with snacks and three large cups filled to the brim with what she could safely assume to be red wine.

Weekly girl's days had been mandatory for the entire eight years Syve and Aimi had been friends. Cameron had only been in the fray for two and a half years—ever since she met Syve through their shared midwife. After Noah was born, Syve quickly determined that when it came to breast milk, she was an overproducer. One chat with the midwife about donating led to a meeting with Cameron, an underproducing mother whose daughter, Kayla, was born a week after Noah. Syve successfully fed both babies for an entire year, and the two mothers had been friends ever since.

"K-drama, Dukes, or Doctors?" Cam asked, tossing the remote to Aimi. Though none of them could likely explain when or why it happened, this one question had always served as the bottle breaking—sending the ship to sea. The ship being a twenty-minute debate over which series was the best choice to turn on—regardless of the fact they never actually *watched* the TV—and always ended with Aimi turning on Twilight. By the time Aimi started arguing about how a purple bedspread *was*, in fact, a safe choice, Cam would have a basket of nail polish out and be well into painting all of their nails. Before the night was over, Aimi would have Syve's laundry in the dryer, Cam would have the loft cleaned up and Syve herself would be asleep on the couch.

"You should totally see if there's a way to lock the thermostat so it can't go any higher than sixty-nine degrees!" Cam laughed, throwing herself back into the couch cushions.

"Gunther would blow a gasket if he couldn't set the temp to match his throne down in Hell," Aimi added, making mock explosions with her hands. "Also, sixty-nine, nice." The two women shared a high-five, giggling like teenagers.

"You are both forgetting he's a total dick and would break it just trying to bully it into working." Syve sighed and threw a handful of popcorn into her mouth.

"Babe, I know he's Erhard's cousin, but you *don't* have to put up with his bullshit," Aimi chided.

"I know, but he's grieving too. Just...in his own way—isn't this what family does? Tolerate each other's bullshit?" Or was it just what she thought she deserved? Who was she to complain about being annoyed? At least she was alive...

Aimi rolled her eyes, waving dismissively at Syve with a fist full of Cheetos.

"Okay, okay," Cam chided, "enough about Gunther and his...*antics*—grieving or not." She aimed the last bit at Syve, who had opened her mouth again to correct her. "Have you still been having that weird recurring dream?"

Syve winced and then slid off the couch onto the floor with a dramatic exhale. "Yeah, every single night still. Why?"

"Because I love you, but you look like hell. I can tell you're not sleeping—more than you already weren't. I'm worried about you, is all." Cam stretched a long leg out and nudged Syve with her foot.

"I'm fine, thank you for worrying, but please don't. No, I'm not sleeping great, but I'm sure it's just stress." Stress—as if you could put a label on the feeling that came with the first anniversary of your family's death. "Maybe I need to lay off the caffeine..."

Aimi gasped and began choking on her wine.

"Decaf, Aimi! I could still drink coffee! Just, decaf!"

The guttural whine that followed let Syve know that actually only made the matter worse.

BASTIEN

"Snow is just a bunch of bullshit," Bastien grumbled as he stomped back into the house, propping the window scraper against the wall before kicking his boots off.

"Oh, quit bitchin' and get in here for breakfast," his mother's voice called from the kitchen. "And thank you for getting the car warmed up, *Mijo*."

"If you would just let me take Del to school in the mornings, Mama, I wouldn't even need to warm the car up for you." His tone gave away how exasperated he was, not that it mattered. This was a conversation they had argued over a dozen times already—and he had never won. Soriah just waved him off with a knobby hand while piling eggs, hash browns, and bacon onto his plate. She wore her winter usual: an old, worn black apron over a chunky sweater, black slacks, and a pair of house slippers. Her once-black hair—long since gone white—was neatly braided and hung well past the hem of her sweater. Soriah had only just celebrated her sixty-fifth birthday, but the years had been unkind, their weight showing in the form of many wrinkles and her now-hunched frame.

"You know what I will let you do, is go wake up that lazy sister of yours." She joked with a light pat to his shoulder. "She could sleep through the end of the world, I swear."

"Honestly, Mama, you spoil her. You should make her get up and get to school herself! What's going to happen next year when she goes off to college?" Bas exhaled and hung his head as soon as the words were out of his mouth. It had been two years and four months since his brother had been killed, but it might as well have been two days and four hours, as far as his mother was concerned.

"Forgive me, *Mijo,*" she bit back. "Forgive me for *loving* my child and wanting to give her everything I have while I still can." She dropped his plate in front of him, the sharp clatter of the ceramic against wood causing him to flinch, then she stormed out of the room.

Dez had left the day after high school graduation and regardless of how much he did not want to leave his twin behind, he never wanted to stay in Montana. Bastien entertained the idea of going with him to North Carolina, that was, until their mother found out. Soriah had screamed, cried, screamed some more and then gone almost a month without so much as looking in Dez's direction. Bas stayed in hopes that it would smooth things out between the two.

It had not.

Señor Yerovi, Bastien's father, had passed away when the boys were twenty-six. Dez had still not been home to visit before it happened. When he finally returned for the funeral, Soriah freaked out, accusing the stress of him choosing to stay so far from home as the reason why her husband had been so sick—as if moving away caused the cancer. Soriah turned to Delanira, who was only eleven at the time, and promised to disown her like her brother if she even so much as mentioned going to college anywhere other than Montana State University. So, when the time came, Del said nothing. When college applications started coming in the mail, Soriah would throw them in the trash and Del would secretly dig them out.

"You talked about college again, didn't you?" A soft voice interrupted his thoughts. Bas picked his head up, meeting his sister's soft brown eyes. He was the only one of the three children to inherit their mother's smokey gray eyes.

"Morning, Del." He pushed his plate across the table toward her as he stood. "Eat. She'll be back down in a few minutes."

"Aren't you hungry?" she asked, tucking a strand of her short, dark hair behind her ear.

"Lost my appetite."

Hal's butcher shop looked like a hole in the wall from the outside, making it easy for someone to overlook. The interior, however, extended through to the other side of the block, making the shop deceptively large. An alley ran the length of the building, where several roll-up doors had been added for bringing shipments in. All of their goods came from local ranches—the only exception being the seafood, which was shipped in from the coast.

Crisp, white walls and polished concrete floors made up the store front, except for one wall painted with black chalkboard paint. That particular wall had been covered from ceiling to floor with all the services, cuts, and prices they offered, along with a few cartoon outlines of the corresponding animals. Hal loved to brag that his granddaughter had spent an entire weekend on a ladder with a box of chalk to make it happen.

A large L-shaped, refrigerated display case spanned the entirety of the back and side wall, with a five-foot stretch of counter for the register nestled in between, directly across from the front door.

Bastien had been desperate when they first moved to Timberfall. After his dad died, they couldn't afford to stay in Billings and were forced south by cheaper housing. Soriah was still getting social security checks, but if Bastien wanted to ensure that his mother could stay at home and out of the workforce, he needed a job. The 'Help Needed Immediately' sign hanging in the window of the local butcher's made it clear that whoever *Hal* was, he shared the same sense of urgency.

Thirty minutes after ringing the cowbell above the door, Bas was wearing an apron and carrying crates of packaged meat from one cooler to another. At seventy-three years old, Hal had no business shuffling hundred-pound crates around, and Bas quickly realized he'd been hired on the spot because of his stature. He wasn't the type to spend hours at the gym, but he did have a quick body-weight routine he kept up at home. Between that and the time he spent in wolf form, running through the woods, he managed to stay in slightly-better-than-good shape.

This morning was cold, as usual; winter was a rough season to work surrounded by freezers. They had to be careful of how high they set the heat, lest they force the ice chests to work overtime to keep the meat chilled. The worst case would be the meat warming and spoiling—Hal *hated* to waste anything. Bas pulled the hood of his sweater over his head, a few wavy, black strands sticking out, as he continued topping off the stock in the display cases. He had been thoroughly disappointed when he was younger to discover that while his wolf form kept him warm in winter, his human form had clearly inherited his climate tolerance from his father's side of the family. Ecuador was a far cry warmer on any given day than Montana ever would be.

His thoughts drifted back to that morning, then to his twin. Thinking about Dez always left him drained—an internal roller coaster of feelings that had become synonymous with his brother's name. He gritted his teeth at the thought of the poacher who had taken Dez away, and at himself for not being able to stop it. His chest threatened to split open over the thought of his mother, who should never have outlived any of her children. The ceaseless urge to reach out and feel for the broken bond—one that had forged long before either boy had taken their first breath—made his skin itch.

Worst of all was the inability to understand why, when he had searched through his brother's things—desperate for anything tangible to feel his brother's presence again—he found a will. It was dated two days prior to the accident and tucked inside an envelope addressed to Bastien himself.

Desiderio had paid off and added Bastien onto the title of his Jeep. He left instructions for how Bastien could help his roommate get out of their lease, and, most surprisingly, he had approved and provided all the information for Bastien to access all three of his bank accounts. Apparently, Desiderio had been investing and saving the majority of his commissions as a real estate agent, and his net worth was rather impressive for a thirty-two-year-old bachelor.

It ate at Bastien's insides to know he might never understand how or why his brother had kept that from him—or if the real reason for his visit had been more than just to see the family.

SYVE

"CHAI FOR KAI!" AIMI called out as Syve stepped into the coffee shop, the smell of espresso immediately permeating every pore of her body. The inside of The Glass Half Full was not what you would expect when you heard Aimi owned it. The contrast between her piercings and her bright wardrobe with the calm, simple atmosphere of her shop was shocking. The front window, which took up the entirety of the south-ern facing storefront, let the sun in through sheer, soft green curtains for the entirety of the day. One wall in the back of the shop was completely covered in shelves, supporting pots of varying sizes with enough plants to make any nursery jealous. The remaining walls were a gentle beige, adorned with a few canvases of Erhard's black-and-white photos.

The wood flooring was Aimi's favorite bragging point. It was made entirely of recycled hardwood she had collected herself, and she paid a handful of local boys in pizza to help her get the flooring down. Afterward, she spent the rest of the weekend sanding and staining, until the dark walnut coloring stood out against the rest of the room. She would puff up like a peacock every time someone asked why she had chosen such a dark floor, then excitedly tell them it was to mask any stains from spilled coffee and tea. It was impossible to argue with that logic.

Syve waved at her friend as she made her way to her favorite seat—a fluffy loveseat tucked in the back corner, beneath a row of spider plants that hung just right to create a little canopy. She always planned her lunch break to line up with the tail end of the afternoon rush. Slipping down into the cushions of the old, sage-green sofa with whatever book she was currently reading while waiting for the crowd to clear had easily become the highlight of her days.

Fifteen minutes later, having finally made it through the long line of java aficionados, Aimi sat a mug on the coffee table next to Syve, then dropped into the seat beside her, kicking her feet up into Syve's lap.

"I'm going to apply for the grant," Syve announced as she absentmindedly retied the laces on Aimi's pink, knee high Converse.

"For real? Babe! That's incredible! I'm so glad!" Aimi squealed, swinging her freshly re-tied feet to the floor to grapple Syve into a hug. "Can I help with anything?"

"That's actually what I was going to ask. I need to find that notebook, and I'm going to need backup if I go digging in that closet." As the only spare closet in the entire residence, it had become a "catch-all" and was terrifyingly full—mostly of ghosts.

"I really don't understand why you even bother asking, when you know the answer is, duh." Aimi rolled her eyes playfully. Syve opened her mouth to respond when her phone started to vibrate across the table.

"Ugh," she groaned, looking at the screen. "Gunther."

"Let me guess—dinner? Again?" Aimi said, raising her brows.

"Mhhm, he's grilling *steaks* this time." Syve raised her brows with a smirk. "Because that's *exactly* what I want."

"Leave it to Gunther to cook steaks for a vegetarian." Aimi sighed. "What excuse are you giving him this time?"

"I'm going to tell him I just started my period and can't leave the house."

"*Can't*?!" Aimi howled, slapping her knee. "Shark week with a twist: when the blood runs, the great white gets kicked out of the water!"

Syve just smiled as she typed out her reply.

"You're sure it's under here?!" Aimi hollered from deep inside the closet. "There's so much shit in here. What the hell!?"

Syve chuffed, still slowly digging through the box of fabric Aimi pulled out earlier. While she wasn't sure if she still wanted to touch the fabric she'd originally purchased, let alone use it, she *hoped* to cut costs by working with things she already had on hand. That included the fabric from Bozeman. She set aside a few yards of a golden yellow plaid and at least a dozen yards in various shades of gray.

"I'm positive I threw it in there, but like...I literally threw it. So, it's probably going to be all the way in the back," Syve called back. She was grateful her friend was willing to dive through boxes for her. Some of them were eighteen years old, left mostly untouched since her parents died when she was ten—their belongings, boxed up and stored away for the day when she was old enough to decide what to do with them, only seeing daylight when they were moved from one closet to the next.

The rest of the boxes belonged to Erhard.

"Oh! Wait! Hold on—I found something—shit," Aimi cursed, and judging by the sound of cardboard slamming into the wall, she had tripped. "All the way in the back, like you said. I found this journal—fuck—on top of this...box?"

Aimi finally stepped back into view, her messy bun knocked loose and hanging limply off the side of her head. She was carrying an old wooden chest with a dusty, leather-bound book sitting on top. With an exaggerated groan, she heaved the box onto the table in front of Syve, sending a cloud of dust into the air.

"Jesus," Syve coughed, reaching across the table to pick up the notebook and blowing dust from the cover. "Why did you bring out *this* thing?"

"Cuz it's locked, and I want to open it," Aimi said with a shrug, as if it were the most obvious thing in the world.

"Locked? I don't remember anything being locked..." Syve trailed off as she flipped open the journal, it was leather-bound and worn from years of use with the silhouette of a deer imprinted on the cover. She'd been using this book for years to scrawl her notes and rushed sketches every time inspiration struck—except, she had not been using *this* book. Syve stared at the first page in confusion, she had not been using this journal because this was not *her* handwriting and these were not *her* words.

"Syve? What's wrong? Is it all there?" Aimi circled the table, carefully stepping around the mess on the floor until she was standing beside her friend, her voice full of concern. "Babe?"

"It's not mine? It's the same journal, but it's not?" Syve flipped through a few more pages until her eyes caught a word that was familiar. "Dearest *Oisín*?" Her voice caught, and her body began to tremble. She turned around, never taking her eyes off the book in her hands, and carefully slid onto the table. Aimi did not hesitate before clambering up beside her.

"*Oisín*? Was that a family name? I thought you had made it up." The severe confusion was written plainly on Aimi's face as she tried to figure out *why* Noah's middle name was written in this twenty-year-old book.

"Dearest *Oisín*," Syve read aloud, her voice shaking. "I've been writing in these journals for as long as I can remember, never knowing who they were for—until now. The rest of my words will all be for you. I guess that is, if you ever want to read them. I'm probably putting the cart ahead of the horse again—your father and I only got the news this morning—"

Aimi gasped and Syve added, "I think...I think this was my mom's? I don't understand. I don't remember ever hearing the name *Oisín* before. I found it by accident when I was Googling baby names and clicked on a wiki page by mistake—you know that part. *Oisín* was the son of Syve in this old legend—I would remember if my mom had called me that, wouldn't I?"

Aimi just sighed, shrugged and snuggled close into her side. "Maybe when you saw it your subconscious remembered it? Maybe she only called you that when you were really little?"

"You don't suppose this chest was Mom's too then, do you?" Syve gestured to the locked box next to her. Now suddenly just as interested in opening it as her friend.

"If I say yes, does that mean you'll let me at it?" She did little to conceal the excitement in her voice.

"Actually, MacGyver, before you get too wild and break your way in—I have this necklace upstairs, it used to be my mom's, it's an old skeleton key and the metal matches."

"The metal...matches?" Aimi deadpanned, giving Syve a you've-absolutely-gone-and-lost-your-mind-now look.

"Oh, shut up! I mean the color and style of the key match the box so I don't think you need to smash your way in like the Kool-aid man." Syve ran up to her room, digging quickly through her jewelry box for the necklace. When she returned, slipping the key into the lock with ease, Aimi groaned.

"Dammit! I really wanted to test my lock picking skills! This feels too easy!"

Ignoring her, Syve gently lifted the lid, wincing as it creaked loudly. Inside were easily two dozen tomes, all leather-bound with the same doe burnt into each cover. Sighing, she pulled out a book at random. A few seconds of flipping through the pages confirmed it was another diary, filled with her mother's words.

"Why was that one left out? What do they say?" Aimi asked the room. "Are you going to read them?" This question was softly directed at Syve.

"I-I don't know." Syve inhaled deeply, placing the journals back inside and closing the lid, "But that's tomorrow Syve's problem. Today Syve still needs to find her own damn notebook." She clapped her hands then turned to face Aimi.

"Back under the stairs I go," Aimi groaned, hopping down from the table and trudging her way back to the closet.

Thirty minutes, ten more boxes, and three distractions later, Syve finally had her sketches in hand.

The gentle whisper of the wind through the trees once again lulled her into a daze as she rested against the headstone, absentmindedly running her nose along the inscription. Syve exhaled deeply, then stood, shaking off the snow that had stuck to her before slowly beginning the trek back to the cemetery gates. The snow was deeper tonight, slowing her steps.

A shift in the wind tickled the hairs along her spine and she paused, tilting her head when a familiar scent wafted past her. Wax smoke, like a freshly snuffed candle. It did not *belong*.

A niggling feeling in the back of her mind urged her to look away from the main gate, and back toward the farthest corner of the graveyard. Her eyes instantly locked onto the mausoleum, its half open door, and the large gray wolf standing unnaturally still in the doorway, bright eyes unblinking.

After what felt like hours—but couldn't have been more than seconds—Syve turned back to the gate.

If this were reality, she might have been terrified. But it was only a dream. And there was nothing an overgrown dog could do to her mind that could possibly hurt it any more than it already was.

BASTIEN

"FUCK!" BAS CURSED, DROPPING his knife in favor of the towel slung over his shoulder and clasping it around his finger, hands tight against his chest. It had been years since he'd last slipped with a knife. "*Dammit*," he hissed. That was at least three pounds of steak that would need to be tossed due to contamination. Hal would be pissed.

That was the fourth time in as many hours Bas had screwed up a simple task because he couldn't stop daydreaming about big, hazel eyes. He had been going to the mausoleum just about every night the last few weeks, reading by candlelight until she would show up, then he would watch her from the mausoleum windows until she left again.

That was until, compelled by a bout of recklessness the night before, he shifted and attempted to slip out of the tomb to get a little closer. Turned out, he must be as sneaky as a train, because he hadn't even made it completely out of the door before her head snapped in his direction. Bastien wasn't sure what he had been expecting, but for her to disregard him and walk away? That was a surprise.

The cowbell above the door rang out, clearing the fog that consumed his mind.

"Sebastian! How ya been, Man?" Cheap cologne permeated the shop as Gunther sauntered in, his wet boots squeaking on the concrete floor despite his pathetic attempt to kick the snow free on the entry rug.

"Bastien. It's just Bastien," he corrected, tossing the bloody towel into the wash basket and reaching for the first aid kit.

"Right, Bas, listen." Bas inhaled deeply, more insulted by the use of his nickname than the mispronunciation. Gunther continued, "What's your protocol on roadkill? Can you guys process it down?"

"In order to process anything, we either need the carcass copy of a legally issued hunting license or we would need to make a copy of your salvage permit—you do have a salvage permit, right?" Bastien probed, one eyebrow raised in doubt.

"Of course I have a permit," Gunther huffed. "And, for the record, I was asking *hypothetically*. For a friend." He stalked over to a display case, slapping a hand on the glass.

Bastien flinched at the greasy handprint that would surely be left on his freshly polished glass.

"Anyway," Gunther said, drawing out the last syllable while he continued to scan the available cuts, "go ahead and wrap up a pair of these New Yorks for me." He tapped the glass above the steaks. "I've got a date."

Bastien fought the urge to roll his eyes until he could see his brain as he slipped on a pair of gloves. The thought that anyone would want to share a meal with this guy was absurd, let alone as a *date*. While wrapping the meat, his thoughts drifted back to the mournful doe and the conversation he'd had with his mother the night before, when he returned home after being seen.

Shivering, Bas eased open the back door. The old hinges ignored his attempt at silence, squealing loudly and causing him to grimace.

"Mijo?" The question came from the kitchen which he now saw was dimly lit, likely by his mother's favorite reading lamp. She was the only person he had ever heard of who preferred to read at the kitchen counter instead of a plush sofa in the living room, always saying something about how the kitchen was the heart of the house.

"Yeah, Mama, it's just me," Bas answered while digging around in the coat closet. Soriah had suggested they keep spare clothes there after he and Desiderio had barreled into the house, buck naked in the middle of her book club's monthly meetup. With a sad smile at the memory, he stepped into a

pair of sweats and threw a towel over his head. He was still roughly drying his dark hair as he walked into the kitchen, where Soriah sat, just as he expected, at the island with her little lamp, glasses perched on the end of her nose and a worn-out paper back laying open in front of her.

"It's late, why are you up?" Bas asked when her eyes, full of concern, met his.

"You'd think by now you'd know that you can't leave this house without me knowing." She raised an eyebrow with a smirk. "Was it the nightmares again?" The question was almost a whisper and most definitely rhetorical.

Bas only ever got out of bed in the middle of the night if he was afraid to go back to sleep, he had been that way since he was a little boy. Bastien shrugged, neither agreeing nor disagreeing, as he pulled out the stool next to his mother and sank onto it with a sigh.

Soriah pursed her lips and rubbed her son's back. "Tea?"

He nodded again, and she rose from her seat, walking around the island to the kettle.

"Want to talk?"

"Actually, yeah." Bastien proceeded to tell her about the doe and how he suspected there may be more to her than meets the eye. "I know there are some of us out there like Papa and Del, herbivore shifters, I just never put much thought into it before, I guess. Have you ever heard of a family of deer?"

"Sí," Soriah replied. *"Your Abuelo used to tell me stories when I was a little girl about all of the different families he had heard of—one was deer."*

"Twenty-seven, thirty-two," Bas said, sliding the carefully packaged steaks across the counter.

"Thanks, man," Gunther replied, impatiently ripping his card from the reader before snatching the meat off the counter. "Same time next week?" he joked, stalking back to the door, not bothering to wait for a response before stepping out into the cold.

"Can't fucking wait," Bas muttered to himself, running his hands through his hair and resting his hand on the back of his neck. He glanced at the clock; it was nearly two and he still had not taken a lunch break—not that he was exactly hungry. Still, Bas made his way to the back office to find Hal.

"Whatcha need, son?" Hal asked when Bas knocked on his office door, not looking up from the journal he was scanning.

The old man was practically buried beneath a mountain of books, his shiny, bald head barely peeking over the top. Even though all the finances, inventory, and sales were logged in the computer and safely saved to the cloud, Hal still insisted on keeping a physical ledger—one he meticulously updated himself. Bas made a mental note to buy the man a printer and show him how to print all the reports. Surely, he wouldn't complain too much about the time saved; Lord knew his arthritis wouldn't.

"Hey boss, I wasn't watching the time. Would you mind grabbing the front for fifteen minutes so I can run down the block to The Glass and snag a bite?"

Hal perked up. "The Glass, huh? Only if you bring me back one of those Elvis Sandwiches!"

Bas chuckled, shaking his head.

"You can shake your head all you want, son. Until you quit being a chicken-shit and actually try one, you aren't allowed to say anything!" Hal scoffed playfully, as he stood and rounded his desk.

Even at his age, the man still stood a touch taller than Bastien and, thanks to his white beard and strong nose, he looked exactly like one of those paintings of The Old Sea Captain.

"You bring me one of Aimi's creations, and I'll let ya tromp over to The Glass as often as you want. Just don't tell Hattie," he whispered conspiratorially, patting his round stomach and glancing over his shoulder as if his wife would magically appear to chastise him.

With a wink, Hal slipped his thumbs into his suspenders and walked down the hall.

"You know I would never come back without one!" Bastien hollered after the old man. "You'd probably lock me out!"

The hearty guffaw that rang back all but confirmed his accusation. Bas shook his head again, then ducked out the back door into the alley.

The Glass Half Full was quite literally just down the block from the butcher shop, on the opposite corner. Though it was not the only coffee shop in town, it was the best, without question, and the constant ringing of the wind chime above the door only confirmed it.

Bas leaned against the back counter, waiting for his order: a 'hot double zinger, one Spicy Chelsea, and one Elvis', which translated to a hot double-shot americano, a four-cheese and chorizo grilled sandwich, and a toasted, peanut butter and banana sandwich.

The chimes sang again.

"Babe! You're late!" the barista with the dual-colored hair cooed to whoever had just walked in.

Unable to remember a time he had ever heard the woman speak so sweetly to anyone, Bas glanced up, searching for the recipient of such honey. Not that he needed to know, but Hattie would love a little fresh gossip and she paid in duck eggs—which his mother called "the magic ingredient" for flan.

Bas could easily be considered a regular at The Glass. At least four out of five days a week, he showed up for his piping hot bean water and, more often than not, Hal's questionable taste in lunch.

So how had he never seen *her* before?

She stood in the doorway, her auburn hair frizzy from the hat she'd just pulled off her head. Bas watched through his lashes as she kicked the snow from her boots and hung her oversized jacket on one of the hooks behind the door.

"You can complain to my boss," the woman replied. "She's had me working all damn day on a project I might not even get paid for." She sighed dramatically, but the slight smile tugging at the corner of her mouth hinted that she was not as exasperated as she sounded.

The barista laughed loudly at that, and Bas furrowed his brows, clearly having missed a joke. He was further surprised when the woman started walking toward him, eyes down as she dug with one arm into the canvas bag hanging from her opposite shoulder.

High cheekbones dusted with freckles, a slender nose still red from the cold and full pink lips pursed in concentration. She was not wearing a lick of makeup, but Bastien felt like that had been a conscious choice—not from a rushed morning.

A look of triumph crossed her face when she pulled a worn book from her bag, and it took everything Bas had to keep from mirroring her reaction.

Then, when she was only two feet away from where he was still propped against the counter, she looked up and met his eyes.

SYVE

IF YOU WERE BRAVE enough to venture out in the morning, just as the sun rose over the wintery woods, you might be lucky enough to witness a cool, gray fog misting through the trees.

Syve saw that fog now, staring back at her from just below a pair of thick, dark brows and some of the longest eyelashes she had ever seen.

She inhaled sharply, mere inches from tripping headlong over a pair of ungodly thick legs.

"Oh. Oh! I'm sorry, I wasn't looking...sorry..." She quickly apologized before ducking around the man, taking the last few steps to her favorite corner seat.

Syve shook her head, mentally chastising herself for not paying attention. In her defense, the man had been preternaturally still as he leaned against the counter, and she had been so caught up in digging out her book that it was a miracle she noticed him at all.

Curling down into the sofa, she sneaked a glance back at the pick-up counter. The man was no longer waiting for his order, but trying to figure out how to get a deli bag into his hoodie pocket without destroying the contents.

She hadn't noticed how tall he was before when he was slouched down, nor had she noticed how broad he was. Based on how he towered over the display counter, he had to be at least a head taller than she was.

How she hadn't spotted the living billboard before smelling him would forever baffle her—and smell him she had.

Where most men carried hints of sandalwood, vetiver, tobacco, or leather, he smelled of pine and sweat—the kind of smell you'd expect from somebody who worked hard—and surprisingly, it wasn't unpleasant.

Syve continued to watch as he made his way to the exit. Having given up on pocketing his food, he held the paper bag between his distractingly perfect white teeth to free a hand for the door.

He hesitated with one foot across the threshold, glancing over his shoulder to where she sat, and their eyes locked again. The thought flitted about the back of her mind, that she should look away, but she didn't. She held his unblinking gaze until he turned and strode out into the snow.

There was something, *familiar*, about him that she just couldn't place.

"He's hot," Aimi stated nonchalantly, setting two mugs on the table before flopping on the couch next to Syve. "You probably haven't seen him before, have you? He doesn't usually come in this late, and he works for Hal." she gestured with her thumb over her shoulder. That made sense. Syve knew who Hal was, but as a vegetarian she had no reason to ever visit his butcher shop. Anytime he needed any mending he always came to her. "You know, he might be single—"

"Would you look at the time? Is lunch really over already?" Syve deflected, jumping to her feet.

It didn't matter if he was single. Just the thought of going to dinner with a man that was not Erhard made her stomach churn—and lord knows Gunther had asked. A lot. If she let her, Aimi would insist she entertain the idea of dating again.

"Oh, sit the fuck down, I'll drop it! We still have fifteen minutes, and I'd rather talk shit about Tyler than waste my time telling you *why* you need to get under someone when we both know you're not going to do it."

Syve only hesitated a second before slipping back down onto the couch.

"Tyler is trash. Cam deserves so much better."

Aimi grunted, jumping in an attempt to knock a box off the top of the cabinets while Toni, the only other employee of The Glass, finished up the closing duties. Dropping her paper onto the coffee table with an exaggerated stretch, Syve huffed in amusement at her friend's antics. There was a step stool literally right next to her.

Syve had gone back to the shop to finish out her day, the only trouble being another visit from Gunther and his incessant griping about the heat. After managing to excuse herself from yet another meaty dinner invitation, she returned to The Glass with her sketch-filled notebook and laptop, fully intending to set up camp on her little sofa and research the average cost of men's shirts.

But when Syve pulled her notebook from her bag, she immediately knew she made a mistake. Groaning, she made a mental note to stash all of her mother's journals back in the closet when she got home—if she kept mixing them up with hers, she was going to lose her mind.

Aside from the few lines she'd read when she first found them, Syve hadn't dared glance at Isla Balko's neatly penned letters. Waxing her entire body sounded more enjoyable than ripping off the metaphorical band-aid of opening that book.

Oh, but curiosity is a fickle thing.

It was not a full minute later, the journal lay open on the table, her mother's steady script beckoning to her.

Dearest Oisín,
I've been writing in these journals for as long as I can remember, never knowing who they were for—until now. The rest of my words will all be for you. I guess that is, if you ever WANT to read them. I'm probably putting the cart ahead of the horse again—your father and I only got the news this morning—pregnant! With you!
I've wanted nothing more than to be a mom for as long as I can remember.
I can't wait to meet you, my little fawn.
More than all the stars in the sky,
Mom

Syve wiped a tear as she remembered the way her mom used to snuggle up and read to her before bed, always kissing her head and telling her, "I love you, my little fawn, more than all the stars in the sky." Reading these journals was going to be more difficult than she anticipated. She read a few more entries. "Dearest *Oisín*, you won't let me eat chicken nuggets.", "Dearest *Oisín*, we heard your heartbeat today...", "Dearest *Oisín*..." She paused when the greeting changed.

Dearest Syve,
Girl.
A girl.

I'm going to have a daughter.

YOU will be MY daughter.

Your Father is beside himself, terrified because you're a girl, and also terribly smitten...because, well, you're a girl. We haven't talked about names yet, but there won't be a debate. Your dad has never been able to tell me no.

You are Syve, just as your Nan knew I was Isla.

Names are powerful things; they carry so much meaning and I've known yours since I was a child.

Maybe one day I'll tell you the story. Our story.

Halfway there, my little fawn.

More than all the stars in the sky,

Mom

"You ready to get out of here?" Aimi's voice snapped Syve back to the present. "Toni already took off for the night—you okay?"

Syve nodded. "Yeah, I was just..." She trailed off in favor of holding the diary up with a shrug.

"Good feels or bad feels? Good, we're getting ice cream. Bad, we're getting drunk."

Syve gave a tired little laugh. "It's Wednesday—actually, you know what? Doesn't matter. Ice cream before bed sounds perfect."

BASTIEN

THREE WEEKS SLITHERED BY. Bastien took every opportunity to run over to The Glass, always searching for hazel
eyes. He couldn't place it, but as soon as their eyes met, he
recognized her—*knew* her from somewhere. The feeling was
infectious, and it was starting to take over. Every time he
would drag himself back to Hal's, coffee in one hand, sandwiches in the other, he looked like a walking storm cloud.
Why couldn't he shake her from his head? Those melan-
cholic, doe eyes had rooted themselves somewhere deep.

Every night, he tucked himself away in the mausoleum,
losing himself to fictional worlds until the creaky iron gate
sang him home. What began with two hesitant steps one

night quickly escalated to twelve the next, until Bas stood close enough that when the doe laid her head on the granite, he could reach out his nose and nudge her rear leg—if he wanted to.

She watched him now. Ever since that first night she saw him, she always looked for him. She would wait, eyes tracking him as he settled nearby, and once he was still, she'd return her gaze to the stone and ignore him completely for the rest of the night. With spring approaching, Delanira had started pestering Bastien to take her to Bozeman to go dress shopping, for both prom and graduation. When he offhandedly suggested she wear the same dress to both events, she'd shrieked, accusing him of *"wanting her to die from social ridicule."*

Soriah, on the other hand, had expertly dodged the subject altogether by simply saying, *"We still have time before we have to think about that,"* before walking away.

Even with the change of season approaching, the mountain air was brisk and the ground still covered with patches of snow. Bas cursed the slick ground as he penguin-shuffled down the alley toward the butcher shop's back door. He had already caught a patch of black ice once when he was running late. The resulting bruise had taken the better part of a month to heal and he was in no rush for a repeat.

Stacks of empty crates lined the walls of the back room. They had received a truck load of carcasses from Hal's supplier, Doug, two weeks prior and now it was time to get everything cut and stored. It was Hal's standard to let the meat hang for fourteen days before doing anything with it, which meant today was processing day and that was Bastien's favorite. He enjoyed having something more challenging than counting change and arguing about why a tri-tip cost more than a chuck-roast. After four years he also considered himself to be decently skilled with a knife and enjoyed the chance to put the skill to use.

"Mornin', son!" Hal grunted as he fought to get the cooler door propped open. "This blasted door—you mind snaggin' that other one?" Bas gave a quick nod before jogging across the wide hallway to open the cooler directly opposite his boss.

Hal was very proud of his rail system, saying it was the best investment he ever made. Tracks started at the bay door, where Doug would stop his cooler trailer, then they ran down the hall to the hanging room, where the meat would age. The track continued back out across the hall to the processing room (that Hal insisted on calling The Carving Room), and then cut straight back out and down the hall to complete the loop. A carcass would be pulled up onto a hook using a ceiling mounted winch, straight from the trailer, then pushed along the rails straight into the walk-in cooler. After tenderizing, that same carcass could then be pushed along the rails across the hall, where it would hang on one side of a nine-foot slab of butcher block. From there, it was easy enough for one person to quarter the carcass, while another cut down the slabs of meat.

"You ever going to invest in the upgrades to have this system motorized?" Bas huffed twenty minutes later as he pushed the first carcass across the hall.

"Bah! Unnecessary expense at my age. Besides, I already have a motor." Hal raised a brow in jest.

Bastien made a show of rolling his eyes as he came to a stop on his side of the counter. Hal let out a hearty laugh and the two set to work.

It only took three hours for the men to fill one rack with steaks and roasts, and a second with miscellaneous cuts for the grinder. Hal cleared his throat as he gestured vaguely for Bastien to wheel over the cart with the vacuum sealer mounted on top.

"I think it's about time I retired."

The cart slammed into the counter as Bas snapped his eyes up to his boss. "What?"

"You heard me, son. I'm not sure if you noticed, but I'm no spring chicken. I think it's time to stay home with Hattie and watch her fuss over those damned ducks."

Bas stared as Hal avoided his gaze and loaded a handful of meat into the grinder's tub.

"Nothing is set in stone, I haven't even told Hattie yet. There would be a lot of details I'd need to work out ahead of time..." He sighed, finally looking up. "I just wanted you to be the first one to know. I feel I owe you that much."

Bas grunted out a thanks before blindly finishing out the morning. He knew from the beginning the old man would likely retire sooner rather than later, but that didn't stop him from being surprised when the prospect of it finally happening came up.

Giggles and the scent of spice in the air greeted Bastien when he arrived home, a sign that Del had company and his mother made her famous cocoa.

"*Mijo*?" Soriah peeked her head around the corner and frowned when she saw his face. "Come sit, I saved you some cocoa." She waved for him to follow and turned back into the kitchen, her long white braid whipping behind her.

"Thanks, Mama," Bas murmured, settling onto a stool at the counter and wrapping his hands around the large clay mug that had been pushed his way.

"Now, tell me what has you so sour." His mother smiled and leaned against the counter facing him.

"It's nothing." Bas sighed, then, noting his mother's raised brow, added, "Yet."

Soriah waited patiently as Bas took a sip of his drink, testing the temperature, before emptying half the mug in one go. He let the rich chocolate soothe the burning sensation the cayenne powder caused before he continued, "Hal is thinking about retiring. I don't know what it means for me—us."

He envisioned the worst: Hal selling the shop to retire, a new owner not wanting to keep him on, repurposing the building.

Then what?

He knew he couldn't make it without the generous salary he earned as a butcher's apprentice.

"Mijo," Soriah called gently, pulling him from his spiraling thoughts. "Patience. Until there is something to worry about," she looked pointedly at him, "don't."

Bas fought to keep from rolling his eyes.

"It's not just the job, Mama. I really like what I do—I'm good at it. I don't *want* another job." And it was true. In the four years he had been working under Hal, he'd grown to love the artistry behind the work.

"You buy it then." Soriah shrugged, as if it was the most obvious answer.

"Buy it?" He scoffed. "With what money, Mama? I make good money, but I can't afford to buy a business. I used my entire savings to get us here." Pushing away from the counter, he paced the length of the kitchen and ran his fingers through his hair, entwining his fingers behind his neck.

"Bastien Artemio, you did not have to use your savings. I could have gone back to work—that was your choice, so don't make me feel bad for it. And we both know that you *do* have the money to buy it. Your brother left it to you for a reason and he would be disappointed in you for not using it. Especially for something like this," Soriah scolded, her voice breaking at the end. Eyes brimming with tears, she turned and walked out of the kitchen.

SYVE

SCRAPS COVERED THE COUNTER and floor as Syve expertly cut various patterns from a stack of jewel-toned fabrics. There were only four months left to have her application completed for the grant, and as of this morning, she only had three of the required pieces done. It had taken her the better part of the last two months to settle on which designs she wanted to use. She'd forgotten her sketchbook was nearly full, with as many as three or four designs on any single page. The application required ten finished products, all crafted by the applicant, to be used to judge her level of skill and determine a general idea of the wares which would be sold by the business. Narrowing roughly two-hundred designs down to ten had been a nightmare.

Setting the scissors down, she stood to stretch her legs and flexed her hands. If she wasn't careful, she would end up with a severe case of carpal tunnel. Cutting was the least favorite part of her craft, so she preferred to get it all done in one go. Sighing, she walked to the front of the shop and flopped down onto the sofa. The action was enough to cause her hair tie to lose the battle it had been fighting all afternoon and fall from her head, her hair cascading in a messy copper curtain around her.

Syve had been spending the majority of her spare time reading through her mother's journals. Currently she was up to her sixth birthday, and she had learned two things. The journals were being kept a secret from her father, and—after years of trying—Isla had given up all hope of having any more children. There was not a clear reason as to why the journals were being hidden, but Isla was convinced her fertility issues were due to 'incompatible genetics' and Syve had less than half a clue what *that* was supposed to mean.

Dearest Syve,
I'm keeping a secret, my girl, one your father doesn't know.
I started out keeping this secret to protect myself and your Nan. You know that before I met Rich, it was only her and I. It wasn't just my secret to keep and after a

while it started to feel like I waited too long to share it. I was scared. I was scared I was going to lose him and I was scared of what could happen if it got out.

See, I had these friends once.

They knew—shared—this secret, and when Rich and I were planning to get married they convinced me to tell him. They told me "if I ever wanted to have children with this man, it would be something he needed to know."

Unfortunately, before I had the chance to say anything, my friends were gone. Dead. Taken from the world because of that very secret I'd been about to share with your father. Someone figured it out, and they were killed because of it.

I couldn't do it. I couldn't risk it. Nan would be in danger, and Rich, just for knowing, would be too.

There is only one problem, my sweet girl. Those friends were right, and it's very possible this may yet be your secret too. Stars above, if that's how your father figures it out...

I pray to whatever gods are listening you take after your father, little fawn, because I could not live with myself if it put you and him in danger.

More than all the stars in the sky,
Mom

Syve let the journal fall to her lap as her face twisted in confusion. She did not think her mom could have left a more cryptic message if she tried. What on Earth could she possibly have been hiding that had gotten her friends *killed*?

Lyrics to FRIENDS by Marshmello and Anne-Marie rang out from Syve's phone, breaking the silence. Quickly digging the device from the pocket of her jeans, she glanced at the screen before laughing out loud. The photo ID was a picture of Aimi flipping off the camera, sticking her tongue out and the name at the top of the screen was 'Nein, Gunny!'. She was never going to be able to leave her phone unattended around her best friend ever again. Clearing her throat and choking down her laughter she answered the call.

"Hello?"

"Hey Doll," Gunther drawled. "I need you to do me a favor."

Syve sighed, rolling her head to the side before answering.

"What can I help you with, Gunther?" she asked dryly.

"I need you to come over—tomorrow, after work."

"Uh, why?"

"Does a man need a reason to ask a girl to come over? I can throw some chicken on the grill; you can get in the kitchen and whip up some of that onion pasta you always make—"

"Gunther," Syve interrupted. "I don't *eat* chicken. And it's leek, not onion"

"Fine, fine. I've got some trout in the fridge. We can have that instead."

Syve closed her eyes and took a deep breath. She was starting to think this man did not know what being a vegetarian meant.

"Gunther, I have plans with the girls tomorrow night. I'm sorry."

Gunther sighed dramatically on the other end of the line. "Syve, I'm trying to do you a favor here, but alright," he relented. "Have a good night with Aims and that tall girl."

"Cameron," Syve interjected.

"Sure. I'll call you later." He hung up before she could respond.

The rest of her day was spent between cutting fabric, pinning patterns, and reading page after page of her mother's words. When she finally closed the shop and went upstairs, she had two more designs fully pinned, ready to sew, and she knew absolutely nothing more about her so-called 'family secret'.

The sound of crunching snow and a soft huff told her the wolf was back in its usual spot— at the foot of Noah's grave. She still thought it odd that it was there, though she had zero motivation to ask why. It was not like she was going to find one of those 'dream decrypting' websites to tell her what a lingering wolf could possibly mean. If it was a bad omen, she would rather not know—not that she had much left to fear from bad luck. Silent as always, her furry companion sat as still as the stones around them and watched her.

After laying against the cold stone long enough for her limbs to feel stiff and numb, she groaned, digging her hooves into the snow to stand. With a quick shake to clear herself of any snow that clung to her coat, Syve moved toward her silver furred companion, or more so the gate behind them. When she stepped past the wolf, she could have sworn she *felt* it touch her, a quick brush of its nose as she breezed past. While a part of her noted the sensation as new and intimidating, the rest of her could not be bothered and she kept walking.

It was not until she was stepping into the street that the hairs stood up along her spine, forcing her to glance over her shoulder. The wolf was trailing her, albeit at a distance, but it *was* clearly following her nonetheless. Maybe she ought to look into dream reading after all.

Cameron squealed, holding up a small hooded poncho.

"Lord help me, this is the cutest thing I've ever seen!"

Syve laughed at her friend as she pulled a similarly sized pair of overalls off of a child-sized dress form. The poncho was made from dark gray cotton duck canvas with a poly-ester lining and had an additional fleece layer that could be attached with a zipper to add extra warmth for the colder months. It sported a matching, removable hood, and little arm slits on either side held shut with little, sewn in magnets—strong enough to keep the seam together to ward off the wind, but not so strong as to keep a child from pushing past them to get their arms free. Cameron was right, it was possibly *the* cutest thing and Syve was incredibly proud of how it turned out.

"Did you notice the pockets?" Syve asked, laughing again when her friend finally found the interior pockets with another bout of squeals. "Kids need pockets...for rocks," she added with a shrug.

"As soon as you're done with this application, I'm going to demand a set of these!" Cam squealed again.

"Jesus, Girl, chill!" Aimi chided as she snatched the poncho from Cameron's hands and set to folding it. "We both know she has to make *me* an adult sized one first! Bright pink, obviously." She screeched, ducking when Cam threw one of her boots.

"You two are out of control." Syve smiled and rolled her eyes at her friends. "I can make *everyone* a poncho *if* I get that grant."

"When," both girls replied at the same time before turning to each other and nodding in agreement.

"Yeah, yeah. Now where is this wine at? Pretty sure when you came down here and disturbed my work you told me there was wine. And those fancy pretzels I like." Syve goaded her friends with her hands on her hips and one eyebrow raised.

"It's upstairs, and probably warm by now, you workaholic," Aimi whined.

"No, I left it on the porch in the snow!" Cam bragged. "I knew better and there was just enough snow to cover all but the neck of the bottle! Kismet." Cam sighed the last bit dreamily, causing Syve to roll her eyes and scoff playfully.

"Cameron Jo, you brilliant bitch—" Aimi cut herself off by stepping up to Cam, grabbing her face with both hands and planting a big, wet kiss on her cheek. "I think your husband doesn't deserve you."

Cameron guffawed and pushed Aimi away. "Oh, that reminds me! What's up with the paw prints? Have you been feeding strays again?"

"It was *one* time! I thought the cat was homeless! How was I supposed to know I was being played by the cute little bastard?" Syve huffed in mock offense. "But wait, what do you mean? I haven't even seen any strays lately."

"You know? The prints all up and down the back porch and stairs?" Cam asked, confusion evident in her tone, and on her face. Syve stared at her for a minute before turning and walking straight to the stairwell leading to her loft.

"What the hell?" she muttered to herself moments later, standing on her back porch.

True enough, there were paw prints, *big* paw prints, leading up the stairs, around the porch, and then back down before disappearing in the shadows down the alley. Syve instantly thought of her dream the night before, about how the wolf had followed her. She'd woken up from that dream and gone straight down to the shop, unable to go back to sleep. It must have been four in the morning before she shuffled back to bed, but she had noticed the fresh snow covering the porch when she walked by the window.

At some point between four AM, when she had returned to bed, and now, half past six at night, some canine had tromped all over. Syve's first thought was how she would not be able to finish her clothing line while on the grippy sock vacation she would surely be taking for suggesting that the creatures from her *dreams* were stalking her.

Maybe I need the vacation, she thought.

BASTIEN

TWELVE HOURS LATER, HE still didn't know why he followed her home after all those nights he'd sat by her side, simply content to share her space and lend silent support. What made it worse was he hadn't even tried to hide his light stalking, and she absolutely noticed.

Last night, he'd followed her to the alley where he sat silently, watching as she walked to a set of stairs as large snowflakes began to fall, quickly covering them both.

He averted his eyes when she started to shift, not sneaking a single glance. Though he was desperate to know who she was and seeing another shifter bare was not uncommon—modesty was rare in large shifter-groups—that was usually in a consenting environment and not a creepy 'I just followed you home' one.

He remained long after he heard her bare feet crunching up the snow-covered stairs, her door squeaking open, then snicking shut. As the sun crept over the horizon, he stood, shook off a layer of snow, and bolted down the alley before padding up to her door.

Bas sniffed around the entire porch, peeked inside the window—the blinds surprisingly left open to reveal the tiny living room and most of the tiny kitchen. What was he looking for? What was his plan? What if she was still there, just inside the door and saw him? A million questions flashed across his mind, not a single one with an answer.

"I think that spot is cleaner now than it has ever been."

Bastien's head snapped up, meeting Hal's suspicious gaze before glancing back down toward the counter he had been very diligently wiping.

"Sorry, Boss. Got a little lost in my head," Bastien replied, wincing as he threw the used rag at the laundry bin, missing by a few feet.

"A little?" Hal teased.

"Hey, are there people who live downtown? Down here? I mean, up there?" Bastien gestured toward the ceiling, a confused grimace spreading across his face.

Hal stared at him for a moment, eyebrows raised before laughing once and responding.

"There are a few shops that have apartments upstairs. The Glass has one," he said pointing down the street. "The post office, the bookstore, my seamstress, that nail salon...Oh! And that little Knick-knack shop Hattie just can't stay out of!" Hal listed each location, counting on his fingers as he went. "Each one of them is lived in by the shopkeeper—except the post office, they made that one into an Airbnb a few years ago."

"Hmm," Bas mused. "I'm not sure how I didn't know that already."

"Honestly, I'm not surprised. It's not like any of them are trying to advertise their home address."

"Hold on, back up, did you say your seamstress?" Bastien asked incredulously. "You mean Hattie's?"

"You heard me, Son! You don't think I've been getting all these aprons and shirts from some big ol' monopoly company, did you?" Hal scolded, gesturing to the polo he was wearing with the shop's logo on it. "Syve's been embroidering everything for me for years! In fact, she's the one who keeps fixing that damn jacket of yours every time you catch it on the meat-hooks."

"If you let me order the motor system, I wouldn't have to shove the carcasses like a fuckin' linebacker," Bastien shot back, smiling as he threw his hands up.

Hal threw his head back, laughing. Shaking his head, he turned and walked down the hall toward his office.

"Always with the motor!"

An hour and a half on the road between Timberfall and Bozeman meant Bastien had ninety minutes of Taylor Swift and his sister's off-key singing to survive before they'd arrive.

Timberfall was not a microscopic town. The number of tourists who passed through while visiting Yellowstone and the surrounding parks made sure of that, but it was not a grand metropolis either. Aside from a few, very specific boutiques and second-hand shops, there was nowhere Delanira could go to purchase two fancy evening gowns.

So, Bozeman it was.

The Jeep slowed to a stop as they pulled into a line of cars at the one toll booth unfortunately placed in their path. While Bas refused to touch any of the money Dez left behind, he couldn't bear to see the borderline obnoxiously large—and definitely obnoxiously lime green—vehicle sitting unused in the driveway. The only thing Desiderio loved more than his family was his damned Jeep, and it showed in every accessory and modification he'd added to it. So, Bas fully relinquished his Durango to Soriah and started driving 'Fiona' full-time.

Silence filled the cab when Del reached out one of her perfectly manicured fingers and turned off the radio. Bas choked on a groan, trying to ignore the burning sensation undoubtedly caused by his sister's unwavering stare boring into the side of his head.

"I overheard you talking to Mom," she stated, "about Hal's."

Bas continued to ignore her. He knew she was going to bring up *something* he did not want to talk about.

The line moved and he crept the Jeep forward.

"I agree with her, for what it's worth," Del murmured, a hint of sadness in her voice. Though still a child, she had already seen so much loss.

"Delanira," he warned, the word carrying more weight beneath the surface.

Bas cut her a quick glance as he eased the car up the last few feet to the teller window. Montana was one of very few states left that still employed people to operate their tolls opposed to the computer operated booths further east. Del huffed, crossed her arms and turned toward her window. The accompanying eye roll was so excessive it could be felt from the driver's seat without ever needing to be seen. Bas paid the attendant, collected his receipt and urged the vehicle back onto the road, merging into the traffic with practiced ease. Del continued to stare out the window even after her brother turned the radio back on, 'Red' playing just shy of too-loud from the speakers.

Six hours, four stores, and two food breaks later, Del had two new dresses hanging in the back, accompanied by two new pairs of shoes and a small bag of jewelry from a shop in the mall. Bas had proved to be even less helpful than Soriah would have been. Every dress the teen had tried on had been too short or too revealing, and Bas had not been afraid to voice his opinion. The odds of Del ever asking either of her family members to go shopping with her ever again were very slim.

That night, Bastien sat in the mausoleum long enough to start and finish an entire book. After every chapter, he stood to check for his doe.

For the first time, she never appeared.

SYVE

Dearest Syve,

Happy New Year, my love! You tried so hard to stay awake, but here we are—11:45 and you're asleep in my lap.

Maybe next year you'll make it.

Gods help me, I can't believe you're already 10 years old! It sure doesn't feel like an entire decade has gone by...

I suppose I only have a few more years left until I know for sure if my little fawn is more Balko or Dorran.

That's vague.

Let me see if I can clarify a little better...It's probably time I do that anyway.

There's a gene, we'll say, that has been passed down in

our family for a very long time. I have it, your Nan has it, your Granddad had it too.

Your Dad doesn't have this gene, and as far as I know, he is the first person to marry into the Dorran family without it. Remember those friends I told you about? The ones who also shared this secret? Well, their family has a similar gene, and they also haven't heard of someone marrying another person without it.

That's to say, it's been passed down for generations without anyone ever knowing if it's a dominant or recessive gene.

Long story short—you, my love, are special—the first born 50/50.

Puberty usually triggers the gene and it...shows up. I have no way of knowing if you have the gene at all, or if it will even manifest—and it's in our best interest not to get doctors involved.

I clearly didn't think about any of this when I met your father, but honestly? I don't know that it would have changed anything. I hope one day you get the chance to see what I mean—to meet someone whose heart beats in time with yours...

Anyway, I've decided I'll tell you all about it soon—here at least—because even if it doesn't show, it's possible you could still be carrying it. You might pass it to your children one day, and I would be the world's worst grandma if I didn't warn you ahead of time.

I suppose this means I should tell your father too...I really should have told him a long time ago.

Wish me luck, little fawn.

More than all the stars in the sky,
Mom

SYVE LET HER HEAD fall back and sighed, her mom just kept dancing around this secret, which was apparently a family secret that her friends—who were not family—also had. Confusing was an understatement.

At least now she knew it was a gene, but that didn't narrow it down much. And what gene could possibly be so secretive people were being killed because of it? It's not like they were fucking vampires—she could barely even *look* at a steak.

The coffee pot chirped, signaling it had done its job, and a fresh carafe of blessed caffeine was waiting for her. Syve leaned onto the kitchen table and pushed herself off her chair with a groan, then picked up her empty mug. Lightning prickled through her muscles as she shuffled to the counter; she'd been sitting in the same spot unmoving for God only knows how long and her legs had fallen asleep.

After they pretended to watch Twilight for the fifty-billionth time, Aimi and Cam stumbled home, leaving Syve awake for once and standing on her front porch staring at what was left of the paw prints in the snow. Two hours of lying in bed staring at the ceiling was enough to know she wasn't going to be getting any sleep. Instead, she curled up in the kitchen with her mother's journals and read.

Syve caught her reflection in the vintage mirror above the counter, a design choice by Aimi that she still questioned. Her hair was a mess. At some point in the night it had been in a braid, but now at least half of it had been pulled loose from running her fingers through it. Dark circles—darker than usual—shadowed her hollow eyes, making her look almost as much a zombie as she felt. She was wearing her favorite nightshirt, one of Erhard's old work T-shirts, so worn and faded she could no longer make out the words on it.

She hadn't pulled an all-nighter since college, back when four hours of sleep and an octo-shot espresso could get her through anything. The ache in her back and legs were side effects she did not experience in her younger years and she suddenly understood the phrase, 'I'm too old for this.'

With a long exhale, she refilled her "I need sew much coffee to function" cup, pivoted to the fridge to add a splash of cream, and then slunk back to her chair.

Dearest Syve,
Okay.
Are you sitting down? I feel like you should be sitting down.
Maybe I should be sitting down...
Well, you probably are, I wouldn't imagine you'd be driving or anything like that. I doubt your father would ever

teach you to drive and make you think it would be okay to be reading a book at the same time...

Right, focus.

If you're not sitting, sit.

I told your father the secret.

I don't know what I expected and honestly, I'm ashamed I thought it would be anything less than what it was.

I should have had more faith in the man, truly. He's not even mad I never told him and that just makes me feel even worse.

I asked him what his thoughts were on telling you. He agrees that while it would be easier, for us, to wait and see if you show the gene before telling you—we should have trust in our little fawn.

Hi, baby girl!

-Love, Dad

Oh, and I also told him about these journals.

I did tell him he needs to get his own and to stop reading over my shoulder (Rich, I mean right now—I love you, but go away!)

Anyway, sweet Syve, we've decided to tell you this year—on your birthday—that this gene? It makes you a shifter.

Syve cocked her head to the side, and mouthed the word *shifter* a few times in utter confusion. What kind of 1990's lingo was her mom using here? Was 'shifter' slang for swinger? Once upon a long-ass-time-ago they stoned adulterers to death...so it was not an awful assumption?

Gross.

Did her dad accept the knowledge so easily because he was into that kind of thing too? But wait, could a gene even affect that?

Syve blinked away her rapidly spiraling thoughts and turned back to the open book, running her fingers through her braid again to prop her head on her hand.

Gods, why was it so much harder to write than to say out loud to your father?

I am a shifter.

Okay, way easier the second time.

Your Nan—your entire family on my side—are all (or were all) deer shifters. Like shapeshifters, but we only turn into deer.

Oh! Your school bus just pulled up—I'll explain more later!

More than all the stars in the sky,

Mom

Syve's hand slid from under her head, causing her to fall forward with her mouth agape. She stared at the paper, reading the entry, over and over while replaying her dreams in her mind.

Suppose they were not dreams after all?

Suppose that made everything worse?

She shot up from her chair so quickly she sent the poor thing tumbling, clanking loudly across the floor. Her heart was thundering in her chest; she couldn't catch her breath and the temperature in the room dropped.

Deer.

Shifter.

Deer shifter.

She backed into the wall with her hand clutched to her chest, afraid her heart would beat straight out of her ribs.

"Deer," she whispered, before the world spun.

"Syve! Syve, are you up here? Bitch, you'd better have a good reason for making me worry!" Aimi's voice echoed up the stairs. "You didn't show up for coffee, you're not answering your phone, and your *worst* crime?! Making me use my spare key on that dicked-up front door of yours! Let's be real, I wasn't going to walk all the way around the back when I was already at the front..." her rambling trailed off when she came out of the laundry room that sat at the top of the landing.

The loft was a disaster.

It looked exactly like someone let a wild animal loose. The entirety of Syve's DVD collection was strewn from the kitchen to the bathroom down the hall, couch cushions flipped off the couch, the curtains were barely hanging above the window, and the TV was lying face down on the floor with a nice hole in the middle.

Aimi stood in the center of the living room with her mouth—all but literally—on the floor. Syve took that moment to make the smallest sound, calling out to her best friend because what the fuck else was she going to do? The damned mirror in the kitchen, which was also a catastrophic mess, already confirmed what had happened, but she was still in firm denial.

When her friend heard the soft bleat, she spun on her heel.

"HOLY SHIT!" She jumped back, tripped over the coffee table and landed solidly on her ass. "HOLY FUCK! SYVE?!" she screeched, glancing over her shoulder toward the bedroom, obviously looking for her *human* friend.

When her eyes locked back onto the deer in front of her, she scrambled back to her feet—equipping herself with the TV remote that had conveniently toppled off the table when she did. Syve repeated her small, panicked sound, flinching and retreating a step when her best friend raised her arm in preparation to throw said remote at *her*.

Aimi's head jerked back in surprise, and she began blinking rapidly.

Syve's teeth were softly clicking as her body was wracked with shivers from the adrenaline flooding her veins.

Slowly, Aimi lowered her arm, dropping the remote to the floor.

They stared at each other a moment more before Aimi pointed at the door. Syve took a tentative step, then another.

"I've officially gone and lost my damn mind," Aimi finally mumbled to herself, as she reached for the door.

The second she threw open the door, Syve bolted, tumbling gracelessly down the stairs.

When the little birds stopped circling her head and she could make sense of which way was up, she stood on shaky legs and began running, the sound of her name fading behind her as she went.

BASTIEN

"YOU'RE LUCKY THERE AREN'T any other butchers in town. I swear, I'd never come back here otherwise. Fucking ridiculous," Gunther complained as he stomped out the door.

Bastien scoffed, rolling his eyes hard enough to make his head ache. They'd spent the better part of the last hour arguing after Gunther had shown up demanding they process some roadkill. Bas could see the roadkill in question, in the bed of Gunther's truck that was backed into a spot out front. Not a soul on this planet would believe the back-half of the elk sitting out there was hit by any kind of vehicle. When Gunther claimed to have 'misplaced' his salvage permit, Bas had seen red. Hal happened to walk out of his office just in time to keep the yelling one sided.

Gunther spun some story about a friend calling him after smoking the animal on the highway and since this friend didn't have a permit, Gunther, white-knight he was, had gone out of his way to help. Only, it seemed he had misplaced his own permit.

Hal reiterated that without seeing the paper, his hands were tied and there was nothing he could do. He suggested Gunther go 'dig around' for his permit and maybe encourage his friend to apply for his own.

"That's not roadkill," Bas growled, as the pick-up squealed down the road.

"No. No, it ain't," Hal confirmed.

Unfortunately, they had no way to prove Gunther's friend had poached this animal—if there even was a 'friend.' The best they could do was to send him away, call Game and Fish and hope Gunther was still in possession of the evidence when they got around to investigating.

"I hate it," Bas mumbled, his thoughts tumbling into memories of the woods and the smell of blood.

"You and I both, son." Hal placed a hand on his apprentice's shoulder, unaware of exactly how badly he needed the comfort in that moment. "Listen, not to further dampen the mood or anything, but I've been talking to Hattie. I'm retiring, officially, next spring. I'm hoping to sell out in January or so..."

"Boss," Bas croaked.

"I want you to take over, son. I don't want to sell to some stranger, just to have them come in here and ruin everything we've built—and don't argue with me, because you know just as well as I do that business has only gotten better since your sorry ass came in my front door. I want you here and I'm willing to break a hell of a deal for you to buy me out. If I had millions in the bank, I would just give it to you, but I can't very well spoil Hattie on social security alone, you understand."

Bastien rolled his neck, running a hand over his beard as he processed everything Hal just told him. His worst nightmare and biggest dream both dancing hand in hand in front of him.

"I don't expect an answer from you right now. You think on it, and we can talk logistics and all that later."

Bastien nodded absently, and Hal gently squeezed his shoulder once before stepping away.

"Now, you go take a break. Go look for your girl at the coffee shop or something. Just bring me back a sandwich!"

"What?!" Bastien gaped back at the man and felt his face flush.

"Oh, come on now. I'm seventy-three—old, not blind. You've been antsy and practically running off at lunch and then moping the rest of the day. Nothing less than a woman could do that, in my experience." Hal stopped, cocked his head to the side and squinted at Bas. "Or a man? I'm not here to judge one way or another, just as long as you're happy."

Hal shrugged as Bastien continued to flounder, opening and closing his mouth like a fish out of water. The old man let out a deep belly laugh, using both hands on Bastien's shoulders to steer him toward the front door.

Instead of walking to The Glass, Bas turned left, crossing the street and meandering down the sidewalk. He only realized where he was headed when he stopped in front of Sew It Seems. This storefront would line up with the loft in the alley, the shops on either side being a one-story soap maker and a two-story wine and cheese business that advertised their second floor as a venue for wine tastings and parties. Bas thought back to his conversation with Hal. This was his seamstress. What had he said her name was?

The curtains were drawn and the sign on the front door read 'CLOSED'. Bastien would have assumed this meant she was not open on Fridays, if not for the hours that were posted on the window to his right which clearly stated otherwise. Stuffing his hands into his pockets, he continued down the sidewalk toward the cemetery.

March was spring as far as the lower states were concerned, but this far north, it was still winter. All the trees were still in hibernation, the grass dead and dry.

Bastien flipped up the collar of his jacket as the wind picked up. Even with the sun bearing down and zero clouds in the sky, the brisk mountain wind could cut to the bone and drag every ounce of heat right out of you.

Bas turned the corner and was only a foot from the mouth of the alley when a brown blur zipped past him, almost knocking him on his ass. He froze, arms raised to defend himself, as he watched a deer run a serpentine line across the empty road and through the large iron gate into the graveyard. It took ten seconds and just as many blinks before his brain caught up.

"Shit."

Without wasting any more time, Bastien sprinted after the doe, eyes darting everywhere trying to catch a glimpse of where she'd gone while he buffered. He only prayed she hadn't gone too far. Finding her in his current form was likely to go over far better than chasing her down as a wolf, but a deer could run laps around a human.

Something told him that, while his sense of smell and ability to track was exponentially better shifted, if this woman looked over her shoulder and saw a wolf loping toward her, she would kick it into high gear and bolt. Weeks of sitting together at night be damned, she would take one look at his predator body and the prey instincts would take over—she was already in flight mode.

Bastien slowed when he was side-by-side with the marble angel, straining his ears and spinning in a slow circle. A flash of movement had him moving again, and he just caught sight of her tail slipping around the corner of his favorite reading nook. The pines that surrounded the cemetery were dense and the midday sun cast odd shadows from the towering branches, narrow gaps between the tree trunks and the foliage, still dead from winter, created a perfect camouflage for a small brown body.

"Please!" Bas called out desperately. "Please, wait!"

He stopped again and scanned the woods with the mausoleum at his back, praying she was close enough to hear. A twig snapped just ahead and he threw his hands up, crouching down to make himself seem as non-threatening as possible.

"Please, I'm not here to hurt you." He took a few tentative steps forward. "You're...You're Syve, aren't you?"

SYVE

"PLEASE! PLEASE, WAIT!"

Syve hesitated, steps slowing a fraction, but did not stop threading through the pines. She hadn't noticed that she was being followed.

"Please, I'm not here to hurt you. You're...you're Syve, aren't you?"

Deer, meet headlights. Slowly she turned her head until she could see a familiar man standing just inside the tree line, crouched low with his arms raised like he was approaching a scared animal. Which, she realized, he technically was.

Recognition dawned on her and she tentatively took a few steps back toward Timberfall. It was the man from The Glass—the one Aimi said worked at Hal's.

Syve was beyond baffled at this point—how did he know? Why was he here? How did he know her *name*? Why did he follow her? How was any of this possible? Why was she a fucking deer right now? How was he not freaking out too?

He knew.

He knew.

But how?

Was he like this too? Did he share the secret like her parent's friends? But...her parents' friends had been killed over this. Was he dangerous?

"Syve, I won't hurt you. You're freaking out right now, aren't you? I can see it in your eyes."

He kept talking softly, but stopped trying to come closer. That was probably because she had unwittingly closed the gap by another three feet on her own, she realized. Syve turned her head, effectively giving him as much of a side eye as her current form could manage. She decided to listen for one more minute, if he didn't say anything convincing, she would resume the flight portion of her emergency response.

"It's not safe to shift in town, so either you have no control, or you are in danger. Based on our previous encounters, I'm going to put my money on the former?"

This garnered him her full attention. He noticed and continued, "Are you in danger?"

Syve shook her head frantically and when his face lit up, she realized she had officially blown her cover.

"Good. That's good. And you can understand me. That's also good." Relief flooded his features, his body relaxing so wholly he almost looked like he was going to sink to his knees. She took another step closer.

Why did she do that?

"Alright. Let's start with the easy questions. Is that okay?" he asked gently, never taking his cool, gray eyes off hers.

She mentally calculated the chances she could outrun this man if he was indeed a threat, and stopped walking completely when they were a stone's throw apart. The odds were in her favor, as long as he was unarmed...She shook her head to keep herself from spiraling into another full-blown panic attack, which more or less just shook her entire body. Human reactions and movements did not seem to translate one-to-one with her animal body. With that in mind she concentrated on her movements to deliberately nod.

"Yes, yes? Yes! Okay!" The man sighed, running his hands through his wavy black hair as he stared at nothing in particular—she could almost see the wheels turning in his mind.

"Would I be correct in assuming that you have no control?"

Another nod.

"You shifted on accident then...Can you shift back?"

She aggressively shook her head 'no' and he sighed.

"Will you let me help?" He stepped forward and she immediately retreated. "Okay, okay. I'll stay right here."

She nodded.

"Do you recognize me?"

More nodding.

"From here?"

He gestured behind him, she tilted her head to the side for a minute, confused, then shook her head no.

"From The Glass?"

Nod.

"Okay, I'm going to take my coat off. I can see you don't trust me. I get it. I'm virtually a stranger. I'm going to give you a reason—show you that you can, okay?"

He unzipped his coat, slipping out of it easily and tossing it next to him on the ground. Syve watched him warily, but nodded. She could not imagine what he could possibly show her that would make her trust him.

She flinched, her eyes wide as saucers. He had kicked off his boots and was actively undoing the button on his jeans.

"Trust the process. I'm not a creep, I promise. It's just...jeans are really expensive, and I just bought these..."

He blushed—actually blushed—and then dropped his pants to his ankles. Syve stumbled back, blinking rapidly as she tried to figure out how she wound up here—in the woods as a *deer* with a *pants-less man* in front of her. A pants-less man, who must be one with the forest if his thighs were anything to judge by—thick as the tree trunks and *clearly* what she needed to be focusing on at that moment.

"You can trust me, because I'm *like* you. Not only that, but we've met before."

He pulled his shirt over his head as he said it, exposing a very tan, fit chest underneath, spackled with dark hair that she *absolutely* did not need to be appraising. There was seriously something wrong with her.

The sudden exposure of his chest succeeded in stalling Syve's brain long enough for the man to toss his shirt on top of his coat, kick his jeans and boots over to the pile and then shift.

Where once a man stood before her, now stood a large—*really* large—smoke gray wolf. The exact same smoke gray wolf from her dreams—her dreams that were not dreams. Syve stumbled, all of the little puzzle pieces finally setting themselves in their places. Instead of acting rational, or as rational as one could be in her shoes, she turned around and ran.

It was easy to zip through the trees on cloven hooves. The extra legs made her nimble, and she was able to dash around trunks and over logs with hardly a thought. A deep growl behind her reminded her that while she may have been able to outrun a man, she was not sure if she could outrun a fucking wolf. She could hear twigs snapping behind her as he gave chase. It triggered a primal part of her, and she found a fifth gear, running even faster.

Syve had gone hiking in these woods a lot before Erhard died. Her late husband had loved being in the woods, which one would expect from someone who chose to work as a cartographer and wildlife photographer, and they had spent a majority of their weekends out hiking, camping, or just *existing*.

She had not been outside of town since the accident. Though, even if she had, her sense of direction was awful. She had no idea where she was or where she was running to. As soon as the mausoleum was out of sight, she was as good as lost. A quick yip both confirmed her pursuer remained and almost distracted her enough to make her trip. Who knew a wolf could make such a cute, innocent sound while literally chasing you through the woods?

Sunlight shone through more easily, as the pines began to thin, but before Syve could consider what that meant for her, she broke through the trees and skidded to a stop. In front of her was a calm lake that mirrored the peak of the mountain inclining away from its shores. She would need to backtrack and skirt the lake to the left or scale the rocky incline to her right if she wanted to keep moving forward—or whatever counted as "keep the wolf to your back".

Before she could make a choice, she heard another low growl and looked over her shoulder just in time to see the massive silver wolf leap out of the trees, tackling her into the dirt. Syve stared up into a panting mouth of dagger teeth, the edges of her vision beginning to fade to black. When he huffed down at her, hot air bursting across her face, she let the darkness take her.

BASTIEN

Syve went limp beneath him, and Bastien mentally smacked himself as he quickly scrambled off her. Clearly he'd, once again, not thought hard enough about his actions. Obviously, she would run from him after he stripped almost naked, then shifted into a full-blown wolf right in front of her. He intentionally followed her in human form to avoid freaking her out, then he went and freaked her out anyway. *Good job, dumbass.*

Bas began pacing beside her limp body. Should he wait here for her to come to and hope she would be willing to...what? Follow him somewhere to talk? Buck naked in the middle of the woods? Did he actually have a plan at all when he followed her into the cemetery? She blazed out of that alley and all rational thinking had gone out the window.

What was it about this woman that possessed him? Why was he so invested in her wellbeing when he didn't even *know* her? Mates were a fantasy. They were just as much a myth as unicorns—much to Del's dismay. There was no physical, spiritual or metaphorical hold Syve could have on him.

Yet, there he was.

A crow cawed somewhere nearby, startling him, and he halted. His gaze landed on the far bank of the lake, the same lake he had been intentionally avoiding for two and a half years. Adrenaline flooded his brain.

Was he thinking before acting? No.

Was he going to do it anyway? Yep.

Fifteen minutes later and only halfway back to the mausoleum, regret began to sink in. Here he was, naked as the day he was born, tromping through the frigid woods, carrying an unconscious deer. Her warm body and the exertion kept him mostly warm—except for the tips of his ears, his feet and his dick, which had absolutely receded so far into his body it was probably aligned with his spine.

Bas almost missed the gentle vibration in his arms, mistaking it for his own shivering, until it happened again more insistently. He stopped walking, loosened his hold slightly before pinning his eyes onto the nearest tree. This was about to get *so much* worse.

Syve's body rippled against his as she shifted but remained limp. Still unconscious, but now a human. A very naked human.

At least this meant she would be easier to carry with her weight distribution more agreeable. Bastien shifted his arm away from her ass to the back of her knees as quickly as he could without dropping her, and without looking down at her. Having managed to stop directly in the center of one of the few snow drifts that still lingered in the shadows, Bastien's feet now felt like clubs as he resumed walking.

He had been ignoring how, and *where,* she was pressed against him—she was unconscious and, all arguments aside, he was not a complete animal. A gust of wind picked up—cold air doing what it does best. Club feet or not, the second she shivered, he took off running. He refused to let her get frostbite or hypothermia because of him. Because he had chased her all the way to the damned lake.

He had to slow down when they reached the back side of the mausoleum, carefully checking for any potential witnesses before quickly ducking inside. The interior of the tomb was far warmer than the outside air, the lack of wind and the heat of the persistent sun creating a giant oven out of the stone walls.

Hurrying to the back wall, Bastien crouched down, careful to keep his eyes on the hanging lanterns as he laid Syve down on the cushioned bench. He blindly reached for one of the many blankets he had stashed. Once she was covered, he slipped back outside to grab his clothes, begrudgingly donning his frozen pants before returning.

As soon as he was back inside, he swapped his cold, dirt-covered shirt for a clean one from his stash—but froze with it caught around his biceps when he glanced at the woman. Long auburn hair, now horribly tangled from the wind, framed her pale face. It wasn't the kind of pale that came from hiding indoors—just genetics. One thing was certain: the doe who haunted his nights was also the hazel-eyed woman who plagued his days.

Bastien turned the page and then turned it back, already having forgotten what he had just read. He was having a hard time focusing with Syve's gentle snores—not that the snores themselves bothered him, but the fact his mystery woman—and mystery shifter—were one and the same. Oh, and she was sleeping naked, five feet away from him, because he had *tackled* her and knocked her out. With his luck, she would wake up, freak out again, and he could not imagine how this situation could get any worse.

A small groan from the corner made him snap his book shut and jump to his feet, back pressed against the wall.

Syve opened her eyes.

SYVE

DUST AND PINE. WHY did it smell like dust and pine?

Syve groaned. Her body was stiff and sore in the same way it always was after she'd fallen asleep on the floor. Only this was not her living room. Quick flashes played in her mind: reading her mother's journal, not being able to open her door...Aimi?

Running and running.

Trees and...him.

Her eyes snapped open, immediately landing on the man standing in the corner. He stood stock still, like he'd been cornered by a lion, watching her while he pressed himself into the wall, as if he was afraid of what she would do. If he could only back up another quarter inch, he could phase right through the wall itself.

Syve squinted her eyes, and was certain when she'd seen him earlier he was the same silent stranger from The Glass, but now...he was different. His hair was disheveled with twigs sticking out of the wavy, tangled mess. Sunken eyes stared at her warily, brows knit and a frown tugging at his surprisingly full lips. She was certain he'd been wearing a black t-shirt before, but was now wearing a dark gray long sleeve. She also noticed he was barefoot, though that took a second glance to confirm, since his feet were thoroughly covered in dirt.

The man cleared his throat, the sound choking out at the end as he winced.

Oh, she had flinched.

He tried again.

"I...there's water."

He pointed and her eyes slowly followed. Two bottles of water, various small bags of snacks, and a handful of candy bars sat in an open plastic tote on the floor. That's when Syve noticed she was lying on a bench, covered with a plush throw blanket. She was confused, tired and so damned thirsty. Questions could be asked once her tongue no longer felt like sandpaper in her mouth. She reached for one of the waters, halting immediately when her raised arm shifted the blanket off her *very* naked shoulder. With a gasp, she snatched the edge of the blanket, pulled it up to her neck and leveled a fierce glare on the man.

"Where are my clothes?!" she croaked. Water would absolutely be necessary if she was going to ask all her questions.

"You didn't...we can't..." He sighed and ran a hand through his hair, pausing to glance down when he pulled free a small handful of pine needles, which he tossed onto the floor. With a shake of his head, he continued, "By your feet, there's a pair of sweats and a hoodie. They'll probably be too big, but it's all I have."

Syve lifted her head again, looking down to see a pile of gray fabric.

The man cleared his throat. "I'll step out for a minute so you can get dressed. I know you have to have a million and twelve questions. I promise I'll answer as many as I can."

He looked at her a moment longer, likely assessing whether or not he could safely turn his back on her, then slipped out the door.

Syve remained where she was, blinking and staring for another thirty seconds before bursting to her feet to savagely yank on the clothes. He was right—they were massive on her. The pants pooled at her feet, and even after cinching and tying them at the waist, they still threatened to slip down. She sloppily rolled up the sleeves of the hoodie until her hands were uncovered.

There was nothing to be done about her bare feet.

Modesty restored, she took in her surroundings, noting the concrete walls covered in plaques, each accompanied by a small vase filled with dried flowers. Oil lanterns hung evenly from the ceiling, and three stained glass windows, a small one on either side of the door and one large rectangular one above the bench she had woken up on, served as the only light source. Dark wood embellished with iron made up the large door that sat slightly ajar, the only way in or out of this...tomb.

Syve felt every last drop of blood in her body run cold as it finally dawned on her.

This was a mausoleum.

Mausoleums were in cemeteries.

She was in a cemetery.

The cemetery.

It was like being kicked in the chest—all oxygen ripped from her lungs, and new air refused to take its place. Avoiding this place had been her top priority, she could not be here. Not in this place.

Not now.

Not alone.

Not alone.

Not. Alone.

Two large hands gripped her shoulders.

"Hey, hey! Are you okay?"

"Wh—where...where..." Her voice did not sound like her own. She sounded like she was underwater.

"A mausoleum, we're in a mausoleum. We're still in Timberfall, in the cemetery. I didn't know where else to take you..."

She already knew, but the confirmation wrapped around her neck, her heart hammering so hard she could *feel* it pulsing in her ears. Her skin itched. It itched, and all she wanted to do was crawl out of it—crawl out and run away.

"SYVE!" Hands on her face forced her to focus on gray eyes. "Syve, look at me. Look at me, you're not alone, it's okay. Breathe." This close she could see the depth of color in his gaze; gray alone was not accurate. All the videos she had watched of melted aluminum sprang to the forefront of her mind. In all of her life she had never seen such a unique pair of eyes.

And then they blinked.

Mystery man was taking deep, exaggerated breaths—breaths she had at some point began to copy.

"I can't be here." A whisper. "I can't—I haven't—not since...since..." The whisper morphed into a whimper with each word, and she felt a sting behind her eyes. Dark brows knit together, blurring when she blinked.

"You haven't? Haven't been here? What do you mean?" Another blink to clear her vision, watching as he searched her eyes. Confusion was clear on his face. "You've been here a lot. Syve, you've been here every night—every night for months."

Blink.

Snow crunching under deft hooves.

Blink.

Full moon peeking through the clouds.

Blink, blink.

Those stormy eyes haloed by silver fur.

Blink, blink, blink.

That silver fur chasing. Trees blurring. Water. The lake. A growl then she was falling.

Syve gasped, pulling away from the man and slipping her hands up to her face where his had just been. He remained there with his hands up, he'd done this before, he ducked his head slightly—a gesture to assure her he meant no harm.

"Who are you? What...how? Did I? Is this real?" She rasped, her throat even more dry than it had already been.

"I think you should sit. Sit and drink some water, I'll give you answers—all the ones I can, at least." He gestured behind her at the bench before sliding down to the floor himself, once again leaning against the wall opposite to her.

Eyes wide, she sucked in a breath and fell onto the bench.

BASTIEN

BASTIEN HAD BEEN PACING and pulling at his hair while he waited for her to get dressed. When he heard the rapid, gasping breaths, he ran back inside to find her having a complete panic attack. Acting on instinct alone he grabbed her shoulders to try and ground her, then he saw her skin slowly begin to tremor. The last thing they needed was for her to shift again.

Without a thought, his hands moved up to her face and he barked her name. That had been enough to get her attention. Enough to stop the shift, before it was too late.

Now, she was sitting across from him, greedily emptying water bottles while absolutely drowning in his clothes.

What a mess.

"So…" he began cautiously. "I don't really know where to start. I guess it might be easier if you just ask questions and I can fill in any blanks where I see them?"

She was halfway through her third water at this point.

"You." Her face screwed up in confusion. "Turned into…a wolf?"

Bastien had to stifle a laugh. She looked like she thought she was crazy. To be fair, if anyone else had heard her, they might have thought the same thing.

"I did," he confirmed and paused, waiting for it to register—to see if she was going to laugh or accuse him of lying. She did neither, only stared.

"That was real." Not a question, a statement. "And I…I turned into—this is insane." She stood, hands shooting up in exasperation, then coming down to rest on the top of her head as she began pacing. "There is absolutely no way—no way—that I," she gestured wildly at herself, "turned into a fucking deer." She let loose a single, "ha!" then dropped down, ass on her heels, and pulled the neck of the hoodie up over her face.

Her voice was muffled by the fabric when she spoke again. "Please just tell me that this is some weird, drug-induced fantasy. Tell me I'm going to wake up in a padded room."

He could not help it; he laughed.

Like an odd little gray cotton turtle, her head popped up just enough to reveal her eyes, which were shooting daggers in his direction.

"I'm sorry, it's just..." He shook his head and pulled his legs up, resting his forearms across his knees. "This *is* insane."

She blinked at him, unimpressed.

"I just can't wrap my head around *how* a shifter could possibly *not know* they're a shifter. It's *insane*."

It took longer than he expected for her to settle back onto the bench and start talking again. Naturally, she started back up with, "How is this possible?" Followed by, "Why me?!" Neither of which he had a good answer for. They spent the next few minutes assessing one another, him waiting for her next question and her, hopefully, thinking of one he could actually answer.

"Oh." She broke the silence. "What's your name?"

Now it was his turn to blink rapidly. After everything that had happened, how had he not introduced himself? If Soriah were here, she'd have an absolute cow.

"Shit, sorry, I'm Bastien, Bastien Yerovi. Everyone just calls me Bas, but you can call me whatever you want. You're Syve, right? I know I already kind of asked you, but you know...Please tell me I haven't been calling you the wrong name this whole time." He groaned and put a hand over his face, splitting his fingers over one eye to look at her.

"Bastien." She said his name like she was sampling a new food, and he decided he liked how it sounded coming from her mouth. "As much as I would love to fuck with you, yes, my name is Syve. Gehring. Though I would *really* love to know how you knew that." She squinted at him skeptically. "And why were you so intent on chasing me down? You tackled me! Wait, how did we even get back here? I ran all the way to the lake!" She was standing again; hands threaded through her hair.

"Whoa! Okay, I'll explain! It's okay." He held his hands up in surrender for the millionth time that day and waited for her to sit back down. "I only followed you because I wanted to help. I chased you because I didn't want you to get hurt—or lost! The tackle was...instinct?" He cringed, what a stupid answer. "And I carried you back here." Syve stared at him, jaw slack in disbelief. "You didn't shift until we were halfway back—I ran after that, and I never looked down..."

He shut up, cheeks heating. Syve looked away, color rising to her face as well. She remained silent, waiting for him to continue.

Bas dropped his head back against the wall with a soft *thump* and stared at the ceiling. He ran his tongue along his teeth while he searched for a way to explain his stalking without sounding like...well, a stalker.

Fuck it.

Starting with an incredibly long sigh, Bas spoke again, "I don't think having you asking questions is really getting us very far. I don't think you know where to start asking questions—obviously, this is all new—it wasn't fair of me to ask that of you."

He proceeded to tell her everything he knew. How he first happened across her, how he could not explain why he kept coming back and why he had kept getting closer. Syve raised an eyebrow at him when he confessed to following her home and he grimaced, apologizing for being a grade-A creep.

"This *whole* time I truly thought I was dreaming. I never cared that a big ass wolf was hanging out because I legitimately thought it was all in my head. If you were like...a *real* wolf I could have literally been eaten." She laughed, a hint of self-depreciation evident.

"Hey, in your defense, I really tried to approach you in a non-threatening way—I'm sure you would have reacted differently if I was like..." He threw his hands up, clawing at the air with a pathetic 'grr' that immediately had him internally face-palming.

Syve slapped a hand over her mouth, poorly concealing her laugh.

"Well..." He cleared his throat. "If I had to guess...I think you've been shifting in your sleep this whole time—kinda like sleepwalking." That only seemed to upset Syve more.

"Great! Now I'm not just a mess, I'm a *sleepwalking* mess! Why did this happen now? I've never had an issue before recently! I've only been having these dreams—or sleep-shifting, whatever, since December."

"Those were your first shifts?" he asked, aghast. "Typically, the first shift follows the onset of puberty—no later than fifteen or sixteen. I'm assuming you're older than that." He raised an eyebrow at her, and she shot him a look that he assumed meant, 'don't be a dipshit,' so he carried on. "Strong physical, hormonal and emotional changes happen around that time...I guess the same could happen later in life? Maybe...maybe you experienced a strong emotional trigger?"

Syve seemed to physically sink away at that.

"Syve, who is Noah?" he whispered.

"So, you're a shifter too? Even though we are different, uh, species?"

She quickly changed the subject and he begrudgingly took the hint. Some questions would remain just that, it seemed. He confirmed they were both indeed shifters, regardless of the fact they did not assume the same form. Yes, it's genetic, yes, there are shifters everywhere, and yes, there are more kinds.

Syve's eyeballs almost popped out of her head when Bastien told her about his family—how his father descended from a long line of horse shifters and his mother from an even longer line of wolves. She asked if that was common, for different 'species' to cross, which led to the question, "Are certain animal genes recessive? Are predators naturally dominant? Is that why you're a wolf like your mom?"

The question caught him off guard, and he laughed. "No, I'm sorry, it's just...you haven't been asking any of the questions I thought you would ask. There is no rhyme or reason behind which animal a child will inherit—at least not one that we know of—and actually, my little sister took after our father. She's a horse shifter."

Syve gasped, then spent a solid five minutes excitedly jabbering about how majestic Del's horse form must be before they could move on.

"I just don't understand *why* your first shift was so delayed. I've never heard of that happening..."

At this she clapped her hands together, pressing them to her nose. "I might have the answer to that...Is it rare for shifters to be with...humans? Non-shifters?" She had his full attention, and he tilted his head toward her, eyes narrowing in suspicion. "My Dad. He wasn't a shifter." She shrugged. "I guess that makes me half-blooded. Do you think *that* could be why I'm so...different?"

Bastien stared at her, mouth agape as he processed her words.

"It's completely unheard of—I didn't know it was even *possible* to have a baby with a non-shifter. I'm sure I would have heard of, or met one by now..."

Syve smiled sadly and told him about the trouble her parents went through just to have her. How they had eventually given up on the idea of a second child after years of trying.

"You're a miracle then, that's incredible," he whispered reverently. "So, if your mom is a shifter, why hasn't she told you any of this? Why didn't you *know*?"

"Was. She was." Syve murmured the words, studying her hands in her lap as she did.

SYVE

"Was. She was." Syve stared down at her hands, mindlessly picking at her nails while she waited for the pity that always came after telling people she was an orphan.

She had referred to her father in past tense earlier and he either missed it or hadn't deemed it important enough to comment on. Honestly, she was happy either way. But this? Now he would have to acknowledge it, and she *hated* this part.

"When did you lose them?" His voice was soft, hesitant even. "You know what, don't answer that. Unless you want to—but I get it if you don't."

It hit her then. She'd been so caught up in her own bull-shit—while he hadn't said anything when she talked about her dad, *she* hadn't said anything when he mentioned his dad in past tense either.

He was just following her lead.

"When I was ten. Car accident," she whispered. "You?"

Bas's face shifted from despair to surprise, then back, as if he was not expecting the question.

"My Father? Seven years ago. Cancer."

Syve sucked in a sharp breath before she could think better of it, then grimaced.

"I'm so sorry, Bastien."

"Yeah. Me too." He cleared his throat. "But my mom is still around. I ended up moving back in after Pops passed so she didn't have to get a job." He huffed a laugh, running a hand through his hair. "Guess I'm a real Momma's boy."

Someone else must have snuck into the mausoleum while they were not looking. There was no other way to explain the hand that just punched its way into her chest, grabbed her heart, and squeezed. Syve pinched her eyes shut and fought the urge to scream—to scream and scream and scream.

Momma's boy.

Momma's boy, Momma's boy, Momma's boy.

"Noah, don't you want to come see Dada? I know you're Momma's boy, but Dada loves you too!"

"Syve? Are you okay?"

"No. But we're not talking about it."

He nodded in understanding. "How do you know all this about your parents and have no idea you're also a shifter?" Zero hesitation. Zero questions. New subject.

Syve could have kissed the man for not pushing it.

Her stomach roiled, sick with herself for even thinking she could kiss this man—she was *married*. A second fist clamped around her heart.

"A journal." She all but gasped, pausing for a moment to take a deep breath. "My Mom, she kept these journals, and I just found them. I was reading an entry this morning where she admitted to being a shifter. It was the last entry before..." She trailed off, sucking her lips into her mouth and releasing them with a pop. "Anyway, I read that and kinda had a panic attack, I guess. It's a little fuzzy between there and when you found me—which never would have happened if Aimi hadn't opened my door for me...OH MY GOD!" She squealed, eyes nearly popping out of her head as she threw her hands over her mouth. "My best friend, Aimi! She was at my house! I never called her back! She came looking for me—she's going to be pissed! I have to go! I don't have my phone—"

She was speaking a million miles a minute, patting her pockets and looking around for who even knows what—it was not like she had anything with her. Why did she not have anything with her? Where was her phone—her clothes, for that matter? She had a thousand more questions, but they would have to wait.

"Whoa, wait! Hold up! Does she know? Does your friend know?" Bastien asked.

He'd stepped closer while she was spinning in circles. There were still pine needles in his hair. Syve just stared at him, taking in his frantic expression.

"Yes? I mean...no? Not exactly? I've told her about the dreams before and she was at my house—she's the one that opened the door and let me out. Oh my god, she's going to kill me—I honestly don't remember when she showed up, it's a little...hazy. I guess she could have been there before I," she gestured wildly at herself. "Went all Animorph."

He rubbed both of his eyes with his palms.

"Okay, listen. If she doesn't know you cannot tell her, do you hear me? You have to keep this a secret, no one can know. It's—"

"Yeah, yeah. It's too dangerous. Telling people could get you killed. I got that from the journals. I *really* have to go." She started for the door as Bastien exhaled with a nod. "But what if she already figured it out? I left the journal on my kitchen table for god's sake, she could have read that by now—especially if she's trying to figure out where I am, or what happened to me."

She stopped when she reached the door, looking back at Bastien who still stood in the middle of the tomb with dirty feet and twiggy hair. He rubbed the back of his neck, staring at the floor as if the cracks in the concrete would spell out directions for how he should proceed. The action brought Syve's attention to a large scar running down to his collarbone. Maybe she could ask about it next time.

Next time?

"Well, first things first. I guess we need to get you home, and then damage control," he finally said.

"We?" She raised an eyebrow.

"Well...I figured you had more questions, but I can just give you my number or whatever and we can talk more later. If you want, that is...Can I at least walk you home?"

He was right, she did have more questions. Whether she wanted to discuss them all tonight or not was yet to be determined. Like he said, however, first things first, she needed to go home. She needed to let Aimi know she was okay and apologize for disappearing. It was a rule, she was never allowed to ghost her best friend, and she had broken it.

So, Syve agreed to Bastien walking her home, even though it was literally across the street. It was obvious he was worried about her, though she was still not exactly sure why.

They were silent the entire walk, aside from Bastien apologizing for not having shoes for her and offering her his boots—ones that had apparently been sitting outside the door of the mausoleum. Sure, it was cold, but she had assured him that she was sure she could walk fifty yards bare foot just fine, she would be making a bee-line for her fuzzy socks as soon as she was done groveling to Aimi.

Loud voices reached them as they made their way down the alley.

"What the hell do you mean she's just *gone*? What kind of best friend are you if you don't know where she is?!"

Shit.

"Excuse the fuck out of me! I don't *own* her; I'm not tracking her every move! I. Don't. Know. Where. She. Is! There is *literally* no other reason in the *world* I would *ever* call you otherwise!"

Double shit.

Syve knew if she didn't intervene soon, the probability of Aimi beating Gunther's ass was *incredibly* high.

"Goes both ways, Sugar. We both know I only put up with you for her sake."

Bastien tossed her a curious glance that she ignored. They didn't have time for her to warn him about what they were walking into. Hopefully he could roll with it, but if not? He *was* the one who insisted on walking her home.

Syve took the stairs up to her loft two at a time with Bas hot on her heels, the door was wide open. Aimi and Gunther must have heard her coming, they both turned toward her the second she stepped in the door. Aimi blinked at her for all of five seconds, eyebrows in her hairline, before she closed the gap between them and slapped Syve right across the face. Bastien let out a startled curse behind her, but she herself was not shocked. In fact, she had expected worse.

"You'd better have the best fucking excuse for..." Aimi trailed off as she took in Syve's appearance before doing a double take over her shoulder at Bastien. "Nice outfit. That adds about seven questions to the ridiculously long list I've made. I hope like hell you have answers for me woman or so help me—" Aimi took a deep breath, let it go and then said, "Spill."

"We're both entirely too sober for this." Syve grimaced, then turned toward Gunther who was now standing next to Bastien.

"Thanks, man, for bringing my girl home."

Syve rolled her eyes and Aimi groaned. *This fucking guy.*

BASTIEN

"GODDAMN!" BASTIEN HISSED.

You could have asked him to name every possible reaction he would have expected her best friend to have and not a single one of those would have been for her to slap Syve across the face. To her credit, Syve barely looked surprised—not surprised that Aimi hit her—no, it seemed she had been expecting more.

What an interesting friendship these two had.

"Sebastian? What the hell are you doing here?" Gunther slipped around Aimi and clapped a hand to Bas' shoulder, squeezing harder than necessary.

Bastien swatted his hand off with a sigh. What was *he* doing here? What the hell was *Gunther* doing here? He was also almost certain that Gunther was calling him the wrong name on purpose at this point. Two could play that game and Bastien was just tired enough to be petty.

"Gunny, weird seeing you here. I was just walking Syve home."

Gunther crossed his arms, lip curling into sneer which he quickly schooled. "Thanks, man, for bringing my girl home."

There was no fucking way.

Bastien felt like someone just dumped a bucket of ice down his back. He always wondered who could possibly be capable of putting up with Gunther, and it never even crossed his mind that person could be *Syve*.

"Your girl?"

"Gunther!" Syve barked. She also had her arms crossed, but she looked pissed. "You need to *stop* telling people that! I am *not* your girl!"

"Come on doll, I don't mean anything by it. It's harmless; don't be so dramatic."

He had the audacity to roll his eyes at her. Maybe Aimi would hit him next. If not, maybe Bas could get away with it...

"Gunther." Syve sighed, pinching the bridge of her nose with her eyes closed. "Please go home. Thank you for helping Aimi—"

"Help?! Help my ass!" Aimi interrupted. A sideways glance from Syve quickly silenced whatever else she was going to say.

"Thank you for helping. I am fine, clearly, and I am home now. Please go."

Syve put her hand on Bastien's arm, gently guiding him further into the loft while using the other hand to flag Gunther out, like he was some unwanted plane and this was the world's smallest runway.

Grumbling the entire way like a petulant child, he allowed Syve to push him out the door where she quickly said good night, before she closed the door in his face. Aimi went as far as to stick her tongue out at him through the window before dropping the shades and Bastien had to bite his tongue to keep from laughing. The humor was short lived when Aimi rounded on him, stalking over to poke a very manicured nail into his chest.

"Now that the asshole is gone—what the hell are you doing with my girl?" Her finger jabbed his chest. "And yes, *my* girl." She pointed to her own chest. "And why,"—back to his chest— "is she..." *poke, poke, poke,* "...wearing," *poke,* "your," *poke, poke, poke,* "clothes?!"

Syve stepped in then. She didn't say anything—just grabbed Aimi by the wrist and gently lowered her arm to her side.

Wonderful. That was all the rescue he was going to get.

He rubbed at his chest, wondering if he'd have a bruise. Aimi was deceptively strong for her size—something he made sure to note for future reference.

"I just...She was...I was—" He stammered, "It was cold?"

Excellent. Real smooth. So intelligent sounding. The urge to slap his palm to his forehead was overwhelming.

"Well? Spit it out, dude. I need to know if I'm spitting in two coffees or just Gunther's from here on out."

That did it. It was so unexpected, and he was too tired to fight it, he laughed.

"I'm sorry, he's just such a dick. The thought of you spitting in his coffee brings me immeasurable joy."

Aimi's eyes narrowed, she seemed to be considering something while Bas tried, and mostly failed, to reign in his giggling.

"I'll be honest though—your coffee is good enough that I would risk it. Especially now knowing that Gunny's coffee would be desecrated as well. Cuz fuck that guy."

Aimi's brows raised in approval.

"Hey, I'm right here and totally capable of explaining myself, thank you." Syve called over Aimi's shoulder. "Let the poor man leave and I'll tell you everything."

"Okay, fine." Aimi relented before turning back to him. "You heard the woman, get out of here before I change my mind."

With that, she ducked around him and began shoving his shoulders toward the door.

"Wait! Wait!" He sputtered, "Syve, can I talk to you first? Just really quick, and then I'll go?"

He hoped that did not come out sounding half as pitiful as he imagined. Syve nodded and stepped out onto the porch with him, pulling the door closed behind her, much to her friend's dismay.

Bastien wasted no time whipping his phone out, unlocking it and shoving it toward her.

"Send yourself a text so you have my number, then you can reach out if you have any questions or anything..."

He ran a hand through his hair, suddenly feeling the same way he had back in eighth grade when he asked Sarah Bernetti to be his date to the school dance. Preposterous! He was offering this woman, who was clearly grieving, some well-deserved answers, not asking her to take her clothes off.

Actually...she would have to take her clothes off for him to help her to some capacity—if he was going to help her master the shifting itself...

"Here."

Bastien blinked a few times, grateful again for Syve's interruption as he pocketed his phone.

"Thank you. For...I don't know exactly what specifically. But thank you anyway." She shrugged.

"Yeah, no, of course. I mean, I want to help...Listen, not to ride your ass or anything, but you really can't tell her *everything*." He emphasized the last word with wide eyes and a sweeping hand motion.

"I understand that, but listen. I know we don't really know each other, but I'm not a complete idiot."

She crossed her arms and pinned him with an incredulous look.

"I'm going to find out what she *already* knows and go from there. Just for the record—if she *has* figured it out already, or if I *choose* to tell her, you don't have to worry. Aimi would literally give up the ghost before doing anything that could hurt me. My secret will be safe with her."

He started to protest and she held a finger up.

"That is what it is anyway, *my* secret. I will respect your boundaries by keeping *your* secret to myself, but you do not get to tell me what to do with *my* secrets."

Bas stared at her for a second, worrying his bottom lip between his teeth.

"You're right. I'm sorry. When we were little, we were always reminded, pretty aggressively, to guard the shifter world with our lives. I need to remember you didn't grow up that way, and even if you had, you're right. I'm not your boss and I don't have any power over what you do. I am sorry."

Syve studied him, clearly taken aback by his apology. Well, obviously, if she was friends with Gunther, she probably wasn't used to men owning up to their faults.

Gunther. How the hell did she know Gunther? Now was not the time to ask, not that he had any right to ask in the first place, but damn if curiosity was not going to kill him.

"I'll text you later? I have more questions, maybe we can get together and you can help me figure this shit out?"

"Of course, I'll help any way I can. I imagine it's overwhelming, it's a pretty big change to literally everything you've ever known." Bastien laughed once then rubbed the back of his neck. "I'm not sure if your...sleepwalking will still be an issue now you consciously know what's happening. If it does and you have *any* control, just be careful? It was way too easy to approach you. Not everyone has good intentions."

"If I have any control of it, I won't go back there."

The haunted look in her eyes agreed. He could not even fathom the pain that place inflicted.

"If I do...if I end up over there again...will you be there?"

Bastien reeled back, blinking at her, questioning whether he heard her correctly. Did she want him there? That was...unexpected.

"Oh, I—yeah, I mean...It has been nice to go for a run every night. It wouldn't be out of my way to swing by and see if you're there...if you wanted?"

Syve smiled. It was a tiny little thing and did nothing to hide the pain in her eyes, but it was beautiful nonetheless.

"If you're in the area. I guess I've grown used to my wolfy companion. Not being alone is oddly comforting." She shrugged one shoulder and looked away from him, turning her head up toward the stars. "I'd better get back in there before Aimi has a coronary," she added, looking back down to him and pointing over her shoulder with her thumb.

"Right, thanks for keeping her from killing me back there. I'll talk to you later."

Syve smiled, waved at him once as he started down the stairs, then she was through the door and gone.

Bastien was certain there was no way the day could get any more chaotic.

"Mama? I'm home!"

Bastien slipped his coat off and hung it on the coat rack.

"Mama?"

He toed off his boots, freezing when he went to nudge them under the bench. There was already a pair of boots there. Men's boots. The hot shower he had been daydreaming about for hours would have to wait. They were not expecting any visitors as far as he knew.

Quickly stepping through the living room, Bas made his way to the kitchen. It didn't matter who was here, Soriah was a creature of habit and that was where she would be. Sure enough, when he stepped through the doorway, there she was.

Soriah was at the stove mixing what could only be her famous cocoa, but what made him stop dead in his tracks was the man sitting at the island stuffing food into his mouth in a way that made it seem like he had not eaten in weeks.

"*Mijo*! You missed dinner, but there should be a little left in the fridge."

Bas grunted an acknowledgement at his mother, watching as their guest wiped his mouth and stood.

"Hey, brother. Long time no see."

Bas met the man with a handshake that turned into a half hug.

"Cyrus. Did they teach a class on showing up unannounced for visits at that fancy school of yours?"

Cyrus Jay Laperle. East coast's wealthiest nepo baby, Soriah's honorary third son, and Desiderio's best friend.

SYVE

AIMI JERKED AWAY FROM the window when Syve slipped back inside, like she was absolutely not peeking through the blinds. The look Syve gave her roughly translated to, 'really?'

"No, you don't look at me like that! You!" She pointed at Syve, her opposite hand on her hip. "You didn't show up for coffee this morning for the first time in a *year*. You didn't answer your phone, you didn't open the shop, and when I let myself in you were *gone*, Syve. Do you have *any* idea how fucking worried I was?!" She threw her hands in the air, her voice rising with each word. "I thought something happened to you. I thought…"

She was whispering now and Syve didn't need her to finish. She knew exactly what her friend thought. After Erhard and Noah passed, Syve had been in a really dark place. Aimi was the one who slept over for weeks, forcing her to eat and bathe, to go to therapy and drink water. Aimi was the only one who knew Syve still struggled everyday with the guilt she felt.

Syve hung her head.

"Aimi, I'm so sorry—" When she looked up, Aimi was rushing toward her with tears streaming down her face. Her friend tackled her with a hug so fierce it almost took them both to the ground. "Oh, Aimi." She shushed her friend and smoothed her hair as she hugged her back.

"Shut up. I'm not crying; I'm just detoxing. And if you tell anyone, I'll tell the world about that one time you drank all that vodka and—"

"Okay! Okay, okay! You're not crying! Don't you dare bring that up!" Syve cut her off in a panic and Aimi erupted into a fit of evil giggles.

"For real though, you've got some serious talking to do. But first, go shower. You smell like a wet dog." Aimi scrunched her nose up. "I'll order food—coffee or liquor?"

She was already headed to the kitchen, scrolling on her phone as she went. Syve noticed the room had been cleaned, the only evidence left that she had in fact trashed the place earlier, was the spider-web of cracks across the TV screen.

"How about liquor in the coffee?" Syve suggested.

Aimi let out a string of expletives, agreeing to the request while also mumbling something about needing to call her therapist after this. Syve shook her head and turned to the bathroom. A hot shower sounded euphoric.

Syve spent a solid thirty minutes standing under scalding water, staring at the wall and replaying the day in her mind. If she went to bed right now and woke up to see the same date on her phone, she would not even question for a minute that the entire day had only been a fucked-up dream.

When she finally ambled back into the living room, Aimi had two giant steaming mugs on the coffee table, surrounded by no less than a dozen takeout boxes.

"Did you really order Chinese *and* wings?" she asked, settling into the couch, one leg folded under her and reached for her drink.

One sniff confirmed it had been spiked generously with her favorite bourbon. Well, Erhard's favorite bourbon. Keeping his favorite things around was a habit she never gave up.

"Listen. I stress eat, you know that! I wanted frickles and fried rice. Sue me." She shrugged, shoveling a massive spoonful of rice into her mouth. "I also got us some of that lava cake from that fancy new pastry shop."

Sure enough, two of the boxes were full of fried rice, another two were full of fried pickle chips and there was a clear-topped box with two massive slices of chocolate cake. Aimi had also gotten an order of lo mein, some spring rolls, orange tofu, a side of white rice, a box full of little sugar donuts, a whole order of fries, and a whole order of tater tots shaped like Tetris pieces. Syve did not even hesitate, popping two tater tots in her mouth before grabbing a fork and the box with the cake.

"Bitch, you're already on thin ice, I swear on my Blu-ray box set, if you eat my half of that cake, I will never make coffee for you ever again."

"Better put down the rice then, this is really good."

With that Aimi dove across the couch, snatched half of the cake up in her bare hand and plopped it down unceremoniously in the top half of her half-eaten rice box.

"Now would be a good time to start talking, b-t-dubs," Aimi chided as she licked chocolate frosting off her hand.

Syve told her about how she had stayed up late reading her mother's journal and how she had finally started getting into the old family history. She told her she had not slept, choosing to binge read instead and that was why she had neglected to show up for coffee.

"Awesome, now I know what you were doing up until you disappeared on me. Now is where you're supposed to tell me you figured out the family secret, freaked out, turned into an animal, destroyed your house and then, when I let you outside, you went AWOL for seven hours only to return with Butcher Boy—oh! And you were *wearing his clothes*."

Aimi, having finally removed all the cake from her fingers, picked back up her rice and began eating again like she did not just drop an absolute bomb. Syve gaped at her for a solid minute before responding.

"I literally told him you were entirely too smart, and way too damn nosy to not have figured it out," she finally said.

Aimi laughed, grinning around a mouthful of rice.

"The notebook was lying open on the kitchen table—it was like you wanted me to read it! What if you left a note for me? Whatever, you know I can't help myself." She gestured dismissively with her fork.

"So...why are you not freaking the fuck out right now? Oh, and don't think you can distract me with this inter-rogation like I'm not going to ask why the hell you called *Gunther,*" Syve said incredulously.

Aimi groaned, ran a hand down her face and slumped back into the cushions.

"Before I figured it out, I was freaked out and assumed if anyone knew where you were, it would be your weird ass stalker cousin-in-law." Aimi sat back up and turned her whole body toward Syve. "As for why I'm not freaking out now? I totally am, you just missed most of it...and I'm hun-gry...and still trying to decide if that brownie I ate this morn-ing was Toni's, not mine, and I'm actually just high as fuck right now."

"Christ, Aimi." Syve shook her head, though she was not truly surprised by any of this. "Okay then. I guess I can start with the fact that those weird ass repeating dreams were not really dreams?"

Aimi nodded, mouth full of fries while her eyes gave her a look that clearly translated to, 'duh.'

Syve took a long drink of her coffee before continuing, "Right, so I don't exactly understand all of it yet, but I guess strong emotions can be a trigger. I kind of had a little panic attack after reading that last journal entry and then...okay, so that part is actually a little fuzzy to me too. I do remember you showing up though. When you opened the door, I ran into the woods."

Syve paused, how the hell was she supposed to explain everything else without *explaining everything else*? She hated keeping secrets from her best friend—truth be told, she had *never* kept a secret from Aimi for as long as they had been best friends.

"And?" Aimi pushed. "Where does the hottie with the sweat suit fit into all of this?"

She narrowed her eyes, searching Syve's face for answers. Syve just stared back, still silently debating how to proceed. She'd promised not to spill the beans about Bastien being a shifter, but while the thought of going back on her word made her want to vomit, the thought of lying to Aimi was infinitely worse.

What if Aimi figured it out on her own? Bastien would just have to understand.

"I guess he saw me before I made it to the tree line." She shrugged. "He found me pacing—do deer pace? Is that a thing?"

"Focus, woman! You're saying he saw a deer running through town and just, what, followed it?"

"Yeah, pretty much." Syve took a deep breath. "He had good reason to believe I was the same deer he had previously seen sulking around the cemetery."

"You are being so cryptic right now." Aimi deadpanned. "What are you trying to say? Or *not* to say?" She tilted her head in suspicion. "Are you saying he's seen you, or deer you—Syve!" She sat up suddenly, her voice raising three whole octaves when she shouted her name. "Are you shitting me right now? Are you trying to not tell me that Butcher Boy is—" Syve waved her hands frantically in front of her friend, shushing her and looking around like someone was going to be there listening in.

"Is he the dog?!" Aimi whisper-shouted around Syve's hand.

"Wolf," Syve corrected.

"Wolf, right, yes, that makes such a difference," Aimi responded sarcastically. "Am I following you right?"

Syve nodded, reaching for the fried pickles.

Aimi slapped her hand. "Oh, hell no. You don't get any of those until I know the rest of the story."

Syve sighed.

"He found me pacing and tried to talk to me. I think he was trying to convince me I could trust him or something, so he straight up dropped his pants and went wolfy right in front of me."

"Oh my god, he *New Mooned* you!"

Aimi screeched, slapping her hands to her cheeks. This woman and her unhealthy *Twilight* obsession. Syve ignored the outburst and continued.

"I don't think he put a lot of thought into the action though, because obviously it freaked me out more."

"Right, fucking magic and shit."

"Not to mention wolves are historically known to *eat* deer," Syve added. "Anyway, my fight or flight reflexes kicked in, and I bailed. So, he chased me down, all the way out to the lake, and then tackled me—fucking *tackled* me! Knocked my ass out. I woke up buck naked in the mausoleum. He had carried me the entire way back. I don't know why he had clothes and food there—I forgot to ask that—but my options were: throw-blanket toga, or monochrome sweatsuit."

Now it was Aimi's turn to look dumbfounded. That was a first, Syve could not remember ever having seen her friend speechless.

They spent the next two hours annihilating the table full of food, Syve taking all of the questions Aimi asked and adding them to the list of things she would have to ask Bastien while Aimi made as many movie references as she could. When Syve started to nod off, Aimi gave her a bone crushing hug, demanded she promise to answer her phone and said she would see her in the morning for coffee, no excuses. Syve agreed while dragging herself off the couch. She hollered over her shoulder for Aimi to lock the door behind her and she dragged her feet down the hall to her room.

As she passed the bathroom door she glanced over, noting Bastien's clothes on the floor where she had left them to shower. Sleepily she gathered them up, backtracked to the laundry room and dumped them in. The least she could do was wash them before returning them. When she finally fell into bed, she fell asleep immediately.

She did not dream.

BASTIEN

IF HE WAS A lesser man he would have called in sick. After coming home and finding Cyrus in his kitchen, Bastien had gotten next to no sleep. His brother's old roommate talked his ear off long after Soriah had gone to bed, explaining how he was visiting Timberfall for a business trip with the interest of possibly relocating. Apparently, he'd had enough of the East Coast and was looking for 'new stomping grounds.' By the time Bastien finally convinced the man to call it a night, it was already after three in the morning.

Bas wanted to keep his word to Syve, to go sit with her again, but it was late enough that she would have returned home and he was too tired to even think about shifting. He barely managed to slip out of his jeans before face planting horizontally across his queen-sized bed.

Calling out to catch up on sleep sounded heavenly, but after he'd gotten Syve back to the mausoleum the day before, he had called Hal and requested to take the rest of the day to "get his shit together." He couldn't justify taking another day off, so when his alarm went off at 6:30am, he rolled out of bed and begrudgingly began his day.

An hour after his feet initially hit the floor, Bastien was walking down the sidewalk to The Glass Half Full. He'd almost considered skipping the coffee shop in favor of Hal's worn-out Keurig, just so he could avoid an awkward confrontation with the town's favorite barista. Alas, there was not a drip coffee on Earth that would keep him on his feet after only three hours of sleep, so awkward confrontation it was.

Luck seemed to be on his side when he lumbered into the cafe amidst the busy morning rush. His order was taken by the only other employee he'd ever seen behind the counter, Toni, according to her name tag, who smelt like Woodstock but couldn't be a day over twenty. When he caught Aimi's eye as he was collecting his order, she let him know she was watching him, pointing two fingers at her eyes and then pointing them at him.

Message received, loud and clear. He smiled back nervously and shot her a two-finger salute.

Bastien's mood improved when he got to work and re-membered it was processing day. It didn't matter how ex-hausted he was, processing day was still his favorite.

When he slid into Hal's office, making a show of present-ing the man with a freshly procured Elvis—because nothing says "sorry I bailed on you yesterday" like peanut butter and banana—he was met with a warm laugh and Hal rustling his hair before they set out for the carving room.

When they broke for lunch Bastien checked his phone and found six messages from Syve which he hastily replied to.

Syve:

Hey, can you come over tonight?

I mean, do you want to come over tonight?

To talk or whatever, in case that wasn't clear

Because I didn't specify

Let me try that again

Hey, I don't have anything going on tonight, if you're free would you want to come over so we could talk more?

> Bas:
>
> That works for me, sorry it took so long to reply, it's been a busy morning. I can walk over after work?

> Syve:
>
> Yeah, of course. I'll leave the front door unlocked; I've got this project I really need to work on so I'll be downstairs.

> Bas:
>
> Okay, cool. See you around six-ish

> Syve:
>
> Six-ish is great

Bastien looked at his watch, 1:00 p.m. Great, he only needed to stay focused for another five hours. Just as he was going to slip his phone back in his pocket it lit up with a call. Cyrus. He groaned, rolled his neck, then answered.

"Yeah."

"Damn, you're just a ball of fucking sunshine, aren't you?" Bas could hear his smile through the phone.

"Just busy, Cy. I'm assuming you need something?"

"Yeah, north, south, east, or west?"

Bastien blinked a few times before asking, "What?"

"I'm feeling pent up, gotta burn off some energy. Which way would you go?"

Understanding registered.

"Doesn't matter around here, really. I usually go west. Just be careful if you go south, lots of tourists with cameras. The entire town is surrounded by National Forest, so it's mostly safe."

Cyrus grunted an acknowledgment on the other end of the line.

"Oh, and Cy?"

With the most mocking tone he could have possibly mustered, Cyrus said, "Eyes up, watch your back, don't be stupid, stay out of the open—" then his tone changed, suddenly serious. "I know." And then he abruptly hung up.

Bastien sighed and pocketed his phone.

Of course he knew.

Without exposing their secret to the world, there was no way they could have told any non-shifter that Dez had been murdered, since he had been shot in wolf form. But, if there was anyone in the world who could understand the pain it caused the Yerovi's, it was Cyrus.

Cyrus, who had been Dez' roommate since freshman year of college.

Cyrus, who paid for an entire kitchen renovation for Mama for her birthday.

Cyrus, who never forgot to send a present for every single one of Delanira's birthdays.

Cyrus understood because he *knew* and he knew, because he came from an ancient line of bear shifters—he was one of them.

Bastien physically ran out the door after closing up, not slowing until he turned the corner and put Sew It Seams in his sights.

Silently, the door pushed open, surprising him. He expected a bell of some kind. He eased the door shut behind him and stuffed his hands in his pockets, taking a moment to catalog the business.

Multicolored walls with black and white photos hung all about and in the center of the room sat possibly the single largest worktable he had ever seen.

It was not until his second pass over the massive island and the mountains of fabric it held, that he even noticed Syve. She was hunched over at the far end, barely visible amongst the neatly folded piles, auburn hair amassed in a haphazard blob on top her head which was ducked low, putting her at eye level with her hands as she deftly stuck pin after pin into what looked to be a small jacket.

This was a side of her he had not yet seen—having only seen her previously in some level of distress. What he saw now was a woman consumed with her craft and she was, without question, breathtaking.

The thought was so sudden it sent him staggering back a step. He had not been so blind as to miss her allure from the first moment he had seen her that day at The Glass, but he'd been so focused on the grief she wore—so thick you could feel its caress just by standing close—he hadn't taken the time to reflect on it.

Syve stuck one more pin into her work with a flourish and sank back into her chair, an accomplished sigh slipping from her lips.

He chose that moment to break the silence.

"What are you working on, Bambi?"

She startled violently, cursing.

"Dammit all, Bastien! You scared the hell out of me!" She groaned, stretching as she stood and setting her work down on the counter in front of her. "Do that again and you'll be getting one of those bell collars they put on cats!"

Bas raised his eyebrows. "You want to put a collar on me? That's a little forward, don't you think?"

Syve gaped at him, cheeks flushing.

He let her flounder a second longer before saying, "Relax, Bambi, it was a joke. What are you working on?"

After she recovered, she responded, "Oh, just some stuff. I won't bore you with it—"

He cut her off. "It's not a bore to me. Besides, I did ask."

With a shrug he stepped closer. It bothered him that she was so quick to dismiss something she was so passionate about.

"Well...if you insist." She eyed him then, no doubt trying to determine if he was being sincere. "You can hang your coat on the rack there, unless you're cold." She pointed just over his shoulder. "I've been keeping it a little chilly in here out of spite and I guess I've gotten used to it."

Eyebrow raised he asked, "You've been keeping it cold...out of spite? For who? Your heater?"

She flinched, recovering so quickly he almost missed it. Odd. He would need to circle back to that later.

"It's kind of a long story, actually. Anyway, come over here if you're serious and I'll show you what I've got going on. I'm really proud of this one."

Again, she abruptly changed the subject. She was good at that. He let it be, choosing instead to relinquish his jacket to the rack before making his way over to her.

Upon closer inspection he was able to make out several articles of clothing in various states of repair—or, assembly, he supposed. In the center of the island was a pair of pants, beside it a dress, clearly meant for a child, and what was possibly the bones of a loose-fitting shirt.

"All of these pieces are part of a clothing line I designed myself a few years ago." She gestured an arm over the collection. "Aimi—my best friend, the one you met—she found out about this grant the state is offering. If I can convince them I'm worth it, the money and support could help me launch this line. It would be huge. I could really use it to keep the shop open and honestly...I've been dreaming of being a household brand." She looked wistful.

"How long do you have to apply?"

"I already applied, but I have to submit a final business plan and give a presentation in August."

"That seems like plenty of time to get everything finished?"

"Oh, absolutely. It helps that I was able to start on the pieces right away. I already had an entire book worth of designs. The hardest part was narrowing it down to only ten pieces to present." She smiled then, a true smile, brilliant and disarming.

"Incredible," he breathed.

She nodded, agreeing while looking over her work, but he was not referring to the clothing at all.

"Well, I can pick this back up tomorrow. I figured I could pluck away at it while I waited for you. I just need to close up and we can head upstairs—if that's okay with you? We can absolutely stay down here if not. I don't want you to feel uncomfortable or anything, but also, I'm just inviting you to the better couch, not my bed..."

His lips quirked up to one side as he dropped his head down, looking up at her through his lashes.

"I'm rambling again, aren't I?"

Bas chuckled as she puffed her flushed cheeks full of air, nodding sharply and stepping past him. He was almost certain he heard her mumbling something about sounding like an idiot as she closed the blinds and locked the door, the latter seeming to require a bit of effort.

"I'm locking this so no one just wanders in, I promise I'm not like, locking you in for nefarious..."

He waved her off, chuckling again.

"Honestly, Bambi, I don't think I would mind if you were."

She scoffed, or maybe it was a laugh, and leveled him with a look which led him to believe she thought he was joking. Only, he was pretty sure he was not.

"Is that going to be a thing now?" she asked.

"What?"

"Bambi?"

"Why? Do you hate it?" He searched her face, if she really didn't like the nickname, he would immediately forget it ever existed.

She grumbled something he wasn't able to catch before she answered aloud, "I wouldn't say I *hate* it. It's just a bit..." She cringed and tapped a finger to her nose. "On the nose, don't you think?"

He laughed again, something he found she was getting him to do often.

"What? Because you're both small and cute?"

Another scoff. No, he was almost certain now it was just an awkward, surprised laugh. Why did he find that endearing?

She started toward him. "Okay, all done. We can go up now."

Bas turned to the side, gesturing with a sweeping motion for her to lead the way.

The stairs were tucked in the back corner; he had truly overlooked them at first. The stairwell was narrow, his elbows almost reaching either side as he walked with his hands in his pockets. At the top was a simple door, as much as you could call a door covered in little blue flowers simple.

Syve paused with a hand on the doorknob and glanced over her shoulder. "My other best friend, Cameron. She paints." She shrugged a shoulder, then turned back and opened the door.

Following at her heel, Bastien stepped into a small laundry room; the space was just large enough for a washer and dryer on one wall with a small open cabinet housing her detergent and what looked like extra linens.

He hesitated when he came toe to toe with a pair of worn boots that were at least five sizes too big to be Syve's, the amount of dust gathered across the laces a testament of their importance to that particular square tile. He gingerly stepped around the footwear-shrine, intending to ask Syve about them later. But, when he looked up, his eyes caught on a canvas hanging on the wall beside her. It was similar to the ones downstairs, but this one was in full color.

Bastien felt as if the rug had been jerked out from under him.

SYVE

SYVE STEPPED INTO THE loft, then to the side to allow Bastien to enter. She closed the door behind him, watching as he studied Erhard's boots before deftly stepping around them. Once he was securely past, he turned toward her, and Syve gasped as his legs seemed to give out beneath him. He barely managed to catch himself against the washer, turning his face immediately toward the ground and covering his face with his free hand.

"Bastien?" She rushed to his side. "Are you okay?"

Worried, she placed a hand on his shoulder, ducking her head so she could see his face. He was taking slow deliberate breaths. Syve looked up, trying to figure out what had happened.

Then, she saw the massive thirty-six-inch canvas and deflated. Daily, literally daily, she saw the picture. She was so used to it, she didn't even think about it anymore.

It was one of Erhard's favorites—a beautiful span of trees and one ethereal, black wolf standing just inside the tree line. The wolf's body blended in with the shadows in a haunting way while its bright, copper eyes all but bore into your soul.

Oh. Now she understood.

"Who is that?" Syve whispered.

Bas took a shuddering breath before muttering, "Brother. It's my brother."

Brother? She thought hard to remember their previous conversation.

"I thought you had a sister?" The question was soft, intending to cure her confusion without distressing him any further.

"I do have a sister, but I also *had* a brother. A twin."

Had. That awful, horrid word she knew too well. He dropped his hand and finally raised his head, looking anywhere but at her or the photo. She reached out and smoothed the hair out of his eyes, not realizing she was doing it until he stilled, slowly turning his head to look at her.

Fingers still pressed to his temple she spoke softly. "I'm so sorry, Bastien."

His throat bobbed and they remained transfixed on each other.

In her periphery, the sight of twisted, faded black ink coiling around her finger registered—and she dropped her hand as if burned. "I don't really want to talk about him," he croaked out, as he straightened himself and faced the dryer.

She supposed she could understand that.

"But…" He cleared his throat. "Where? Where did you get this?" How the tables had turned.

"My husband—" She curled her lips between her teeth, noticing as his eyes grew wide, "My husband is, or rather, *was* a photographer."

She exhaled a shaky breath, one side of her mouth pulling up into a forced smile for half a second.

Bastien's shocked expression immediately morphed to one she was all too familiar with seeing.

Pity.

"Syve." Her name came out in a breath.

She *hated* that look—like she was broken. Though she could not argue against it.

"I don't really want to talk about him." She parroted his words then swiftly stepped past him, pulling open the door to the living room. "If you want the picture, it's yours. Living room's right through here."

She left him standing there and made her way to the kitchen, calling over her shoulder as she went, "I have water, wine and coffee. Want anything?"

She almost felt bad about walking away, but it seemed like neither of them wanted to continue that conversation.

"Water would be great, thank you." His answer preceded the soft click of the laundry room door closing.

A few minutes later, they were sitting on either end of the couch, each holding a glass of water.

"I'm sorry about last night, I got caught up with some stuff at home...I didn't mean to stand you up—I said I would be there, and I wasn't. I don't like going back on my word, I swear it won't happen again." Bastien met her gaze with a surprising level of guilt written across his features.

"Oh, no, please. Don't feel bad, you're fine. I honestly...I'm pretty certain I just *slept* last night. I don't think I...you know."

It was weird for her to sleep dreamlessly. Waking up with socks still on her sweaty feet, right where she put them before bed, had been all the proof she needed to know she had never left her bed unawares.

"Really? Bambi, that's great! I mean, I'm glad—you'll be able to sleep better now, I hope. Maybe *knowing* is enough to keep you from sleep-shifting."

She agreed and an awkward silence fell over them.

"So," Syve said as Bas took a drink, "Do I like...need to start planning around full moons now?"

He choked, coughing on the water and a mouthful dribbled down his shirt.

"Sorry," he laughed, wiping his short beard with his hand then drying his hand on his jeans. "I'm not laughing at you, I promise."

"Sure, sounds like it." Syve pouted. "It's not my fault I don't know anything."

She crossed her arms, dejected.

"I'm sorry, I really should have seen that one coming. No, you don't need to worry about lunar interference. All the stereotypes you see in books and movies are mostly false rumors spread by shifters to help keep us hidden. There are a couple books that have a few things right..." He trailed off then shook his head like he was trying to force himself back on track.

"Alright, then I guess I can assume I'm not at risk of turning the entire town into deer by accidentally biting them?"

"Do you usually make a habit out of biting the towns-folk?"

Smart ass.

"Yes, I obviously go around biting everyone I meet as a form of greeting," she deadpanned, and he laughed.

"Just making sure I don't need to watch my back around you."

"You're not worried about your front?"

What the hell was wrong with her? Was she *flirting* with him? Her stomach turned.

He opened his mouth to respond, studied her a moment and then seemed to change his mind. Instead, he set his glass on the coffee table and leaned back, throwing one arm over the back of the couch while the other rested in his lap.

"Can I ask a question now?" he finally said.

She nodded, angling her body toward him and tucking her legs under her.

"How did you and Aimi meet?"

"Oh." The only other person to ever ask her that was E. "We met in college. She's wicked smart—she also got her BA in business, so we had some classes together. She's actually three years younger than me."

Bastien tilted his head to the side, eyes wide, shocked. Not that she could blame him, it had shocked her too.

She had been sitting in her first college class, a month away from her eighteenth birthday, when Aimi had bounced into the room and taken the seat next to her.

"Hi! I'm Aimi, and we're meant to be best friends."

Syve blinked at the literal child sitting next to her.

"Oh—guess I should explain instead of sounding like a complete psycho. You and I are the only two people in the entire class with pigtails. Kismet."

"She seems like a good friend."

"The best. She's my anchor—she's kept me from drifting, on more than one occasion. I can't imagine life without her." She sat up a little straighter. "That reminds me, I obviously talked to Aimi after you left last night…"

Bastien crossed his arms. "I'm not going to like what you say next, am I?"

"Yeah, probably not. She knows everything."

"Everything? As in..." He pointed at himself, then to her and back again. "*Everything*, everything?"

"*Everything*." She grimaced. "I told you she was smart! She's basically a genius and she had most of it figured out before we even got back here."

"How did she figure out my part of it?"

"You don't think it's weird for a dude to randomly chase a deer into the woods and start talking to it? You were acting pretty chill for a dude who just spent the afternoon being waterboarded with the paranormal—and who stashes clothes in an abandoned crypt? She knew about the dreams." She made air quotes. "She did the math—it wasn't exactly calculus. Though, she actually called you a dog."

Syve covered her mouth to hide her smile, while Bastien placed a hand to his chest, feigning offense.

The two continued talking about everything and nothing in particular, stopping just long enough for Syve to order take out—explaining her kitchen was basically just for show because she was an *awful* cook.

When Syve started yawning, Bastien glanced at his watch and winced.

"It's one in the morning."

Yawning again she nodded. "That explains why I'm fighting for my life to stay awake over here." She rubbed her eyes with her palms.

"I should go. You should get some sleep."

Syve hummed in agreement, and he stood up. "I'll...talk to you later?"

Syve yawned yet again, wanting to walk him to the door but lacking the energy to extract herself from the cushions. "Later, yes."

He smiled at her and bid her goodnight. Fumbling with the doorknob, he slipped out into the early morning air and pulled the door closed with a soft click. He'd made sure it was locked behind him.

She marveled at how considerate the action was, nuzzling deeper into the couch before sleep finally took her.

BASTIEN

Bas watched through the windows as Cyrus jogged across the street toward him. He rolled his eyes, rubbing the back of his neck with a yawn. There was not an ounce of regret in his body for having stayed up so late with Syve, but he was running too many consecutive days with no sleep and the accumulated deficit was starting to take its toll. Thankfully, he only had a few hours left of work, then he could go home and straight to bed.

It was girl's night, so Syve would be spending the evening with Aimi and Cameron—he could silence his phone and sleep for twelve straight hours, guilt free. She texted him that morning to make sure he had gotten home alright, apologizing for not asking sooner because she'd fallen asleep on the couch as soon as he had left. She also said she was certain she didn't shift in her sleep again. That had to be a good thing.

The cowbell jingled as Cyrus stomped into the storefront with a face-splitting grin.

"Hey, Pup!"

"You're insufferable. What are you doing here?" Bastien gave Cyrus a once over, squinting before asking, "Are you—is that *coffee*? Why are you covered in coffee?"

"You've been holding out on me with this town, brother. I just met the most fascinating woman—and yeah, it's coffee. She dumped two whole cups on me."

He looked entirely too proud of that fact, grinning like a mad cat.

"Why are you smiling about that?! Where were you?"

"That coffee shop across the street—" He pointed his thumb over his shoulder. "That barista, she's so damn feisty, can't be taller than here." He held his hand up to his chest. "And she's got this hair that makes me wanna hide my dog."

Bastien cut him off, "First of all, you don't have a dog." Cyrus made a tsk sound and waved him off. "Secondly, what the hell did you do to provoke Aimi?"

"Aimi?" Cyrus hummed. "I didn't manage to catch her name, thanks." He winked.

"Cyrus," Bastien scolded.

"It's nothing, really, I was just helping out." He shrugged.

Bastien tilted his head to the side, calling him on the obvious lie.

"I was! She might not have asked for it, but I was more than happy to deliver." Cyrus waggled his eyebrows then, with a devious grin he said, "I can't wait to go back tomorrow."

"If she even lets you in." When the look on Cyrus' face indicated confusion Bas elaborated, "Cyrus, she's the fucking *owner* of that coffee shop."

"Well, fuck. No wonder she was so pissed."

Bastien made a gesture widely interpreted as 'no shit'.

"God, that makes her so much hotter, gotta love a woman in charge." He gave a mock chef's kiss.

"Jesus, Cyrus."

Bastien shook his head, he was far too sleep deprived and under-caffeinated for Cyrus being...well, Cyrus.

Hal strode in from the back then, asking Bas about a bulk pick up order they'd been prepping that morning. He stopped mid-sentence when he saw Cyrus who had turned back toward the door, looking out with both hands on the glass like a child searching for Santa. Eyebrows raised, Hal looked between the two men.

"All good out here?"

"Yeah, Boss. This is Cyrus. He's an old family friend. Cy, quit being a creep and come here."

When Cyrus peeled himself away from the glass and dragged his feet over, Bas continued.

"Cy, this is Hal. He owns the place."

"Hopefully not for long," Hal corrected, reaching out to shake Cyrus' hand.

"If you don't mind my asking, sir, what do you mean not for long?" Cyrus asked as he shook the man's hand, shooting a glance over to Bas, who slapped a palm to his forehead and sighed loudly.

"I'm trying to convince this knucklehead here to buy me out so I can retire and spend all my time spoiling my old lady. Awful hard sell though, maybe you can help me wear him down." Hal chuckled and stuffed his hands into his pockets, rocking back onto his heels before turning back toward his office. "Nice to meet you, son. Bas, take a look at this before you head home, would you?"

"You too, sir." Cyrus called back at the same time Bas said, "Yes sir."

They watched until Hal turned out of sight, then Cyrus turned fully to face Bastien.

"He wants you to buy him out?"

Bas rolled his eyes and nodded. "Yes, he does. Now drop it."

"I think you should." Bas barked a laugh and Cyrus responded, "What? You think Mama hasn't told me about how much you love this job?"

At that Bastien's face fell.

"I can't afford to buy him out, so drop it." Agitation flooded his words.

"That's an awfully bold lie." Cyrus squared his stance and crossed his arms. "Try again."

"What the hell are you talking about?"

"I know damn good and well what you can afford, Bastien." Cyrus' tone hardened.

Bas glared at him. "Why don't you mind your own business, Cyrus. I don't know what you *think* you know—"

"Who the fuck do you think gave him the idea?" Cy unfolded his arms to point at Bas, who flinched. "Who do you think sat down with him and made sure nothing was overlooked?" His voice raised, words coming out angry.

Speechless, Bastien stared at the floor.

"I was twenty years old—" he seethed, just above a whisper. "I watched animal control take down a bear that had been caught, 'wandering' through town." He emphasized his words with air quotes. "They made the call, right there on the spot—said a bear found in town would always come back and that made it a threat to the people. They shot her while her mother screamed from behind the tape line."

Bas looked up in horror and the look of anguish he found made his stomach turn. He opened his mouth to speak, but nothing came out.

"You never truly know when your ticket will be punched. I told *him* that. I know Dez left you every goddamn thing he owned because *I told him to,*" he growled.

"I—I can't—"

"Don't be fucking stupid. You can. Get over yourself." Cyrus clapped Bas on the shoulder before turning to leave the shop. "Oh, and Bastien?" He called from the doorway, "Happy Birthday."

Then he was gone.

It may have been the anniversary of the day he entered the world, but it was not his birthday. That died with Dez.

Syve

Aimi thought she was really funny for cueing up New Moon the second she stepped into the loft. She kind of was. The two women were curled up on the couch waiting with the movie on the title screen when Cam came running up the stairs.

"I'm here, I'm here! Tyler stopped for a drink on the way home because he forgot it was girl's night. I literally had to call him a million times before he even fucking answered his phone—he's out of his mind if he thinks he's sleeping anywhere other than the couch tonight." She rapidly fired off, still slightly out of breath from the stairs.

"Girl. I'm going to say this again, because I have to. Tyler is a piece of shit. If he doesn't pull his head out of his ass, you and the kids can just move in with me and he can suck eggs."

Aimi fumed. This was not the first occasion Cameron's husband had forgotten something important in favor of going to the bar with his coworkers.

"I love you, and if he decides being married to his job is more important than being married to me, I will kick his ass out and you can move into the spare room. Then no one has to live in that tiny ass studio apartment of yours," Cam promised.

"Hear, hear!" Syve added.

'Studio apartment' was rather generous for the glorified closet above The Glass.

"Oh! Okay, so as much as I would love to sit and talk shit about Tyler all night, because I would, I've got a tale to tell."

Aimi clapped out the last words and sat up taller, crossing her legs under her. Syve and Cam both grabbed a bowl off the table, immediately shoveling their chosen snack into their mouths as they settled in for 'Story Time with Aimi'.

"You guys know how busy the three o'clock rush is, right?" She waited a second for acknowledgement before continuing. "So...Toni and I are slogging through it, when we run out of cup sleeves—I don't even know how that happened, but it did. So, Toni runs back into the storage closet to grab more, but it takes like, God only knows why, fifteen whole minutes. The *second* she walks away, I hear the chime ring and this guy walks in. I'm mad already, because he is disgustingly attractive. Seriously, tattoo's, piercings, man bun and he is *huge*—like someone plucked this man right out of my wet dreams."

Cam started choking on her pretzels.

"I'm not even kidding! So, anyway, he gets in line. I make two whole drinks before this man just *jumps over the counter* and starts man-handling my espresso machine." She eyes Syve and Cam, to make sure they are listening.

"I'm just standing there like...what in the actual fuck, right? So, I say to him, 'Excuse me, can you not?' Because what the hell else do you say? And I'm not even kidding you, this man—" She paused, inhaled and exhaled quickly, closing her eyes and held up a hand. "This. Man. He says to me, 'I'm not waiting four years for a mediocre cup of coffee, Daisy. You should tell your boss to hire more help.'"

"No! What?!" Cam screeched.

"You didn't call for bail money, so you obviously didn't throat punch him," Syve added.

"I was so dumbfounded, I just stared at him like a fucking idiot. So, then he says, 'I can show you how to make a real coffee—I bet your boss would thank me.' I can't make this shit up."

Cameron was gasping along with the story, hanging on Aimi's every word. Syve could not keep from shaking her head at her friend's animated retelling.

"So, what *did* you do?" Cam probed.

"Well. I was holding a cup in my hand, just about to hand it over to Jasper, one of my regulars, and instead, I walked over to this guy and dumped it on him."

Cam burst out laughing again.

"No, you did not!" Syve was pretty sure there were tears in Cam's eyes now.

"I fucking did! But this man is undoubtedly a whole-ass foot taller than me, so the best I could manage was to splash it on him." She rolled her eyes.

"Did he bail with his tail between his legs?" Cam asked between giggles.

"Oh, no. No, it gets better—worse? Whatever, now I'm triple mad, because what a fucking *waste* of espresso that was, and this *fucking man*!" Aimi squealed. "He wiped the coffee off his face, says, 'God, you're hot when you're mad,' and fucking *sucked the coffee off his fingers*."

Cameron made an animalistic sound and fell off the couch. Syve put a hand over her mouth in shock, she'd never heard of *anyone* giving Aimi such a run for her money.

"I. Can't. Breathe!" Cam cried from the floor.

Aimi continued, speaking a little louder to be heard over Cam's hysterics.

"He did that—*he did that*, and then says, 'You know, that's actually pretty good.'"

There were more squawks from the floor.

"That honestly pissed me off more, so I grabbed the cup out of his hand, the half-made drink he was working on, and threw that on him too." She was beaming. "He wasn't expecting that one. Then I told him to get the fuck out before I kicked his ass." Aimi rolled her eyes again. "He laughed at me, like I was kidding, jumped back over the counter, the cafe door is *literally* right there, but he still jumped over the counter and just *left*! I still don't know what the hell..." She shook her head, now giggling along with Cam.

"And Toni was gone the whole time?" Syve couldn't help but laugh with her friends.

"The whole time! She came back up front and was confused as to why there was coffee all over the damn floor." Aimi shrugged.

"This has literally just made my entire day." Cam sighed, wiping her eyes.

Aimi mocked a bow. "Happy to serve my people."

They were still giggling when Cam's phone chimed from the coffee table. She quickly snatched it up—she was always quick to check messages when she was not with her kids.

She unlocked her phone and quickly read the screen. Cam groaned.

"Of fucking course. Mom just texted me—apparently that dude she's been talking to just invited her on a cruise. Tomorrow. She's supposed to watch Kayla tomorrow so I can take the boys to their baseball day camp!" She visibly melted into herself, shoulders slumping in defeat.

Syve hesitated a minute, knowing what she wanted to do, but not knowing if she could stomach it. Her mouth made the choice before her brain could interfere.

"I'll watch her. I mean, if you want, I can come over and watch her…"

Aimi and Cam both froze and turned to look at her.

Cam thawed first, asking, "Are you sure? Would you? She would love that and I would owe you big time!"

"You don't owe me anything, what are friends for? I love Kayla, I can watch her for you so you can just focus on the boys."

Syve had spent a lot of time around Kayla and the boys—they were a package deal with Cam—but she never volunteered to babysit, and Cam never asked. Not that she could blame her, it was hard to be around kids since the accident and her friends knew that.

Surely one night could not hurt…right?

It was just after four when Syve knocked on the front door of Cameron and Tyler's big yellow house.

"Come in!" Cam hollered, quickly followed by, "Zachary! Do *not* fart in your brother's face! Where are your shoes?"

Syve turned the handle and pushed, quickly jumping back as Bryce, Cam's middle child, bolted out the now open door—his little arms snuggly hugging a pair of shoes that were most certainly not his.

Stepping into the house Syve hollered, "Hey Cam, it's me! How can I help?"

"Hey, girl!" Cam cheered, diving out of one doorway at the end of the hall and into another one across from it. "I've got this handled, unless you've seen a pair of cleats since you walked in?"

Off Cam went, back across the hall and into a third doorway.

Unable to keep from smiling at what looked like a reenactment of Scooby Doo, she answered, "Pretty sure Bryce has them in the front yard."

A groan came in return, then Zach was zipping down the hall and out the still open door.

Cam reemerged a second later with a duffel bag slung over each shoulder, her crossbody hanging around her neck.

"I'm sorry, I'm in such a rush! Can't ever get out of this house when I want to—you know where everything is, Kayla's watching a movie in the den, bedtime starts at 6:30. She'll walk you through her bedtime routine and we should be back around ten. Text me if you need anything! Thank you, love you, bye!"

The last five words came out as one as the door slammed shut.

Syve made her way to the den where, true to Cam's word, she found Kayla sitting in a tiny beanbag in front of the television.

"Hey, baby girl, whatcha watching?"

The little girl turned her head entirely toward her before taking her eyes off of the screen, but as soon as their eyes met, Kayla's big, green eyes doubled in size.

"Annie Sy!"

Curly blonde pigtails bounced as she scrambled out of her seat, running and jumping into Syve's awaiting arms. Syve sighed with a smile and returned the child's hug, holding her tightly and waiting for her to let go first. Her heart warmed and broke, all at once.

She thought of Noah, of how he should be this big now.

Not for the first time she wondered what would have happened had she been home that night. Could she have saved them? Or at least been given the mercy to join them?

With one final, big squeeze, the toddler pulled back.

"Hi!" She smiled up at Syve. "Are you gonna play with me?"

Quickly wiping her eyes before any traitorous tears could make it to her cheeks, Syve nodded.

"I am going to play with you! Do you want to finish your movie? Or do you want to show me all your super cool toys?"

"TOYS!" Kayla squealed, jumping up and down a few times before spinning around and dashing across the room to the stairs, bear crawling her way up. "Come on Annie Sy!"

An hour later, after going over the names of every single stuffed animal the toddler owned, the two found themselves in the kitchen. According to the tiny human it was dinner time, which meant ice cream and noodles.

Syve was certain that was a little bit of a stretch and instead asked if chicken nuggets or mac and cheese would be okay. A short lesson followed in which Syve learned that mac and cheese is actually made with noodles and because of that, it would be okay to have for dinner.

Which was perfect.

Cooking was one thing Syve had *never* been able to do. In fact, she failed a culinary class in high school after she attempted to boil water but forgot about the water, which led to the pot running dry and burning the bottom. The pot was ruined and so was her grade.

Luckily, there was a fantastic vegetarian restaurant in town that just so happened to make the best mac and cheese to ever exist, and they delivered. Syve set her charge up with crayons and a stack of coloring books before pulling her phone out to call in an order for an obscene amount of pasta.

"I'm sorry, we've had two people call out today—we're too short staffed and can't fulfill any delivery orders right now. If you'd like we can do a pick-up order?"

A chaotic cacophony in the background forced the girl on the other end of the line to need to yell to be heard.

"Oh, no, thank you. I wouldn't be able to pick up the order."

"Sorry again, have a good night."

Click.

Now what was she supposed to do?

Her phone lit up with a text from Bastien—they'd been texting off and on all day. She swiped open to a picture of him holding four baby ducks in his cupped hands.

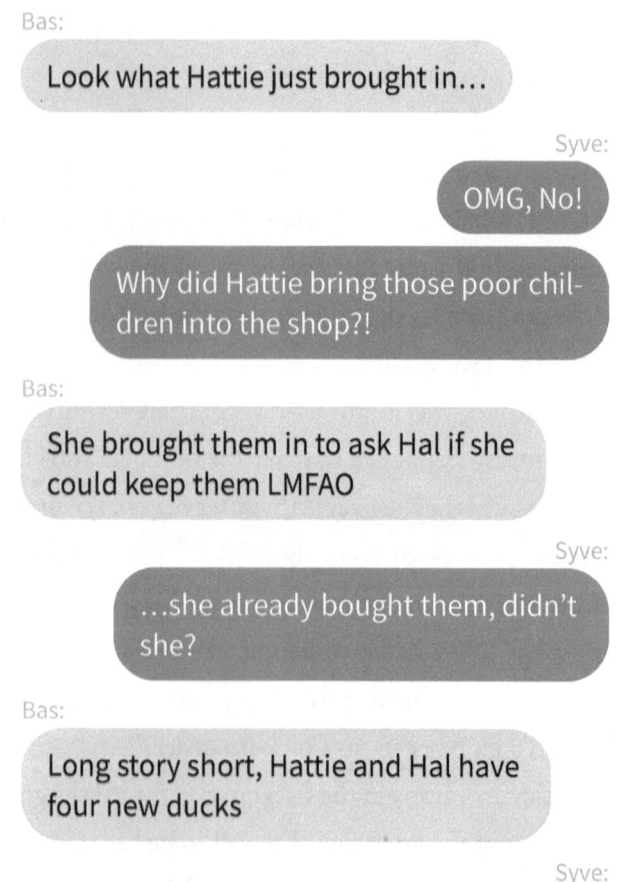

Bas:

Look what Hattie just brought in...

Syve:

OMG, No!

Why did Hattie bring those poor children into the shop?!

Bas:

She brought them in to ask Hal if she could keep them LMFAO

Syve:

...she already bought them, didn't she?

Bas:

Long story short, Hattie and Hal have four new ducks

Syve:

ROFL

She scrolled back up to the picture, saved it and set it as Bastien's photo ID.

Bas:

So, what are you up to tonight?

Syve:

Wallowing.

What about you? Anything fun planned for after work?

Bas:

Why wallowing? What happened? I'm just supposed to go home and play host for a family friend.

Syve:

Thyme to Eat can't do deliveries tonight

It's basically a national emergency.

I'm crushed and I'm about to severely disappoint a toddler

The same toddler I had to spend twenty minutes convincing that mac and cheese was REALLY made with noodles.

Also, yikes. Unless you like to play host-with-the-most?

Bas:

Mac and cheese is made with noodles?! Since when?!

Syve chuckled, eyes fixed on the little dots bouncing at the bottom of the screen—pausing, then starting again.

Bas:

I've seen a disappointed toddler before, they hold grudges forever. I could pretend to be a delivery driver in fifteen minutes…

If you want?

Syve blinked at the screen. Going to Thyme to Eat and then driving all the way across town to get to Cam's just to deliver food was no small favor. Why would he offer to do that?

Bas:

> Don't feel obligated to accept

> I would honestly rather play delivery man over going home though. This family friend really doesn't need to be babysat anyway.

Syve:

> Ah, so it's a "help me, help you to help me" kind of thing?

Bas:

> Pleaseeee, I'll beg on my knees if I have to!

Syve shook her head, smiling and looked around the kitchen. It would not be the end of the world if she had to make a peanut butter sandwich for dinner—actually she loved peanut butter—but Kayla might not agree.

Surely there would be no harm in taking him up on his offer—and he *was* offering; it was entirely his idea.

Relenting, she shot a quick message to Cameron asking if it was okay to have a friend swing by with dinner. Cam immediately replied.

Cam:

Friend?!

That's…suspicious.

Wait! It's that mysterious man Aimi keeps talking about, isn't it?!

You better let that man bring you food, Syve Aislin or I swear!

Kayla sleeps like a rock

Guest room is open…just saying…

Syve:

OMG Cam

Cam proceeded to send a slew of obscene gifs and strings of suggestive emojis to which Syve physically face palmed.

Syve:

Okay.

I'll call in the order, do you want anything? My treat

Bas:

Don't be mad…

I've never eaten there before

Syve:

Excuse me?! I take personal offense to that.

I'll order for you.

I hope you're hungry.

BASTIEN

A SMILE HAD PERMANENTLY glued itself to his face. Bas could not remember the last time he smiled this much. After sneaking home to roll the Jeep out of the driveway so he could start it down the block and avoid having to talk to Cyrus, he drove across town to Thyme to Eat where he had been a little shocked to find three entire bags waiting with his name on them.

He slid out of the Jeep's seat, arms laden with bags of food, and started up the walkway. He had taken advantage of the slowly warming weather and taken the doors off the vehicle, a decision which was now proving to be quite handy.

The door opened as he got closer. Syve was standing in the entry with a little girl on her hip and a genuine smile on her face. Her copper hair was in a messy ponytail—one that looked like it had started at the back of her head but was now well off to the side.

Bas deduced the reasoning for that when the child reached out and latched onto the dangling strands where they hung over Syve's shoulder and began rubbing the hairs between her fingers absently as she stared at him.

He kept walking until he was directly in front of her.

"Hi."

Why did he sound so out of breath?

"Hi."

That smile.

"Hi! Are you mac and cheese man? Annie Sy, is he the mac and cheese man?" the toddler basically hollered, sending Syve into a giggling fit.

"My name is Bas, and I guess, yeah, I'm the mac and cheese man."

He chuckled. Syve looked down at his arms, eyes widening and then jumped back a step to give him room to enter the home.

"Sorry! Come in! I didn't realize I had ordered so much..." Her cheeks reddened and she spun around leading him to the kitchen. He smiled, shaking his head as he followed.

Bas was reclined into the couch cushions, waiting for Syve to come down once Kayla was asleep.

After demolishing some of the best pasta he had ever eaten, though he would never admit that to his mother, the toddler had proclaimed herself 'Kayla the Unicorn Princess' and demanded everyone play castle with her until bath time.

Which they did.

When Syve finally looked around, asking what time it was, it was almost eight.

"Baby girl!" she gasped. "We're late for the underwater ball!"

Both girls ran dramatically to the bathroom.

Twenty minutes later they emerged, Syve nearly soaked through with a sleepy toddler blinking slowly in her arms.

"Nigh-nigh mac and cheese man."

She had mumbled as Bastien backed out of the little girl's room and switched off the light, leaving only the lamp to illuminate the room.

"Goodnight, Unicorn princess," he had whispered back.

Soft footsteps sounded and then Syve appeared in the den.

"Thanks for waiting. She didn't even make it through one whole page of her book before she was out."

She made her way over and sat on the couch, not exactly the opposite end, but not quite next him either.

"She's adorable," he mused and she nodded with a smile. "You're really good with her."

Her smile dulled a fraction, her eyes looking suddenly unfocused.

"I've known her since she was about four months old. As far as she knows, I'm her aunt for real."

Now she was studying her hands in her lap.

"Lack of blood doesn't make you any less her aunt for real." He cocked his head, studying her as if he could figure out all her secrets if he looked hard enough. "Four months old...I guess I just assumed, after all the stories you've told me, that you knew Cameron a lot longer than that. How did you meet?"

Syve shrank into herself, pulling her knees up to hug them to her chest.

Brows furrowed, he replayed everything he'd just said over and over again, failing to see what could have made her shut down.

After a long moment she finally whispered, "Long story short? Kayla is a week younger than my son. She needed a little help and I was capable of doing it, so our midwife connected us."

Son.

Bas flashed back to the first night he had seen her, when he inspected the tombstone after she had left.

Her *son*.

He felt a crushing weight settle over his body, his heart aching from pain that didn't belong to him. How had he not made that connection on his own?

Sitting forward and resting his elbows on his knees he whispered, "How?"

She took a shuddering breath and he immediately regretted his question.

"I'm sorry, don't answer that. That was insensitive," he amended.

Deep inhale in and slow exhale out, then she said, "You already know I lost Erhard, my husband." Her voice broke.

Bastien waited patiently, understanding the amount of effort it would take to tell this story.

Syve cleared her throat.

"Noah...my son."

It was impossible to miss the quiver in her words.

"Both of them—" She sniffled.

He wanted to stop her, to tell her she did not need to continue, then she looked straight at him, unshed tears filling her eyes—she needed to tell their story.

"There was an issue with our heater. We never had it serviced—didn't even know that was a thing. We'd only ever rented before the loft...They said there must have been a crack in the vent or something. We must have had a small carbon monoxide leak for who knows how long and...one day, it just *broke*—split wide open and flooded the house. They couldn't explain why it happened." She shuddered.

"I wasn't home that day. I had gone to Bozeman with Aimi—I just wanted to pick out some fabric. It was really cold that day, the heater would have been running non-stop to keep the apartment warm—they told me it might not have happened so fast if it hadn't been running so much." Tears were freely running down her cheeks. "Routine checks of your furnace are very important, at least once a year, and if you don't have any CO detectors in your house, you should really fix that immediately," she concluded, sniffling and raising her arm to wipe her face with her shoulder.

No wonder she flinched when he joked about her keeping her shop cold out of spite toward her heater—and CO detectors? He could honestly say he had never once even considered whether their house had carbon monoxide detectors. Actually, he couldn't be sure he even knew they existed before that very moment. Well, he was absolutely planning to check for them as soon as he got back home.

It occurred to him that he was silently staring at her.

"Bambi. I am so sorry—I know that doesn't mean anything, but still."

He wanted to scoot over and hold her, to wipe away the tears that were staining her beautiful face.

"Is that why you don't want to talk about your brother? He's gone too, isn't he?"

Bas ran his hands over his face and up onto his head, then sagged back into the couch.

"Yeah. He's gone too." He sighed. "His name was Deside-rio. We shifted and went for a run...there was a poacher. I didn't notice in time."

Syve covered her mouth with her hand, a look of horror in her eyes.

"You were there?"

Leaning to the side, he pulled down his shirt collar, show-ing her the scar that covered the right side of his neck from spine to collar bone.

"I noticed something was off—I saw the glint from the gun...I was too slow. He gave me this trying to get me to leave him."

He froze when he felt her trembling fingers tracing the scar. He hadn't noticed that she had moved close enough to reach him. Without thinking he reached back, covered her hand with his and turned his head just enough to meet her gaze.

They stayed that way, neither moving an inch, until the sound of Syve's phone vibrating on the coffee table made her jerk away before she reached for it.

Groaning, she swiped her phone open and began rapidly typing.

"Sorry, it's Gunther."

She aggressively finished sending her message and then slapped her phone back down on the table.

"I was going to ask the other day; how do you know him? Pardon me for being so blunt, but he's kind of an asshole. He's not exactly the company I would picture you to keep."

Syve scoffed, "Oh, there's no *kind of* about it. He's a raging asshole, but he's family, kinda. I guess that's why I put up with him. He's Erhard's cousin."

"You poor thing."

They both laughed at that.

"But I get it. I told you we had a house guest—it's my brother's best friend. He annoys the hell out of me, but he's basically family too. You know, he said Aimi baptized him in coffee the other day."

"No way!" Disbelief slowing her words. "I can't believe that's who that was!"

The song of their laughter carried on, playing until Cam returned home, and then Bastien drove home, still humming the melody.

SYVE

Six pieces done.

Syve only had four pieces to finish and a presentation to plan. She still had four months until the deadline to submit—she could do this.

Midway through attaching a sleeve to a shirt that she started that morning, her phone rang, the picture of Bastien with the ducklings filling the screen.

"Hello?" She held the phone between her ear and her shoulder and resumed her stitches, running the sewing machine a little slower so she could hear him speaking on the other end.

"Hey, Bambi. I know you're working, but my little sister's prom dress is...broken?"

He paused as there was frantic yelling in the background.

"I'm sorry, not broken, Del accidentally burnt it with her curling iron and she's freaking out. Is there any chance—"

"When does she need to leave the house?"

He repeated the question—she assumed to his sister.

"She needs to 'be walking out of this house at five exactly or my social life is toast'," he quoted dramatically.

"You do know how fragile a teen girl's social life is, right?" Syve chuckled. "Send me your address—I'll leave now and see what I can do."

She heard him repeat this for his sister, who in turn began screaming thank you.

Five minutes later, she had everything shut off and locked up in the shop and was bolting up the stairs to get her truck keys.

Syve dashed through the laundry room, skidded to a halt then walked backward, stopping directly in front of the canvas of Desiderio. She considered it for five whole seconds before she pulled it off the wall and took it with her.

Erhard's Chevy whined its way down the street—no doubt from disuse and poor maintenance. It was bigger than she needed, not that she drove much anyway, but she didn't have the heart to get rid of it.

When practicality said she should get rid of one of the cars, there was no hesitation before she handed over the keys to her hatchback. Changing oil, rotating tires, replacing wiper blades—these were all things she knew had to be done, but Erhard had always taken care of it. Add 'get the truck checked' to her ever-growing list of shit that had to be done.

Syve pulled up in front of Bastien's house, putting the truck into park behind a very expensive-looking white Range Rover. She had just barely stepped out—slamming the driver's door with both arms (because anything less never actually closed it)—when a short-haired teenage girl came barreling out the front door and straight toward her.

"Oh my God, thank you for coming! You're the best, please help me!" she sobbed as she collapsed into Syve's arms.

"Hi! Don't thank me yet—" Syve returned the hug and tucked one of Del's curls behind her ear as she pulled away. "Let's go see what we can do about that dress first, yeah?"

Del nodded violently then snagged Syve's hand and dragged her across the yard and into the house.

Bastien was leaning against a doorframe across from the entryway when they stepped inside, an apologetic look on his face. Syve assumed it was for his sister—until she heard clanging coming from the room behind him.

"*Mijo*! Is that her? Is she here?"

An older woman with perfectly white hair braided down to her waist came around the corner wiping her hands on her black apron. She looked first at Bastien then turned to the door where Syve stood, hand in hand with Del.

"Mama, this is Syve. Syve, this is my mom, Soriah."

Soriah tsked and swatted her son.

"*Mija,* you can call me Mama, like everyone else. Please, come in, come in!"

She mumbled something else in Spanish as she turned and walked back through the doorway she had first appeared from. Bastien pushed off the wall quickly and stepped over to her, gesturing he wanted to help her out of her jacket.

Del let Syve step out of her untied boots before dragging her along after Soriah. The room was separated by a long island; to the left was a plain wooden dining table surrounded by an entire wall of waist high bookshelves, the rest of the wall covered entirely with pictures.

One picture in particular caught Syve's attention, an eight by ten portrait of a family of five—a mother, father, two teen boys and between them a tiny infant girl swathed in pink tulle. Syve stepped closer, immediately distinguishing Bastien from his twin; Bastien looked so much like Soriah, with his sharp chin and silver eyes, while his brother looked so much more like their father with his strong, square jaw and copper eyes.

Syve smiled softly as she wrote the missing Yerovi men's faces to memory, so she could picture them when Bas spoke of them later.

To the right of the island was the kitchen—if you could even call it that. Calling the room a mere kitchen would be like calling the Library of Alexandria a *mere* library. A six burner stove sat beside a double oven, and across from them was one of the largest refrigerators Syve had ever seen. The counters were lined with appliances she couldn't even name, and she'd bet money the door at the far end of the room led to an equally impressive pantry.

"Wow," she breathed.

"Mama likes to cook." Del shrugged like it was no big deal.

"I will make some food; you girls go ahead. I'll put this one to work so he stays out of the way."

Soriah smiled and winked, gesturing to her son who uncrossed his arms, putting his palms up in a clear 'what did I do?'

Syve was barely able to say thank you before Del was, for the third time, dragging her through the house. They had just reached the top of the stairs when a man stepped out in front of them, Del jumped gracefully to the side just in time to miss a collision.

Syve did not.

"Whoa, sugar. Where's the fire?"

One look was enough for her to confirm that the man before her must be the family friend and the asshole that Aimi had mentioned.

"Has to be a fire, cuz damn. You're hot." He winked.

Yep, definitely the asshole.

"Cyrus," Del whined. "Don't be gross! Why don't you go do something helpful? Like...I don't know...go outside or something?"

"Actually," Syve interrupted. "I *could* use your help. I have a box in the back seat of my truck—I need it to fix the dress. Would you be willing to bring it in for me?"

She honestly expected him to scoff and deny her, so she was surprised when he dropped into a dramatic bow and then set off down the stairs two at a time. It was not until she heard the front door close behind him she remembered the canvas that was also occupying her backseat.

"You okay?" Del asked.

"Um, yeah. I just...Bas can handle it, I think. Show me this dress."

Syve hoped Bastien would forgive her for bringing the picture over. She intended to cover it with one of the spare blankets she kept in the backseat and then give Bastien the option to put it in a closet or something. It belonged in his house, not hers.

Del's dress was beautiful. Rich, cobalt blue satin draped to the floor, a stunning mermaid silhouette with one thick strap over her left shoulder. Syve winced, the strap had a very large burn across it, large enough she wondered how the girl had managed to do it without completely burning herself in the process.

"How attached are you to this dress having a strap?"

Del hesitated, "I'm not, but the school dress code for formal dances demands at least one, or I'll have to wear a shawl all night."

Syve rolled her eyes. "Of course they do. Okay. I can fix this; I just need you to trust me."

Del nodded with tears in her eyes.

There was a knock at the door and Syve turned to see Bastien standing in the doorway with her emergency sewing kit in his arms. She opened her mouth to speak, but he beat her to it.

"It's okay, Bambi. Cyrus is having a...moment...but Mama stepped in when she saw it. She just made him hang it up in the kitchen."

He stepped into the room and set the box on the bed next to her.

"Thank you," he added.

"I know you said you didn't want it but—"

Bas shook his head.

"Mama is really happy to have it, and I shouldn't have been so quick to turn you down. It's just...hard."

He didn't need to explain any more, she understood.

"What are you talking about?" Del interjected. "What did Mama hang in the kitchen? Why are you being weird?"

"Don't worry about it, Del, I'll show you later. Aren't you supposed to be getting ready for some dance or something?"

"Some dance?" she screeched.

Bas winked at Syve over his sister's shoulder and slipped out of the room.

Syve was sipping on some of the best hot chocolate she had ever had, sitting with one knee up to her chest on a barstool at the island in Soriah's kitchen.

Bastien was right, Desiderio's wolf form watched from his new spot on the wall next to the probably-a-pantry.

Soriah had pulled her into a rib crushing hug when she had gone back downstairs, thanking her once in Spanish and twice in English. She then insisted on making cocoa, despite Bastien's grumbling. Soriah had leveled a look at him that could surely end wars and he shut his mouth so fast his teeth clicked.

They were alone now. After pouring the cocoa for Syve, his mother had kissed her on the cheek, told her she was always welcome in her home, then left the room—a mug of cocoa in one hand and a worn paperback in the other.

"That was amazing, what you did for Del. Thank you again for coming over." Bas said, rubbing the back of his neck.

Syve thought calling it amazing was being a little generous. All she had done was cut off the burnt strap and replaced it with seven strands of silver ribbon, braiding an inch of each ribbon to the ones next to it to create a honeycomb effect.

Del had been thrilled, and on time. That was all that mattered.

"Happy to help." She smiled and took another sip.

"You wanna go for a run?" Bas blurted.

Syve blinked up at him, then furrowed her brows. "A...run?"

"Yeah." He shrugged one shoulder and looked away. "I haven't been out in a while and I'm feeling a little antsy. I wonder if you might feel the same?"

Her mouth formed an O-shape as it dawned on her. He meant *to go for a run*. As in...

"I—but...*how*? I don't even know how I did it before."

Bastien's eyes lit up. "That's not a no? I can try to walk you through it? It's really not as hard as you think."

She hid her face with her hands for a few seconds then split her fingers to reveal one eye.

"I guess it wouldn't hurt to try. That's probably something I should know how to do, right?"

The words were hardly out of her mouth before he was up and pulling her by the hand. Must be a family trait, to drag people around. Syve giggled as she did her best to keep up with him without tripping.

He led her down the hall to a little mud room with a set of French doors that overlooked an unfenced backyard that faded into the trees.

A perfect yard for a family of shifters.

Bas walked them to the tree line before letting go of her hand.

"I'm not sure how this will work out. You've subconsciously mastered shifting, so your body knows what to do, but your brain doesn't. I'm just going to tell you what I was told when I was little. Just close your eyes, take slow, deep breaths and imagine yourself melting away into a puddle. Relax all of your muscles and then imagine stretching up out of that puddle, *changed*."

Then his shirt was over his head and on the ground before she could blink.

"What are you doing?!" She squeaked.

"Taking my clothes off?"

He sounded genuinely confused, one hand absently scratching his chest—his very well-defined chest, dusted with the perfect amount of chest hair. She vaguely recalled as much from the day he had tackled her, but seeing it when she was not in the middle of a panic attack was...*different*.

"Obviously, I can see that, but *why*?" Syve felt her cheeks growing warmer as she realized she was staring and averted her eyes.

"So...I can...shift?" he spoke slowly, like the answer should be obvious.

She stared blankly at him, blinking a few times with her mouth ajar, but said no more.

"I would really rather not destroy my clothes if I don't have too." With that, Bastien began unbuttoning his jeans.

Syve spun around, putting her back to him. "Right, be-cause that's a thing. I forgot."

That was something that he had mentioned to her already, after she'd woken up naked and freaked out.

"Do you...do you have to watch me? To help me?"

Silence.

"Bas?"

She timidly glanced over her shoulder, but Bastien was gone and in his place was a massive silver wolf. No, he was not gone, she had to remind herself, this *was* Bastien. She turned fully to face him and greedily ran her eyes over his shifted form.

"Your wolf is beautiful," she said excitedly. "Your fur is the exact same color as your eyes!"

He wagged his tail in response, causing her to giggle with glee.

"Can I...?" she asked, shifting her weight from foot to foot and holding her clenched hand against her chest.

He stepped forward, ears forward and head lowered. His tail never stopped wagging as she timidly reached out and sank her fingers into the long fur on top of his head. A content sigh left her as she scratched behind his ears and his eyes drifted shut.

A moment later, Bas pulled away to sit back on his haunches. He jerked his snout up in the air once—it was her turn.

Anticipation gnawed at her insides.

After casting a quick glance over her shoulder, noting the many windows along the back side of the house, she took a few more steps into the woods. A low chuff behind her made her turn, walking backward as she looked.

"I'm not going far, just trying to get a little privacy."

With an exaggerated nod, he turned to face the house. She smiled widely at his back, then side-stepped behind a fairly large tree—not quite big enough to shield her entirely, but it was better than nothing.

Quickly, she slipped out of her clothes, hastily folding them and dropping the pile by her feet. She shivered, it was not exactly a cold day in May, but the light breeze paired with the shade from the canopy of branches left her naked body to collect goosebumps. The violent swirl in her stomach wasn't helping either.

Syve shook her arms out, leaving them to hang by her side, palms out. She rolled her neck from side to side, then with a long exhale she closed her eyes and recalled Bastien's words.

Close your eyes.

Check.

Take slow, deep breaths.

Check.

Imagine yourself melting away into a puddle.

She let her shoulders slump, imagining water trickling from her head, down her neck...over her shoulders...along her arms, until it dripped from her fingertips. She sank into the metaphorical pool gathering at her feet, sinking deeper until only her head remained above the surface. Then she tipped that back, surrendering.

Relax all of your muscles and then imagine stretching up out of that puddle, changed.

Syve pictured herself rising from the water, pulled gently upward by an invisible rope.

She could almost imagine that the ghostly tingling she felt on her limbs was from millions of tiny hairs growing along her body.

That was all Bastien had told her to do, so she opened her eyes.

When the landscape around her came back into focus, she deflated. Nothing looked different, nothing *felt* different.

Playing ice-cube-in-a-sauna was surprisingly peaceful, sure, and she would be keeping that exercise filed away for the next time she was stressed out—but it appeared to be useless for shifting.

She opened her mouth to say just as much to Bas, but jolted when all that came out was a pitiful bleat. She snapped her head down, looking at her legs—legs in the plural sense of four and not two.

Holy shit.

She did it.

What she did not do was account for her new center of balance. Or how operating her animal form was far more difficult now, than when she had been running in primal-flight mode the last time she had seen his wolf. One second, she was counting *hooves* and reveling in her success, the next she was crying out as she went ass over teakettle into the dirt.

BASTIEN

PATIENTLY, HE WAITED WITH his back to the woods. Syve made it clear she did not want him to see her strip, and the least he could do was respect that.

He jumped when he heard, what he could only describe as, one of those toy cans that mooed when you inverted it.

He was still questioning whether or not he was imagining things when he heard the sound again, followed by a loud thud. He risked a glance back toward Syve to find the doe flipped on her back, legs tangled over her body.

If it was possible to laugh in his current form, he would have been in hysterics. Instead, he chuffed and shook his head.

The look in her eyes screamed excitement. Apparently, she was just as impressed as he was that she had gotten the hang of things so quickly.

Bastien trotted over to Syve as she gracelessly flopped onto her stomach, and he stood beside her for support as she stood on shaky legs. She leaned into him for a beat as she found her balance. When he no longer felt her weight, he swung around to stand in front of her. When he caught her attention, he wagged his tail, dropped into a playful bow, and then hopped a few yards away. She seemed to understand his intentions, and after a handful of wobbly steps, she started bounding toward him—looking very much like a drunken rabbit.

The two carried on this way—him chasing her and her chasing him—until Syve pulled ahead and slipped out of sight, bursting past the brush edging the lake. Bastien followed a second behind. When he leapt from the woods, skidding to a stop beside her, he startled a small herd of deer that had been drinking from the crystal water. The lone buck had been approaching Syve—an act that spawned a low growl in Bastien's throat. He scolded himself for the act of possessiveness he had no right to show, let alone feel.

Together, the shifters watched as the does urged their spotted fawns into the trees opposite them, the buck the last to disappear after casting one last perplexed look in Syve's direction.

Once the clearing was theirs alone, Bas watched Syve tip-toe over to a patch of wildflowers—the same flowers that were painted all over the door at her shop. He followed her movements as she ducked her head low, nosing the little blue petals. When she raised her head again, eyes closed as she faced the sun and looking like a giant brown sunflower, he was struck with an idea.

Bas whined to get her attention. When she looked his way, he gestured with a jerk of his head, asking her to follow him.

He led her through the flowers to an odd pile of both living and downed trees. At least four fallen trunks were propped up by one sturdy green pine, creating a natural lean-to that looked just large enough for two people to hide under. Various smaller logs and branches blocked off the opposite side, creating a perfect wall and further adding to its likeness to a tiny shelter.

She watched over his shoulder as he rooted around be-neath one of the logs and pulled a simple brown backpack free. He turned around and dropped the bag on the ground. Hazel eyes followed the pack's movement, then snapped back up to stare at him again. Bas raised his brows, glanced down at the pack, and when she continued to stare at him, he mentally shrugged, then shifted. What else he could possibly do with a backpack without thumbs, he wasn't sure—she had to have realized he was going to shift back.

Oh well.

If she *wanted* to see him, he would let her.

Years of practice lead to a speedy transition and he was now standing right in front of her—very naked. A minor oversight, he realized, was that his human height compared to Syve's deer form left her precisely eye level with his hips. With a startled bleat, she fell back, turning her head up and away.

"Tried to warn you, Bambi." Bas chuckled as he crouched and dug around in the backpack. "I thought you might like to feel the sun on your skin. If you ask me, the fur dulls the warmth." He pulled out a pair of black sweats and quickly pulled them on. "I'm decent. I have a shirt for you too—I'll turn my back so you can shift. It's the same concept as before, just in reverse. Oh, and you should do it under here, just in case."

He stepped out from under the little tree shelter so she could take his place. Most people that went hiking around Timberfall did so south of town, closer to Yellowstone, but there was always a chance someone might be milling around the lake—he knew firsthand.

He shook his head to clear the thought.

Syve turned away from him, facing the rotting logs and he took that as his cue to do the same.

"I won't look, but I'll be right here if you need me," he assured her and settled down in the dirt.

While he waited, he dug out the two shirts he had packed and the second set of sweats, pulling on one shirt and folding the remaining clothes over his shoulder.

A few quiet moments passed with Bastien sitting contentedly, watching the water ripple under the gentle breeze. The gentle touch of her fingers against his shoulder as they wrapped around the clothes startled him, and it took everything he had to keep his eyes forward.

"Awfully convenient stash of clothes you found," her tone was suspicious and mocking.

"After last time, I decided I should be a little more prepared," he teased, lacing his hands behind his head, a cocky smirk taking up residence on his face. "I've hidden a few caches in strategic places. Next time I have to carry you out of the woods, at least I won't freeze my—"

"Okay, okay. First of all, who said there was going to be a next time?" She guffawed. "Secondly...that's a pretty good idea—oh my god, Bastien! You're bleeding!" He felt her grab onto his right arm, one hand at the shoulder, the other on his elbow.

"Bas! You might need stitches! How did you do this?!" she scolded.

Dropping his hands from his head, he twisted his neck to look at the back of his arm, a gash, easily five inches long, ran the length of his bicep.

"Oh, I must have caught it on a rogue branch." He shrugged and she let go. "It's really not that bad; it'll heal pretty quick." He placed his hands on his thighs, rolled forward to stand, then walked to the water where he crouched down and splashed his arm to clean the cut.

"Are you out of your mind? You're using dirty *lake* water to clean that? What if it gets infected?" She sounded close, like she had followed him to the water.

"Nah, it'll heal fast enough—" He pivoted on his toes to face her, and the words died in his throat. Syve was standing there, in nothing but his shirt. The pants she had taken from him were hanging forgotten in one hand.

What was it about seeing a woman in his clothes? Some primal, claiming instinct? At least two sizes too big, the shirt hung nearly off one of her shoulders and down to the top of her thighs.

"Are you trying to tell me that you have super healing or something?" She gestured wildly with her empty hand, and it pulled the shirt higher up her legs.

Bas cleared his throat and stood abruptly, making every effort to keep his eyes on her face while also slipping a hand into his pocket to cover what would be a very embarrassing reaction to her attire.

"I wouldn't call it super. But...accelerated?" He pursed his lips, brows furrowed. "Have you ever noticed—do you heal faster than expected?"

Stepping closer to him she said, "No, probably a downside to only being half..." She gestured vaguely at herself, which he noted from his peripherals because he was still doing his best not to look at her body again.

Especially now she was close enough that he could touch her, if he wanted to.

"I guess so, that's unfortunate. It's one of the better perks if you ask me," he mused.

Suddenly her hands were on his face, pulling him down to look her right in the eyes.

"Are you sure you're okay? You're not just acting tough because I'm here, right?" Her eyes darted back and forth between his, searching for a lie.

"I promise," he murmured, grabbing her wrists and stepping flush against her, "I'm fine and I'll be fine."

Syve sucked in a breath, and he almost regretted acting on impulse—but then she glanced at his lips—there and back, so quickly he could have missed it if he had blinked. Bastien closed the distance and pressed his lips to hers, gently, an invitation she gingerly accepted. When her eyes fluttered shut, his followed suit.

Just as he parted his lips for her, she gasped and jumped back.

"No. No, I'm sorry. I can't, I'm sorry," she stammered, one hand covering her mouth, the other wrapping around her middle.

Shit.

"Syve, it's okay—that's on me. I'm sorry. It's okay, you don't need to apologize." He took a step back, giving her more space. "I'm sorry, I shouldn't have done that. I don't want you to be uncomfortable."

"I just...I'm married? I can't..." She was spiraling; he recognized that.

He diverted. "How did you meet?" When she blinked up at him, perplexed, he amended, "Your husband? How did you meet?"

"Oh." She paused and took a deep breath. "College. We met in college. Erhard was here as an exchange student and he just...never left," she scoffed with a smile. "He called his parents a few weeks after we met and told them he was applying for citizenship so that he could stay here with his future wife. We weren't even dating then." She shook her head. "His parents were already pissed that he wasn't staying home to run the farm, pursuing a cartography degree instead of milking cows, but then to say he wasn't coming home?" She grimaced. "I never did win them over...Made it worse when I wouldn't let them take him home to be buried in the family plot..." Her face fell.

"Cartography? Like, maps? I thought he was a photographer?" He asked, shifting the subject again.

"Yeah, actually he did both. He worked for the state as a cartographer and freelanced as a photographer on the side. That's why we moved here—" she waved her arm around her, "—the state job. I didn't care where we lived and then Aimi followed without question."

She relaxed a little, and he relished that she could still talk normally with him. He was going to spend the rest of his life feeling obtuse for misreading the situation, but at least she did not seem entirely repulsed by him.

Syve shivered, he resisted the urge to go to her to lend his body heat. Instead, he said, "We should head back before it gets dark."

She looked at the sky like she had not noticed the sun was setting.

"You shift first—you'll be warmer. I'll pack the clothes away and then we can head back?"

Five minutes later, Bas had the pack back under the logs, and they were running side by side through the darkening forest.

SYVE

AIMI SETTLED ONTO THE green couch next to Syve, handing over one of the two mugs she was holding. Syve took the proffered drink in both hands, bringing the steaming cup up to inhale the aroma deeply, eyes fluttering closed.

"I swear if you ever stop making coffee, I'll cry," Syve groaned.

Aimi shot her a smug look over the edge of her own mug.

"So..." Syve continued, "I went over to Bastien's house on Saturday..."

With a shocked hum and a dramatic head tilt that almost landed her blonde pigtail in her coffee, Aimi demanded,

"Excuse me? Why am I only hearing about this now? On *Monday*?"

Her incredulous tone rose an octave with each question.

"Bitch, spill the beans! Ha, get it?" She raised her mug between them, grinning, "Beans?"

Syve playfully swatted her friend, rolling her eyes and complaining about her bad jokes, then launched into the recap of her weekend.

"He *kissed* you?!" Aimi shrieked, causing most of the patrons to glance in their direction.

"Shut up!" Syve scolded, using her eyes to gesture toward the rest of the mostly full cafe. "For real though, I just told you I managed to turn into an animal on purpose, and you can't get past that one little detail?"

"Little?!" She was still squawking a solid thirty decibels higher than she needed to be.

Syve sighed deeply. "Yes, he kissed me. It was a mistake, and he apologized—can we move on please?"

"A mista-apologized?! Baby girl, with all due respect, what the fuck?"

"Aimi. I'm married." She dragged out the last word, thinking her friend obviously forgot to pack her brain cell when she left for work, because that was not new information.

Pity instantly flooded Aimi's features. "Oh, love."

"Don't look at me like that. I know, okay? I just...can't do that to him. It's only barely been a year—I shouldn't have let it happen." Her voice cracked.

"Syve." Aimi leaned across the couch to tightly hug her friend. "I understand." She squeezed Syve once and then let her go, sitting back into the cushions. "So, is it super-weird now between you two?"

"That's just the thing," Syve replied, wiping the inner corner of her eyes to wick the tears she managed to prevent from falling. "I freaked out, he changed the subject and then it was like it never happened." She shrugged. "We've even been texting all morning and I was planning to take him coffee after this..."

"God you guys are so cute." Aimi groaned. "Okay, I have to get inventory done. Let me get you a coffee for Butcher Boy and then you can get out of here—but you have to text me later! No more waiting *days* to fill me in on things! I'm too nosy, I'll wilt away." She swooned dramatically.

In no time, Syve was headed out the door, with an Americano in one hand and a deli bag in the other. Aimi insisted on sending the sandwich along, prattling about extra brownie points and how Bas never got coffee without one.

When Syve opened the door, hollering goodbye over her shoulder, she stepped right into a wall of a man. Unable to prevent it, a little of the espresso she was holding splashed onto the man's crisp white shirt.

"I am so sorry!" She looked up and all the guilt she felt immediately faded. "Cyrus? What are you doing here?"

"What is it with you Timberfall girls and coffee?" he teased, wiping uselessly at his shirt. "I'm not here to cause any trouble, Doe Eyes—you can relax."

She felt the blood drain from her body.

"What did you just call me?"

"Ah, so the pup didn't tell you?" He stepped closer to whisper, "You and I have more in common than just a java addiction." He pulled back, winked, and then slipped past her into the shop.

Bastien's coffee would now be delivered with a side of interrogation.

Syve made her way across the street to Hal's, carefully juggling the deli bag to push open the door. The shop's namesake was standing behind the counter with Bastien, the two men appearing to be in the middle of a serious debate. Bastien was the first to look her way when the cowbell above the door rang out her entrance.

"Bambi." His entire demeanor brightened as he made his way around the counter.

"Hi, Bas." She smiled in return, adding over his shoulder, "Hey Hal!"

"Hey, pretty girl! What brings you here of all places?" the older man asked, leaning across the counter.

"I was leaving The Glass and thought I'd bring this one some coffee." She shrugged as she handed over the coffee and sandwich to Bastien, who was now standing just to her side. "I saw Cyrus, by the way. You failed to mention that he *knows,*" she whisper-hissed. Bastien had the decency to grimace.

"Shit, sorry Bambi, I wasn't sure if he wanted me to share that—it's okay though, he's *one of us,*" he murmured back, booping Syve on the nose as he lifted the deli bag to inspect. "What's this?"

"Oh, Aimi sent that. She said you usually get it with your coffee?"

Hal gasped and dashed from behind the counter to snatch the bag out of Bastien's hand. "You tell Aimi she's a real gem, will you?" he said enthusiastically, then leaned over and kissed Syve on the cheek. "You've just made my whole day!"

Bastien rolled his eyes.

"Not that you were having a rough day anyhow, I just agreed to close up so you could go home early."

"You did, and Hattie will be very happy to have extra help with the ducks—but you still haven't agreed to buy me out." He looked pointedly at Bas.

"Buy you out?" Syve interjected, "Why would you need someone to buy you out, Hal?"

"I'm no spring chicken; I need someone to take over so I can retire—which I'd like to do by the end of the year. I've been trying to convince Bastien to be the one to do it. Maybe you can persuade him?" Hal raised an eyebrow at Syve, both of hers raising in return.

"I don't know how I could do that." She laughed.

"Hal, you really don't have to tell everyone that you're trying to bully me into buying."

"Sure I do." He winked, clapping Bas on the shoulder.

Then he said goodbye to Syve, who demanded he tell his wife hello for her, and started down the hall to the back door.

After jiggling the knob once to ensure the door was securely locked, Bas stuffed his hands in his hoodie pocket and turned toward Syve.

"Thanks for waiting around while I locked up. I feel like those tasks went faster having you there to keep me entertained." He smirked, looking her right in the eye. "Can I walk you home?"

Syve nodded, unable to look away. He stepped closer and she thought for a second he might try to kiss her again, but before she could react one way or the other, he stepped past her. He took a few steps down the alley before stopping to wait for her.

There was no reason for her to be disappointed—she should *not* have been disappointed. *So why was she?*

"Can I ask a question?" she said when she caught up with him. Bas side-eyed her and hummed in acknowledgement.

"What's stopping you from buying out Hal? Is it finances?" She badgered, gasped and then amended, "Sorry, that's none of my business—Damn, Hal! I let curiosity get the better of me, forget I asked."

Chuckling, Bas shook his head. "No, you're fine. It's complicated. I technically have the money...I just..." He sighed. "Dez left me everything. I have the money to buy out Hal; I just feel like trash for even thinking about spending a single dime."

Syve nodded, knowing the feeling all too well. When she had finally needed to dip into Erhard's life insurance to start paying the bills she promptly heaved the entire contents of her stomach into the kitchen sink.

"You should do it. You should use the money, and you should buy Hal's."

Bastien stopped walking and turned to blink at her.

"I have a feeling Desiderio would want you to. He left everything to you for a reason—he *wanted* you to use it. I think you know he would want you to do it. Especially if it makes you happy."

Bas opened his mouth, likely to object, and she cut him off.

"Bas, I also know what it feels like to survive. It will be okay." She reached out and grabbed his wrists.

It has to be. Maybe she was not just talking to him.

Slipping his hands out of his pocket, he twisted them to hold her hands and murmured, "How do you know?"

"I guess, I'm just being optimistic." She smiled sadly, squeezed his hands once and then let go. They still had two blocks to go, so she turned and started walking again.

Bastien sighed behind her. "You're incredible, you know that?"

"Incredible?" She laughed, watching over her shoulder as his long legs quickly ate up the distance between them. "Why do you think that?"

"I have never met anyone with a heart as big as yours, that's all. That reminds me, I have pictures, from Del, she literally won't shut up about how you saved her life—you're her hero." He dug his phone out of his jeans and began swiping across the screen.

With a content hum, she replied, "I'm hardly a hero, but I'm glad I was able to help her."

He held his phone out to her, nodding for her to take it when she hesitated.

"You can swipe through them; there's at least fifty."

Syve side eyed him, surprised he would just hand his phone over like that. Most men were weirdly protective of their phone, yet here Bas was—not even looking over her shoulder while she was about to scroll through his photos.

She flipped through a dozen of the pictures, all mostly identical with the same four girls in various poses—but Del undeniably stood out the most. Not because her dress was more extravagant than the others, no, it was the absolutely radiant smile on her face. Syve shivered, hairs rising along her arms. That feeling, that was why she loved her job. Knowing there were another few dozen pictures yet to see, she passed the phone back to its owner before she could do something as silly as get emotional.

"Thank you for showing me, will you tell Del thank you too?" She swallowed the lump in her throat.

"Of course. But I should be the one thanking you, again. You had no reason to drop everything to come over. Still, you did. Thank you for helping my baby sister."

She met his gaze, those slate-gray eyes. There was no mistaking the admiration emanating from them. Syve could only nod dumbly. They were now standing at the base of the stairs leading to her loft.

"One last thing," he said, reaching into his back pocket and retrieving a slightly creased, shimmery, gold envelope. "Shit, sorry, I probably should have put it in a different pocket...Del wanted me to give you this. It's an invite—she's graduating the first of the month. I—we would all love it if you came. If you're not busy, or if you even want to go...obviously..." he trailed off, scuffing the cracked concrete with his boot.

Syve flipped the envelope in her hands, her name scrawled across the front in blue ink, decorated with little hearts.

"I'll be there."

BASTIEN

THE FOLLOWING TWO WEEKS went by in a blur. Bas had been texting back and forth with Syve every day, they met up for mid-day runs on their lunch breaks, and when their schedules did not align, they met up after work and frolicked in the woods until the sun set.

Del tagged along for a few of the runs, after which Syve could not stop gushing about how she was right about Del's horse form. Cyrus had attempted to join for one, only to promptly make a crude remark about Syve's tattoo while she stripped behind her tree. Bastien, unaware of any tattoos, immediately revoked Cyrus' invitation.

Syve had been a little disappointed when Bastien informed her they would be running alone since Cyrus had an urgent family matter to tend to. She had been looking forward to seeing a bear up close.

Bastien shuffled into the kitchen early on graduation day, surprising his mother who was slumped at the counter, blotting tears with a tissue.

"*Mijo*, you need a bell!" Soriah scoffed, cursing in Spanish as she shifted her arm awkwardly in front of her.

"So I've been told." He closed the gap and slung his arms around her. "Why are you up so early, Mama?"

From where his chin rested atop her head, he noticed something sticking out from under the flowy sleeve of her blouse and deftly swiped it before she could stop him. It was a photograph from Dez and his graduation. The twins in their matching cap and gowns and little three-year-old Del held up in the middle, one arm slung around each brother. Bas sighed softly and kissed Soriah on the forehead.

"I should go make sure your sister is awake." She sniffled, patting Bastien's hand where it rested on her shoulder, then slipped off the bar stool and out of the kitchen.

Bas hoped, for his sister's sake, their mother would be able to at least pretend to be happy for her, that they would be able to take a picture together for Del to take with her to college, and that the day would not end in another fight over her leaving.

A few hours later, Bastien had managed to wrangle a very excited Delanira and a very morose Soriah into Cyrus' Range Rover. He sent off a quick text to Syve letting her know they were on their way to the school, apologizing in advance for his mother's sour mood in hopes she would not take it personally.

Cy let Bas and Del out in the front of the school, promising to meet them inside with Soriah after finding parking. Hoping Cy could say something to alter his mother's mood, Bas nodded, closed the door to the car, and led Del into the building where his sister immediately abandoned him in favor of her friends.

"We're going to head in and get to our seats early!" the teen called over her shoulder as she was swept away among a crowd of her peers. Bastien sighed, one hand slipping into his pocket, the other rubbing at his beard.

"I didn't think pets were allowed in the building."

With a dramatic roll of his neck, Bas' eyes landed on Syve and Aimi walking through the main doors.

Chuckling, he quipped, "Only on Saturdays."

He spoke to Aimi, but his eyes never left Syve. She was wearing a simple lavender sundress that looked like it was made just for her. It likely *was;* she probably made it herself. Thick straps topped with little bows showed off her freckled shoulders, a heart shaped bodice hugged her chest and waist until it met the skirt that flowed down to her knees. While he was cataloging the cute, little white heels she had paired with the outfit, she cleared her throat, forcing him to drag his eyes back up to her face.

Syve quirked a brow and grinned, "Bas."

"Bambi," he rumbled, shocking himself with the amount of gravel embedded in his words. "I'm glad you could make it."

"Right." Aimi clapped. "If you guys are going to eye-fuck each other can you at least tell me where we're sitting first so I can go?"

Syve swatted at her while Bas willed the heat he felt rising all over his body to cool.

"There isn't really assigned seating, so it doesn't matter. If you guys want to go find a spot you can. I'll come find you when my mom catches up."

"We're going to find the best seats, dead center—best view in the house! I don't care if there's already someone sitting there either, I'm not afraid to push them out of the way!" She grabbed Syve's hand and started toward the open door to the auditorium.

"Actually," Syve said, stopping short and pulling her hand free. "Give me a minute? I'll catch up with you."

Aimi glanced between Bas and Syve with a devious smirk, raised her brows up and down, and then with a salute, backed through the doorway and down the hall.

"Everything okay?" he asked her.

"Yeah, I just wanted to give you a heads up that she doesn't know Cy is going to be here." She winced. Right on cue, Cyrus walked in, ushering Soriah ahead of him.

"Well don't you look like a ray of fucking sunshine after a week of rain," Cyrus praised, flinching when Soriah swatted his arm, calling him a fool and chiding him for cursing in a school.

"Hi, Cy." Syve rolled her eyes playfully. "Hi Mama," she added, turning to Soriah.

Something about her calling his mother that made his chest feel tight in a not-exactly-uncomfortable kind of way.

"*Mija*, it's always so good to see you! You know you should come inside and eat after you go off running with my son, it's not fair that he's keeping you all to himself." Soriah swooped in to hug her.

Bastien left the women to catch up, leading Cyrus to the side and speaking low, "Aimi doesn't know you're here. Can you please, for Del's sake, *behave*?"

As it turned out, the 'espresso baptism' had not been the only altercation between Cyrus and Aimi—the former seemed incapable of leaving the latter alone.

"Aw, come on, pup, you know me! I'm always on my best behavior."

Bastien scrubbed a hand down his face. "That's exactly why I'm asking you to be good. Just today, just for Del."

Cyrus heaved an exasperated sigh, rolling his eyes dramatically.

"Fine, fun sucker. I'll be a good boy." He threw his hands up in defeat then turned and retreated into the auditorium.

When Bastien turned back around he found his mother and Syve hugging, tears sneaking down both of their faces. *What the hell?*

"Syve? Mama?"

"Worry about yourself, *Mijo*." Soriah waved a hand in the air dismissing him. "Where did that trouble making *osito* go?"

Gesturing with his head toward the door, Bas said, "He went in to find Aimi, Syve's friend. You remember me telling you about her?"

Soriah's eyes went wide.

"I should go in and make sure he doesn't do something to get us kicked out."

She swiped her hands across her cheeks once and dashed through the door with more grace than anyone would ever assign to a woman her age, though Bastien knew better.

Turning back to Syve, he took in her face. The only evidence of her emotional encounter was one stray tear still sitting at her jaw line. Without thinking he reached up and brushed it away with his thumb.

"Are you okay? What happened?"

"It was nothing, really. You mentioned your mom was in a mood, so I wanted to see if there was anything I could do to help. I don't think either of us realized how much we had in common before...I just told her something Aimi said to me once, that's all." She didn't give him a chance to ask any more questions before she grabbed his hand, interlacing their fingers as she started walking. "We better go catch up; it'll be starting soon."

Bas looked at their intertwined hands and smiled as he followed her into the auditorium.

When it was her turn, Delanira walked confidently across the stage to shake the principal's hand and accept her diploma. Before she made her way off the stage, she stopped, looked right up to where they were all standing, and blew a kiss. Bastien could not think of a single moment in his entire life where he had been prouder of his baby sister.

Directly after, the new graduates filed into the gymnasium for a celebration, where they would be surrounded with games, raffles, fountain drinks, and junk food until the sun came up.

After hugging Syve goodbye, Bastien's mother went with Cyrus to bring the car around, leaving the two of them a minute alone.

The longer the night had worn on, the more solemn Syve had become and Bastien was concerned. At the risk of being annoying, he asked for the third time, "Bambi? Are you *sure* you're okay?"

She sighed covering her face with her hands.

"I'm sorry, Bastien. I feel selfish. This is supposed to be Del's big day and I'm over here making it about me. This was just a lot harder for me than I thought it would be."

He stepped closer, pulled her hands from her face and ducked down to be eye level with her.

"You are the least selfish person I have ever met, Syve."

She laughed, then sniffled, blinking back tears.

"Thanks." She took a steadying breath. "It probably doesn't help that Noah's birthday is next week—" Her voice broke, cutting the sentence short. She stared at the ceiling, her throat bobbing as she swallowed hard.

"I can't even imagine how challenging today must have been, Bambi. I'm sorry, I didn't even think about that when I invited you—"

"No, it's okay, I really wanted to be here for Del, and for you." She sniffled again.

"What do you need right now?" He released one of her hands, cupping her cheek as he straightened, bringing them chest to chest.

"Will you come with me next week? To see him? You've been there with me a lot..." She tried to look away but he didn't let her.

"Of course, Bambi. I'll be there." She slipped her face from his hand and burrowed it into the front of his shirt, snaking her arms around his waist in a crippling hug. He forgot how to breathe, but only hesitated half a second before he was hugging her back.

"Thank you, Bastien," she whispered—just before a car horn blared relentlessly, Cyrus hollering along with it.

SYVE

SYVE WAS LYING IN bed, still dressed—shoes and all—from the night before, hugging a small green crocheted blanket when Aimi arrived. Her friend had crept in well before sunrise, crawled onto the bed behind her, and held her tightly—brushing her tangled hair away from her face as Syve sobbed into her pillow.

The past week had gone by in a blur, with hardly any work getting done. It was impossible to focus on finishing anything when it took all of her strength to breathe. Still, at least this year, she planned to get out of bed. One could call that progress.

When her dehydrated body refused to cry any longer, Syve rolled off the bed and took a few steps to gently drape the blanket over the edge of the crib. She reached for Aimi, her hand paused on the crib, anchored there by a grief too heavy to lift.

Aimi gently ushered her into the bathroom, started the shower, and helped her out of her shoes and socks before slipping into the hall with a vow to return in a few minutes with coffee.

Syve didn't step out of the shower until the water ran cold. But when she did, she found a pile of clean clothes and a blissfully hot thermos full of coffee. She forced herself to towel-dry her hair, got dressed, and then hugged the thermos close as she shuffled out to the living room—where Aimi waited on the couch with a brush and her favorite vampires playing baseball on TV.

A knock at the door came just as Aimi tied off the Dutch braid she'd woven into Syve's hair. Cameron entered without a word and sat across from Aimi. The three of them sat in silence, curled up together, until the credits rolled.

"Alright love, the birthday boy is waiting for you." Cam coaxed her friend off the couch and Aimi helped her into her boots, then they set out.

Syve lost count of how many times she wanted to turn around, but with Aimi and Cam on either side of her—linked arm-in-arm—she had the strength to continue.

A few new tears fell down her cheeks, but her heart, though it ached, was warm.

The trio slowed when they drew near the marble angel. Bastien sat in the grass beside Noah's headstone, one knee bent, propping up an arm while he toyed with something in his hands. She tore her gaze from his hands to find him assessing her.

Concern. Grief. Comfort.

That familiar storm brewed in his silver eyes—the same one that had always been there when they'd sat paw to hoof in this very spot.

But this time, when Syve sank to her knees before the granite, he reached out his hand and held hers.

They sat in silence for a while, her fingers curled around his. Then Bas gave her hand three gentle squeezes. She nearly protested when he let go—until he returned a moment later, holding something out to her.

The offering, a toy no bigger than her hand: a coal-black wolf with copper eyes.

Syve examined the small wolf for a moment, before tossing a questioning glance toward Bas. She recognized the wolf instantly, but the meaning behind it was lost to her.

Without a word, Bas shifted onto his knees, their thighs pressed together. He held his hand out. Syve placed the figurine into his palm and watched as he nestled the wolf into the grass, posed to howl—its back turned to the stone.

"Wherever they are...I hope this will help them find each other. I know he has his dad watching out for him, but maybe they can keep each other company while they wait for us," Bas murmured.

Syve looked from the little wolf up into his misty eyes.

"Thank you," she whispered.

A choked sob reminded them Aimi and Cam were still behind them. Syve reached both hands behind her—one on either side—and, leaning into Bastien while holding the hands of her best friends, Syve led a tearful rendition of "Happy Birthday".

"I asked her what she wanted, and she insisted on uni-puppies. *Uni-puppies!* Now I have to deliver and—shocker—*uni-puppies* aren't a thing! So please, oh wonderful, brilliant, smart, beautiful brains—help me."

On her knees, Cameron literally begged.

Bastien looked like he was about to cry from the effort he was putting into hiding his smile while Aimi literally rolled on the floor, in hysterics.

It was going to be a new tradition, but already it was becoming a favorite—after going to see Noah, the three re-grouped at her loft to prep all the decorations for Kayla's birthday party the following week.

Bastien, lucky as he was, volunteered to help before fully understanding what exactly he had signed up for.

So, there he was, sitting on the floor under a pile of paper, still slightly warm from the printer with a pair of scissors in hand—primed to cut out, God-only-knows, exactly how many dog bones and paw prints, because Cam insisted it would be recyclable and therefore 'cooler than traditional confetti'.

She had a point.

Daunting as the pile seemed, the man had yet to complain.

Pouring her broken heart into creating smiles for Cam's soon-to-be three-year-old helped keep Syve together. Odd as it was, sitting on the floor next to Bastien while he soldiered past paper cuts also soothed her.

When Cam informed him that attendance to the party was mandatory lest he incur the wrath of the birthday princess, he didn't even balk—instead he assured her he would catch a ride with Syve, and refused to miss it for the world.

Another work week toiled past. Any free time Bastien had was spent on Syve's sofa at Sew It Seams, tirelessly working on the uni-puppy confetti.

While he was battling hand cramps and dancing a fine-line with carpal tunnel, Syve was plugging along, having fully completed another piece for the grant submission.

Though they were working in parallel, she kept catching herself sneaking glances over her sewing machine. More than once, their eyes locked. She'd blush and silently scold herself—only to rinse-and-repeat all before another fifteen minutes could pass.

When the day of the party came, the birthday princess was very much looking forward to Bastien's arrival and presented him with the title of 'birthday knight'. The little girl forced him to wear a tiara and stand guard over her until she passed out on the couch in a cupcake-induced coma.

BASTIEN

FROZEN AIR NIPPED AT his exposed skin while Bas shuffled stacks of crates around in the cooler. His phone chimed in his pocket, requiring him to utilize all his self-restraint to keep from dumping an arm full of the crates onto the concrete floor. Quickly as he could, he freed his arms and dug his phone out to reveal one notification—an email, and the exact one he had been waiting for all morning.

Cyrus and Syve were right. Dez would want him to be happy. He'd want him to use the money he left behind if that's what it took to get there.

Bastien had never set out to work as a butcher, it was not a lifelong dream of his, but once he was there, he could not imagine leaving. After years of working with no goal, he could confidently say he could picture himself in Hal's shoes one day—nine to five at the shop and then home to his wife.

Maybe he was getting ahead of himself...Hal's made him happy. Owning the butcher shop had become his goal and he knew he would regret it if he let the opportunity slip past him, so Monday morning he called the bank. Now it was all dependent on the message sitting in his inbox.

"You in here, son?" Hal called, peeking around the door. When he didn't get a response, he stepped all the way into the cooler. "Everything okay?"

Phone held up in front of him, a broad smile on his face, Bas turned around and said, "Hal, I'm ready to talk numbers. Let me buy the shop."

Syve answered the phone on the second ring. "Bastien, hey, everything okay?"

He could hear her sewing machine whirring in the background.

"Bambi, I did it." Despite the warring emotions bouncing around in his body, his voice clearly held all of his excitement.

"Did it? Did what?" Syve asked. The sewing stopped, he had her full attention.

"I talked to the bank, and I told Hal I'd buy the shop." He stopped pacing and covered his mouth with his free hand, waiting for her reaction.

A gasp. "Bas! That's amazing! Congratulations! What happens now?"

"Well, nothing right now," he chuckled. "We've still got to sit down and talk real numbers, get the bank involved—Hal said he's got a friend who can help with the legal end. It'll take a few months, but the ball's at least rolling."

"I'm so happy for you—both of you! Hattie's going to love having Hal home all the time. It's about time he retired, and this will be so good for you! Should we celebrate? Is that bad luck? Should we wait?" she rambled.

He just listened for a moment, relishing in her excitement.

"I wouldn't be opposed to celebrating now. Actually, that's part of why I called. It's because of you and Cyrus that I finally went through with it. Come to dinner with me. A celebration—but also a thank you, for encouraging me."

She hesitated, but before he could say anything else, she answered, "Okay, yeah. I'm in. When and where?"

He let out a breath, muscles relaxing. "Would tonight work for you? I could pick you up after work, say, six-thirty?"

"That's in forty-five minutes; you know that right?"

"Well...I could be there sooner?"

"No, no! Six-thirty, I'll see you then. Bye, Bas!"

Click.

Bas thought back to earlier, sitting in Hal's office.

"Well, I'd better have Hattie help me pick out some flowers to send Syve."

"What? Why? What are you talking about?"

"You aren't sitting here talking to me just because you woke up and changed your mind. She said something to you, you and I both know it was her, and I intend to thank her."

Bas laughed. "You're not entirely wrong."

"You'd better spoil that girl, you hear me? She has a heart of gold. You're a good man, I think you two could be good for each other."

A replay of the nine-to-five daydream skittered back to the front of his mind. This time, when he lumbered home after a long day behind the counter and opened the front door, he allowed his mind to keep wandering. He imagined walking in to find his wife sitting at a table in the sitting room, auburn hair, streaked silver with age, a near constant whir from her little machines...

"Why don't you roll on out of here a little early? Seems like you might be able to use that extra time to...I don't know, swing by Maggie's? Maybe call and make sure there's a table waiting for you, wherever it is you plan on taking her?" Hal goaded, leaning against the corner.

"You eavesdropping, old man?"

Bas smiled, but he knew he was right. Asking Syve to dinner had been a spur of the moment decision, and he needed to make sure they had somewhere to go, at minimum.

Timberfall was not an outrageously big town, but by six o'clock, one could safely assume there would be at least a short wait for a table. Stopping by Blooming Pleasures to snag a bouquet from Maggie wouldn't be a bad idea either...

"I'm capable of locking up. Tell Mags I said, 'hi,' and I'll see her next Tuesday," his soon-to-be not-boss insisted, all but shoving him out the back door.

Bastien laughed as he turned to jog the few blocks home to grab the Jeep.

Securing a table at Thyme to Eat was simple enough—he called on the way to the flower shop and managed to claim the last open reservation for the night at 6:45 p.m. Some might call that kismet.

Blooming Pleasures promised to be more of a challenge. For a cute little shop, Maggie managed to stock dozens of different flowers, all on display in various glass-doored refrigerators. In spring, it doubled as a nursery—any orphan plants were popped in a bucket and housed right there in the shop for the entirety of their life cycle. Cut flowers, potted plants, vegetables, saplings—you name it. There was even a contraption, in the back corner, used for growing tubers in a vertical fashion.

An idea struck him while he was greeting the florist and passing along Hal's message. "Maggie, I'd really love a specific flower—but I actually have no idea what it's called." If he had the time, he could easily run out to the lake and pick a bouquet of his own, but for now, he would have to hope Mags really did have everything.

"If only someone here made it their life's mission to know every single flower possibly attainable in North America," she deadpanned. "Do you at least know what the flower *looks* like? Can you describe it to me?"

Bastien raised his hands in surrender, earning a laugh for his troubles, then did his best to describe the flowers painted on Syve's door.

"Hmmm...maybe comfrey? Or morning glory? No..." She muttered to herself, tapping her chin while walking around, searching her cases. "Ah-ha! Wildflowers, of course—here!" Maggie pointed to the glass door she had stopped in front of. Sure enough, in the far corner, a vase brimmed with little blue flowers.

"Those! Those are the ones! Thank you. Can you make something up with those please? Oh, and what are they called?"

"Forget-me-nots, special little things...Do you want any other flowers mixed in? Peonies, perhaps?"

With a shake of his head, he declined, and she set to work arranging a miniature bouquet in a small blue vase. Once the flowers were paid for, plus another order he would pick up the next day to take home for his mother, he checked the time. Cursing under his breath, he gathered the flowers, thanked Maggie again, and bolted out the door.

Syve

At 6:28 p.m., the sun glinted off Bastien's Jeep as he pulled in front of the shop and caught Syve's attention.

She looked up from the pants she was pinning, just in time to see him jump out of the driver's seat, cargo shorts doing him every sort of favor as his muscles flexed upon landing. He cleared the sidewalk in three large steps and pushed the door open before she could clear her lap to stand. His eyes landed on her immediately—a look passing across his face too quickly for her to gauge what it was. She probably looked like a complete mess; she could feel the hair that had slipped from her bun and she was perched on her chair like a little bird—though that part may have been obscured by the table...

"Bambi." The way he breathed her name made her skin tingle—how could he make such a silly nickname sound like a prayer? Why did he keep saying it like that? Why did she like it so much?

Finally, detangling herself from her work, she stood and stepped around the island to meet him. In his hand he held out a small glass vase overflowing with her favorite little wildflowers.

"Bas?" She took the vase, gently running a finger along a few of the pale blue petals. "They're beautiful...for me?"

A glance up caught his nod. "These are my favorite," she whispered, though she knew he heard by the smile on his face—you'd have thought she had just handed him a gold star.

"Why are you giving me flowers if this is a dinner to celebrate you?"

"I told you, it's also a thank you. I needed to be pushed; you're a very efficient pusher."

He cringed at his own words, and she giggled. *Giggled*? What was it about him that made her act like she was fifteen?

"Well, thank you—and you're welcome?" Her brow furrowed in thought, her voice rising an octave with the question. That had them both laughing.

With a mostly gentle shove, Syve cleared a space on the island then reverently set the vase down.

"We have a reservation for 6:45, how can I help with closing?"

One look at his face and she swallowed the debate she was starting. This was not a question he was asking to be polite, he genuinely wanted to assist, and who was she to turn down an extra hand?

Choosing to have him vacuum would end up being the highlight of her week. It would be a lie to say Syve had failed to notice before how muscular the man was, but the things that black t-shirt did for his forearms were *criminal*.

Seriously, what was wrong with her?

With the extra help, the shop was closed up in a few minutes, Bas watching quizzically as Syve fought with the front door to get the lock to engage fully. When she explained to him that the latch only caught when approached with the exact right amount of aggression, he laughed—but she noticed his stare lingered on the old door.

"It'll stay locked just fine, don't worry," she assured him as they walked away from the building. Bas just hummed in response, following Syve to the passenger side of the Jeep.

Blue skies meant a topless ride—at least that was Dez's motto. Bastien dutifully kept the tradition alive, which is why the top and doors were all tucked away in the Yerovi garage.

Before she could even wonder why he hadn't gone straight to the driver's side, she found herself staring up into the bucket seat—questioning whether her jeans would stretch enough to allow her to climb into the damned thing.

Strong hands landed on her hips just as she began to lift her foot. A squeal slipped from her lips, both hands snapping down from the seat to clutch at Bastien's wrists while he effortlessly picked her up and placed her in the Jeep.

She gaped at him, getting only a cheeky smile and a wink in return while he jogged around to climb behind the wheel.

"A little warning next time?" She huffed in mock annoyance.

"Nah, you make fun sounds when you're surprised." He smiled, slipped one hand behind her seat and expertly backed out of the parking space.

It was not until they stopped at a red light that Syve finally asked, "So...where are we eating?"

"I got us a table at Thyme. I hope that's okay?"

"Oh, yeah! I mean, it's my favorite restaurant, I just didn't think everyone else would like it."

"Everyone else?"

"Yeah? Aren't we going out to celebrate?"

"*We* are." Bas gestured between the two of them with his pointer finger.

"Oh." She blushed again. When he'd asked her to dinner earlier, she'd just assumed she'd be tagging along with the whole family—not that it would have been a bad thing. Spending time with Soriah and Del *was* always fun. Honestly, she couldn't bring herself to hate Cyrus either, much to Aimi's dismay.

Blushing over the concept of dinner alone with Bas was ridiculous—how many times now had just the two of them gone for runs or sat together in her empty shop?

She was acting like she had a crush.

Oh, God.

"We're here." Bas' words drug her out of her spiral. After parking and insisting that she let him help her down from the cab, they made their way into the restaurant.

They were greeted by a young brunette wearing a floor-length white dress, cinched at the waist by a deep red corset that was barely visible behind her dark green apron—an apron that matched all of the employees—with *Lettuce Serve You* embroidered across the top.

Syve openly gawked at the girl's attire as she led them to a booth in the back corner.

Once they'd both slid into their seats and were handed menus, the girl introduced herself. "My name's Addie. I'll be your server today. If you need anything, please don't hesitate to ask. Can I start you both off with some water while you look over the menu?"

"Yes, please. Thank you, Addie. Actually, can I ask you where you got your dress? I love the cottage core vibe—I've been hunting for a dress just like that for ages."

"Oh, um, this one was custom made for me back where I'm from...sorry." Addie smiled, then excused herself to fetch the waters.

"If you like it, why don't you make your own?" Bastien asked over his menu.

"I've tried, but I can't get it exactly right. The balloon sleeves are a nightmare and I'm just missing something—I was hoping I could get my hands on one like that," Syve motioned toward where the waitress had disappeared. "So that I could tear it apart. If I could deconstruct it, I bet it would be easier to replicate..." She looked up to see him staring. "Sorry, I was rambling, you probably couldn't care less about a silly dress."

"Don't do that. I asked, and I absolutely do care about a dress that is anything *but* silly. I love when you ramble, you should see yourself—when you're talking about your job you just...come to life."

She blinked at him; not exactly sure what part of his admission affected her most.

Addie returned, setting two cups with ice and a pitcher of water on the table, then she took their orders for drinks, appetizers, and entrees before dashing off again.

"Tell me a story," Syve prompted. "Something you wouldn't tell to just anyone." She raised an eyebrow, leaning forward to fill both of their cups.

"A story?" Bas dramatically stroked his beard, humming in thought. "Oh, I've got one! So, back when Dez and Cy were still in college, I flew out to The Keys with them for spring break—"

He went on, animatedly recounting a wild, drunken adventure in which the three boys were kicked out of no less than a half of a dozen clubs, Cyrus was detained for stripping at the beach, and Dez *shifted* in the ocean.

"We bailed Cy out just in time for them to catch their flight back to North Carolina, but I missed mine and had to sleep in the airport until the next one left the following morning."

Syve laughed so hard her stomach muscles ached.

"Oh my god! How much trouble did you all get in?"

"A shit load. We thought we were in the clear, Cy paid everyone off. It pays, literally, to have a rich ass friend, I guess. But then a news article went out with a *picture* of a big ass wolf running across the damn beach."

Syve gasped, "No!"

"Oh, yeah—'New photographic evidence of the long believed extinct Florida black wolf: is it real? Or a hoax?'" he dramatized, waving his hand with a flourish.

They continued to share more stories while they ate, laughing the entire time.

It was almost ten o'clock when Bas put the Jeep in park under the stairs to her loft, leaving the vehicle running while he hopped out to walk her to her door.

"Thanks for going out with me—to dinner, out to dinner." He closed his eyes, wincing.

When he peeked one eye back open, she was trying—poorly—to smother a smile. "Thank you for taking me out...to dinner."

He rolled his eyes at her, one side of his mouth quirked up. "You bully all your friends?"

She shoved his shoulder playfully, but her hand lingered, running down his arm to his elbow. Goosebumps rose up under her touch and she noted how close they were standing as she looked up into his eyes. Seconds passed with neither of them moving even so much as to blink.

Then his gaze drifted slowly to her mouth, and back again. She held her breath.

His shoulders slumped, and he straightened, pulling back just a fraction.

"I should let you get to bed," he breathed.

She wasn't sure if he was speaking to her or trying to convince himself to leave.

Indecision tore at her.

His retreat was her fault, and she was disappointed—but *why*? She should *want* him to retreat.

But she didn't. Not really. And she couldn't ignore it anymore.

Before he could back up any further, she slipped her hands around his neck, pulling him down until their mouths crashed together. Taking advantage of his shocked gasp, she darted her tongue inside, licking at his.

His surprise only lasted a second before his hands were on her—one winding into her hair, the other clenching the back of her shirt at the small of her back.

He kissed her like he was diffusing a bomb, careful and deliberate.

She pulled his bottom lip between her teeth. He groaned, his hand at her back flattening as he pulled her closer.

Then, with a devilish smile, she released his lip and planted a quick peck on his cheek. Just as quickly as she had grabbed him, she let go and stepped back, fingers brushing lightly over her lips.

"Goodnight, Bastien," she whispered, then quickly slipped inside, leaving Bas dumbfounded on her porch.

BASTIEN

MOUNTAINS OF FOOD WERE piled high, covering the entire counter. Soriah and Del worked quickly, setting out paper plates and napkins for the last-minute party they decided to throw.

Okay, so Cyrus had decided they were having a party—and when he unloaded a trunk full of groceries, no one argued. Especially when he suggested they invite the girls.

Bastien was starting to think his mother and sister liked Syve more than him—though honestly, he couldn't blame them.

Not that he had the brain capacity to do much of anything since he left her place a few nights ago.

She kissed him, closed the door, then turned the porch light off.

It had taken him a two-hour run and a *very* long, very cold, shower every night since before sleep was even an option. When he finally was able to drift off, he dreamt of her and those damned teeth scraping against his—

"Hey, Pup! You gonna stand there all night or are you gonna come out here and help me start this fucking fire?"

Fire?

"Fire? What do you mean, *fire*? Cyrus? What do you mean, fire—there's no fire pit out there!"

Bastien was right—there wasn't a fire pit. But he was also wrong, because by the time he stumbled out onto the deck, there was a giant hole right in the middle of the yard. *Perfect, he dug his own grave.*

"Great, now that you're out here, you can pour the kerosene." Cyrus wiped his forehead with the back of his hand, leaning his weight against a shovel.

Where the hell did he get kerosene?

Flames licked at the sky as they danced across a mound of scrap wood and dried branches. Though he was loath to admit it, Cyrus had crafted a really nice fire pit. The depth of the pit paired with the large ring of stones had seemed excessive at first, but it did safely contain the entire bonfire.

Thankfully, the girls arrived just as Cyrus struck the match, so there were other witnesses when the idiot lit his pants on fire. He managed to drop his pants in time to avoid any serious burns, the denim continued to burn on the grass and had to be stomped out. Aimi, of all people, volunteered to help Cyrus inside to clean up and tend to his minor burns. There must have been a decent number because they were gone for quite a while.

Syve had been in his house, in his line of sight even, for twenty whole minutes before he even got the chance to talk to her. The second she stepped through the door his mother and sister pounced. It didn't seem to bother Syve in the slightest, however, she smiled happily, listening to every word they had thrown at her.

At least, almost every word—there were a few times he caught her staring at him and when she would turn back to the others, he was almost positive she was asking them to repeat themselves.

When she was *finally* standing next to him, hands stretched out toward the fire, she asked, "How did you guys manage to get the pit put in so fast?"

"You'd have to ask Mr. Flammable about that," he joked.

"Somehow, I had a feeling he was responsible."

"I hate to admit, but it was a good idea."

"The fire? Or the party?"

"Yes," he answered with a smirk.

Syve laughed, reaching out to trail a hand up his arm.

"I can't believe I've never asked you about this before," she said, thumb ghosting over black ink—a crescent moon full of stars atop three stone-tipped arrows crossed at the middle covered the underside of his left forearm.

"It's the symbol of Artemis—or a variation of it, at least. Dez had one too, except his was the symbol of Apollo and had the sun instead of the moon. These stars make up the constellation Canis Major. That was Dez' idea, he thought that would be funny." He raised his arm up as he spoke, and she traced the lines with her fingers.

They were close enough that all three of his arrows, though not parallel, pointed only at her.

Glass shattering came from inside the house, startling them both. Yelling followed and they shared a quick glance before running up the back steps.

"You can't keep me here, Mama!" Del screamed, tears running down her face while she shook a ripped piece of paper in the air. There were glass shards covering the floor at her feet.

"*Mija*, I am your *mother*. I can do as I please!" Soriah stood in front of the doorway, blocking his sister in the kitchen, punctuating each of her words with her own torn sheet of paper.

"Whoa, Mama! Del! What's going on here?" Bas demanded, resting his hands on his mother's shoulders so he could step past her to stand between them.

"Go on, Delanira, tell your brother *what's going on here,*" Soriah spat.

"Del?" He turned toward his sister who deflated, lip quivering.

"I got in."

She got in.

Six months of busting her ass and applying to colleges in secret had paid off. Bas stomped over and scooped the girl up, hugging her tightly and spinning her around.

"You got in!" He planted a loud kiss to her temple.

"You *knew*?!" Soriah seethed, interrupting their moment with her vitriol now aimed at him.

"Mama—"

"No!" She threw the paper she had been holding on the floor then pointed a finger in his face. "*No.*" Then she spun on her heel so fast her braid whipped into the wall with a crack as she stormed off.

Cyrus held up a hand to stop Bas from following. "I've got Mama. She needs you more," he gestured to Del with a tilt of his head, and Bas relented. Cy disappeared around the corner.

"Why don't you guys go out and sit by the fire? Aimi and I can clean up," Syve said with a soft smile, ushering them out while Aimi crouched to pick up the larger pieces of the punch bowl.

"Thank God this shit was empty—you ever try to get fruit punch off tile? PSA, it *stains,*" the barista griped.

Bas shook his head with a smile as he led Del out the back door.

Once again, he sat before the fire. He dragged a second folding chair over with his foot and motioned for Del to sit. The fire, now burning low on fuel, cast more shadows than light across his sister's hunched form.

"So, which one did you get into?"

Del sighed. "Actually? All of them."

"All of them?!" He turned toward her. "How long have you known? Why didn't you tell me?" He couldn't mask the hurt in his voice.

"I only started getting the letters this week—I wasn't hiding it! I just wanted to wait until the last one came in to show you...I was hoping you would help me look at them and pick one? I got distracted today with the party and didn't check the mail before Mama got to it. She was reading the letter from Cornell when I went in to refill the punch." Her voice was low, defeated.

Carefully, he pulled her chair closer so he could wrap his arm around her shoulders.

"I'm sorry, Sis. It's not fair to you. She has her own shit she's never worked through, and that's not your fault. I hope you know how proud I am of you though, and I know in my soul, Dez is somewhere watching over us right now and he's proud as hell too."

Del sobbed into his shoulder.

"I want you to do what makes you happy—what makes you feel fulfilled. If you want to go to college in California, or New York, or Colorado, I don't care. Just please, don't worry about Mama, be true to you, Bug—Mama will be fine. I'll make sure of it, okay?"

Sniffling, Del leaned back and wiped her eyes with her sleeve. "Thanks for always being there for me."

Bas nudged her shoulder with his. "What are brothers for? I can't just pick on you *all* the time." That earned him a real laugh.

"You know, I've missed this. I like seeing you smile again," she said.

He chuffed, one corner of his mouth curving up slightly while his eyes drifted to the house.

"I like her. A lot," she admitted, her tone leaving no room for doubt. With his eyebrows in his hairline, he turned to look at her again.

"Just saying, if I had to pick between you two...It would be *really* hard." She shrugged one shoulder, doing a poor job of hiding her smile.

Laughing loudly, he pushed her chair over.

SYVE

GURGLING FROM THE COFFEE pot echoed through the loft as Syve stretched her arms above her head, then threw the sheet off her body and swung her legs over the edge of the bed.

With a mug of coffee securely in her possession, she made a lap of her home, collecting an arm load of things that needed to be put away as she went. In the kitchen, she collected a few of her mother's journals that were still lying out. After shelving the journals in the living room, she ventured to the bathroom, where she caught her reflection and distracted herself with a much-needed shower.

Afterward, she dug out her dusty blow dryer and, for the first time in ages, she blow-dried her hair.

Once she was showered and dressed—in a pale yellow sundress with daisies trailing down one side, pulled from the deep recesses of her closet—she dragged her laundry basket from the hall to the washer.

While separating the clothes from the towels, she tripped over Erhard's boots.

Syve stared at the boots—still where they had lain for over a year and a half.

With a deep breath, she closed her eyes, turned back to start the wash, then stooped down to pick up the boots. Tears pricked at her eyes, but she smiled as she hugged the dirty leather footwear.

Ceremoniously, she walked them to the closet, where she nestled them among the sneakers and dress shoes of the same size, and gently closed the closet door.

Clouds darkened the sky and thunder rumbled in the distance as Syve made her way down the alley.

It was a Tuesday, so she waited until lunch to walk to the cemetery. Asking Bastien to join her had crossed her mind, but this visit felt like one she needed to make alone.

This trip was not for her, and it was not for Noah. It was Erhard's thirtieth birthday.

Passing by the ever-watching Angel statue, she habitually counted her steps, taking the usual thirteen, then two more. On the back of the stone writ with her sons name, another was etched:

E

July 16th, 1989
December 5th, 2017
Loyal Husband, Loving Father.

Buried beneath her feet was the box holding his remains. Other than her, only Aimi knew he was there.

Everyone believed he'd intended to be buried on the Gehring farm, but when he died without leaving behind a will and Syve was given the power to keep him close—she did. She was too ashamed of going against his wishes to admit it to anyone—her soul sister excluded.

The left side of the stone was empty—meant for her. One day. A day she suddenly realized she wanted to be far, far in the future.

"Alles Gute zum Geburtstag."

She sank down into the grass as she wished him a happy birthday in his first language. Sighing wistfully, she added, "It's going to rain—just like it does every year for you."

As if on cue, thunder rumbled again.

She told him about the grant and all the pieces she finished and she told him about how well Aimi was doing with The Glass. Past a stifled sob, she told him about how well Cameron, Kayla, and her brothers were doing—scoffing when she mentioned the deadbeat husband, Tyler. Next came the story of Del and her prom dress, and of Soriah—who had lost just as much as Syve had.

Last but not least, she told him about Bastien.

"I met someone." She cringed, hating how that sounded but unable to call Bas *just a friend*. "I think you would've liked him—you two would've been friends. He's patient and thoughtful...he got our boy a birthday present." A lone tear dripped down her cheek—or maybe it was a raindrop. "He's been really supportive...and incredibly understanding," she added, tucking away a strand of hair the wind had whipped into her face.

"Erhard. I will always love you." She sucked in a deep breath. "But...I think I have a little more love to give in this lifetime." Her voice was thick with emotion. "I tried so hard—God knows I tried—to ignore it. He makes me smile, E. Really, *truly* smile. And I don't know that I've been able to do that since you left me. He's just been there. Selflessly. I know he has feelings for me—if he's been trying to hide them, he's done a piss-poor job."

She hiccupped a laugh and wiped her eyes with the backs of her hands.

"I care about him. I want him to succeed, to enjoy life and get everything he dreams of. Most of all, I want to be beside him when he does. I feel like I'm failing you. I've felt like I'm dishonoring you, disrespecting you and spitting on your memory."

She was sobbing now; there was no blaming the rain that had yet to fall.

"I know," she paused, struggling to swallow the emptiness. "I know you'd want me to be happy. That's all you ever wanted for me. You're probably out there somewhere shaking your head because I've been so stubborn about this—"

Lightning lit the sky, thunder booming a split second later, and she laughed.

"Point made."

Eyes down, she toyed with the hem of her shirt.

"I will miss you up to the very day I see you again, but I will try to be happy until then. I'll make sure to live the full life I know you would wish for me."

She brought her fingers to her lips, tears slowing as warmth washed over her. Then, parting with a kiss, she pressed her fingers to the granite.

"I'd have to agree with you."

Syve jumped, a hand flying to rest over her heart. "Jesus Christ, Gunther. You scared the hell out of me! What are you doing here?"

She took a second to catch her breath, trying to ease the adrenaline rushing through her veins. Gunther was leaning against a headstone, maybe ten feet away, with his hands in his pockets. He had one ankle crossed over the other and was looking at her down his nose—one eyebrow raised, and one side of his mouth pulled up in a smug smirk. It was clear he had been standing there a while.

"I thought I might run into you here." He pushed off the stone, sauntering over to where she still sat on the ground.

The wind had picked up, the thunder becoming more frequent. Lightning flashed over the trees again, illuminating Gunther's silhouette as he now hovered over her.

Scrambling to get her feet under her, Syve stood, retreating in an effort to put more space between them and finding herself now backed against her Husband and Son's headstone.

"Happy Birthday, Cuz." He leaned down, throwing the phrase around her as if the words were insignificant. When his attention returned to her, he added, "My dear cousin always did prioritize your happiness."

"Is there a reason for you being creepy and eavesdropping today, Gunther?" Syve asked, crossing her arms in front of her. "Or, is that just your personality?"

"Creepy? Come on doll, you're going to hurt my feelings." He reached up, slipping a finger around a loose strand of her hair and tugging.

She swatted his hand away.

"I didn't realize that was possible. How did you know I would be here?"

"You think you could bury my own flesh and blood without me knowing where?" he asked, voice dripping with condescension.

Syve fought the urge to cringe. "My lunch break is over; I need to get back to work."

"I'm sure your boss wouldn't mind if you were a few minutes late."

"Goodbye, Gunther." She stepped around him, walking backward, not wanting to turn her back to him just yet.

"Alright then, Doll. See ya later." He winked, and she turned away to hide her look of disgust.

Torrents of rain began to descend from the sky as she jogged through the cemetery's iron gates.

BASTIEN

AUGUST HAD BEEN UNUSUALLY hot that year. Bas found his runs with Syve ending more and more at the lake so they could dunk their furry bodies into the cool water. In fact, he had been considering asking Syve if she wanted to add a swimsuit into the clothing stash—the only thing stopping him was his own reaction to the thought of her in a bikini.

Something changed in the last few weeks, though he wasn't sure what exactly it was. They went from running together at lunch nearly every day, to making out on the shitty little sofa in her shop, almost always failing to save enough time for food. He never pushed further than that, afraid even a wayward hand would be too much, and she would pull away. He felt like a teenager again.

This particular day was the first where they had planned to *actually* get out into the woods. Usually when they were meeting up for a midday run, they would walk over to the mausoleum from Sew It Seams. Any other time, like this one, she would drive over to his house.

They both agreed it would be silly to go anywhere else when leaving straight out of his backyard was the best chance to go unnoticed by anyone. Anyone, that was, other than Cyrus who was annoyingly only ever in one of two places—the Yerovi house or The Glass.

"Hey Pup, we going for a run?"

Think of the devil.

"We," he drew the word out, gesturing between the two of them, "aren't doing anything. Syve is coming over. Don't you have a coffee to chug or something?" Bas checked his watch in annoyance, not at Syve—she still was not supposed to come over for another twenty minutes, but at the man in front of him who was almost impossible to bear.

"Sourpuss. I already got kicked out today, for the record."

"Cy, It's not even ten," Bas deadpanned.

Cyrus shrugged, smug as ever and walked back into the house.

Right on time, the back gate opened and Syve skipped through, looking every bit a teenage boy's Daisy Duke wet dream, just in unlaced hiking boots instead of a pair of Frye's.

Curls fell down around her. He had never seen her hair curled before, and the ringlets changed how the sun made her hair glow.

"Bambi," he called out to her as she jogged over to the base of the steps to join him, satisfaction flooding his mind when she smiled in response.

Once before, she had asked why he kept calling her Bambi, *that* was the reason.

Openly feasting on her appearance, he grumbled, "We are supposed to be running for real today, and you show up here looking like that?" He licked his teeth with a groan.

"Here, I thought you would *want* me out of my clothes," she crooned back, flipping her hair over her shoulder as she slunk past him to head toward the trees.

Bas bit at his lip, contemplating all the ways this woman would be the death of him, as he followed her.

Crossing her arms in front of her to grab the hem of her tank top, Syve slowly lifted the garment off her body, all before she even reached the edge of the yard.

No bra.

Lord have mercy.

His brain short circuiting in surprise, he just stopped and watched.

Anger reignited toward Cyrus as he took in the cherry blossom branches that stretched from under her arm all the way down her left side where they disappeared beneath the waistband of her denim shorts. That had to be the tattoo Cy mentioned before, and Bas had every intention of beating the memory out of him.

Syve slid her thumbs into the waistband of those little shorts, looking over her shoulder at him with a wicked grin. Then she shimmied them down over her hips, letting them fall to her ankles. She stepped free of both her boots and the clothing, standing now in nothing but a thin black pair of panties.

He was certain he was about to come in his pants.

She snickered and he begrudgingly removed his eyes from where he was memorizing every inch of her ass. When his eyes met hers, she winked, blew a kiss and then shifted, bounding off into the trees.

"Son of a bitch," he laughed, tearing off his own clothes as he dashed after her.

After losing sight of her for the third time, he made his way to his little log-shed, sniffing around, only to find himself alone. Twigs snapped behind him, and before he could fully turn his head, a brown blur side-swiped him, sending them both rolling across the ground.

Syve jumped up, prancing in a few proud little circles before dropping her head behind the logs to dig for the pack—which she then carried over in her mouth and dropped on his chest.

He growled playfully before rolling off his back, shifting in the process and leaving his entire backside bare before her. With a surprised bleat, she turned her head, but he didn't miss the glances she kept stealing as he watched her over his shoulder.

Black shorts, gray T-shirts—he really needed some diversity in his wardrobe. With a quick toss he landed one of the shirts directly over Syve's head, laughing as she shook it off and shot him a glare. When he had his shorts pulled over his hips he turned around.

"Are we even now? No more tackling—" words failed him and his sentence died on the spot.

Syve was finger combing her curls over one shoulder in nothing but his shirt—obviously, since the other pair of shorts were still lying at his feet. She really would be the death of him and he was so, absolutely lost to those long, bare legs...

"Oh, we're even—for now. But I would be lying if I promised you no more tackling." She drawled, making a show of glancing down at his very obviously tented pants. "I actually like to play a little rough," she teased, leaning back against a tree.

Growling, he stalked over to her, watching as her eyes widened—but so did her smile. When he was close enough, he placed both hands on the bark behind her head, looking down at her while she toyed with the hem of her, *his*, shirt.

"How did I not know you had more tattoos?" She asked innocently.

"You never asked, and I guess until now you've never looked."

He raised an eyebrow at her, red flushing across her freckled cheeks. The way she was staring into his soul had the power to capsize him. Bark rained down from where he clenched and unclenched his fists against the pine before he gave in to temptation—moving to run a thumb along those freckles until he could bury his fingers in her hair.

A soft gasp escaped her lips when he gently pulled her head back, just enough to meet her lips with his. Her hands found his hips, sliding their way across to his abs before ascending up through the dark hair on his chest and lacing behind his neck.

Bastien leaned in until their noses and foreheads were touching. He brought his other hand down to her shoulder, running it along her ribs slowly, thumb grazing the side of her breast on its way.

When he reached her hip, he dug his fingers in, inhaling sharply when she arched into him in response, pressing her body into his with a whimper.

Primal need shot through his body at the sound, his mouth crashing to hers with a ferocity he didn't know existed.

She matched it instantly. Nails clawed at his neck, his back, his chest—anywhere she could reach, tugging him closer as they took turns licking and sucking each other's tongues, teeth and lips.

Soft pants filled the silence of the woods as they broke for air. He immediately trailed down her jaw to her neck, nipping along her collarbone before licking a slow deliberate path back up to her ear.

"Bambi, *fuck*." He growled, licking her earlobe into his mouth and rolling the skin between his teeth. She shuddered beneath him, urging him on.

Without warning, he bent low, slipping his hands under her bare ass, lifting her and slamming her against the tree trunk. Her legs wound around his waist, sending his eyes rolling into the back of his head as not even the summer air separated their bare skin.

Heaven had a name, and it was *hers*.

"Bambi." His eyes found hers—blown wide, lids hooded but locked on him. "Tell me to stop, and I swear to God, I will."

Syve pulled her lip between her teeth and nodded slowly.

Bastien inhaled deeply and the blood in his veins turned to ice.

"Bas? What happened? What's wrong?"

"Can you smell that?" he asked, brows furrowed as he eyed their surroundings. Searching.

Beneath him Syve sniffed the air. "Is that...tobacco?" she asked, perplexed.

Unceremoniously he dropped her legs, holding her hips just long enough for her to find her balance before backing away with a deep growl.

"Stay here," he ordered, spinning on his heel and shifting, shorts be damned.

Last time he caught *that* smell on the wind, he hesitated and paid the price. Now, all he could think was vengeance.

"Bastien!"

Her panicked cry was not enough to stop him as he sprinted away, following his nose deeper into the woods.

Rust began mingling with the tobacco stench and Bas knew he was getting close. He had forgone stealth in his rage, crashing through the brush like an enraged bull.

Tearing through a copse of new growth, Bastien found himself standing in the middle of an old logging road twenty yards shy of a man hovering over a massive, dead bull elk.

Poacher. He fucking knew it—he had no doubt in his mind this was the same man who robbed him of a brother.

Clearly having heard him coming, the piece of shit was standing behind the elk, silenced rifle in hand. Not that his rifle would do him any good against anything approaching the way Bas had. Between the full camo—balaclava and face paint included—Bastien could only make out the man's hauntingly green eyes.

A violent snarl tore loose from his throat as he stalked closer, begging the man to lift his gun—to give him another reason to rip his throat out.

Ask and you shall receive.

Just as the barrel pointed his direction, Bas launched himself forward, swerving in a serpentine trajectory. Realizing how useless his weapon had become, the man stumbled back, dropping the rifle to the ground and fumbling with his belt.

Bastien leapt, clearing the last few feet, noticing the man's movements too late. He made contact, knocking the poacher onto his back. The deafening crack of the man's head against the ground left Bas' ears ringing. Beneath him the man was limp, unconscious or dead, he wasn't sure. The pounding of his own heart took over as the ringing subsided and his vision blurred. Just one bite, one swipe of his paw and the asshole would be done for with no doubts.

But something was wrong. Blinking rapidly Bastien tried to stop his vision from swimming.

"BASTIEN!"

Syve? Why did she sound like that?

His head lolled to the side, searching for her but the motion cost him his balance and he stumbled. Searing pain licked out like lightning across his body, legs buckling before he slammed into the dirt. He fought to open his eyes when he felt her hands on his face, succeeding just long enough to see her beautiful hazel eyes full of tears.

Then, darkness took him.

SYVE

"STAY HERE."

The order shocked her. Bastien had never talked to her so aggressively before. He turned, not even bothering to remove his shorts before shifting and he was gone.

"Bastien!" she cried after him, watching as he sprinted along the lake.

How was she supposed to just stay there? Panic set in as he broke away from the water's edge, angling toward the trees. A few more seconds and she wouldn't be able to see him at all.

There was no way she was going to stay there.

Whipping his shirt off, she focused on shifting as fast as she could—not daring to take her eyes off the wolf for even a second. Shifting under pressure proved to be frustratingly difficult and took her far longer than she had time for. When this was all said and done, she was going to start practicing—literally shifting back and forth until she could do it as fluidly as he just had.

Hooves finally on the ground, she tore off, aiming for the gap in the pine where she last saw him.

Adrenaline fueled her as she flew through the woods, praying he continued to run a straight line and she was not going in the wrong direction. She slowed when she entered a section of reforestation, the smaller trees making it harder not just to see, but to move at all. Fierce growling to her right had her jumping back into action, fighting her way past the low branches.

The pines gave way, spilling her out onto an old dirt road. The scene before her played out in slow motion. Bastien was going after a hunter, the hunter was reaching for something at his waist, a pistol, but it was too late to intervene.

Wolf and man collided, a shot rang out as they crashed to the ground and slowly, blood began to stain his perfect silver fur.

"BASTIEN!"

Her own voice startled her, not knowing exactly when she had returned to her human form. Rocks dug into her feet, yet she ran anyway, watching as Bas staggered then slumped into the dirt. She dropped to her knees when she reached his side, carefully grabbing his head, begging him to look at her.

One blink and then his body went slack.

"Bas! BAS! No!" she sobbed, eyes darting everywhere desperately searching for a solution. Aside from a wounded wolf, a naked woman, a dead elk and a camo-clad man, of whose current state she was neither sure of nor cared, there was nothing.

"I'll be right back—I can't carry you. I have to get help! I'll be right back. I *swear* I'll be right back!" she promised, pressing her forehead to his. Gently, she laid his head down, shifted quicker than ever before, and ran.

Two miles. That is how far the lake was from the Yerovi house, Bastien had told her that once. Syve had no idea how far from the lake she had chased after him.

She stormed into the back yard, cleared the steps to the porch and slid to a stop. Cyrus was just stepping out of the back door, a tray laden with a variety of meats clearly meant for the grill, his brows furrowing the moment he noticed her.

Modesty be damned, she shifted—just a dirty, bloody mess on her knees.

"Bas—" she rasped, still sucking in air from the run. "Shot." Her voice cracked, but it did not matter.

Message received.

"Soriah!" Cyrus boomed, ripping his shirt over his head. "Talk later, take me to him."

Syve nodded, shifting back as Soriah appeared in the doorway, a hand over her mouth.

Cy looked at her, vowing, "I'll bring him home, Mama. Be ready."

Then he stepped around Syve, threw his shirt into the yard and shifted as he leapt from the deck. The bear landed with a *thump*, bent his head to grab the shirt up in its jaws and started running.

When she was told Cyrus could shift into a bear, she imagined a cute little black bear—not a whole ass grizzly, like the one she was currently leading through the trees. Not that she could complain, his size was about to come in handy.

The return trip seemed to take twice as long, the fear of what they would find when they got there was eating her alive. She hadn't checked the hunter before leaving.

What if he was not dead? What if he woke up and finished the job? What if he took Bas and they never saw him again? What if, what if, what if and it was all her fault for not looking?

One 'what if' she dutifully ignored.

What if Bastien was dead?

As the grove of baby pines came into view, Cyrus let out a low growl and Syve let him pull ahead. He could probably smell the blood. It was far easier to pass through the trees when she was following in the wake of a massive bear, not to mention the security it provided when they reached the other side—if she needed it.

Cyrus broke out onto the road, head snapping from side to side before standing on his hind legs, dropping the shirt and letting loose a roar that rattled Syve to her bones. When she trotted around him, she sagged in relief, Bastien was still there, chest visibly rising and falling—albeit barely.

Cyrus' anger was aimed at the hunter, who was nowhere to be found.

With all due haste, Syve shifted, snatching Cyrus' shirt off the ground and running to Bastien's side. Cy came up on the other side, delicately rolling the wolf with his giant paw, exposing the wound.

Syve swore aloud, pressing the fabric into the scarlet fur as she pleaded with whatever deity might be listening. *Please,* she begged silently, *just let him be okay.*

Carefully, Syve helped Cyrus shoulder Bastien onto his back, hesitating for a second when the big beast inclined his head insinuating he wanted her to climb on as well. Between the snapping maw that came far too close to her leg and the understanding that Bastien's wolf form would simply slide off with nothing holding him, she relented.

Scrambling onto the great bear's back, she clung to golden and silver fur alike.

"Go!"

And they did.

SYVE

SORIAH STOOD WRINGING HER hands in the doorway as they came through the trees. Instead of rushing to her son, she surprised Syve by turning instead and disappearing into the house, hollering for Delanira as she went.

Cyrus carried them all the way to the door before shifting—likely because he wouldn't fit through the door otherwise. Grizzly one moment, man the next and somehow managing to spin and catch Bastien before he could hit the hardwood. Syve was not afforded such luxury, and landed in a heap. Cy slipped into the house leaving her to scramble after him.

Fabric covered her face the second her feet hit the tiled floor. Del grimaced apologetically, arm still outstretched from her toss but said nothing before turning into the kitchen.

Syve followed the young girl, stopping in the doorway to slip the T-shirt on. As worried as she was for Bastien, she knew she would only be in the way right now, and there was no point in standing around cold and naked.

Papers, spices and other miscellaneous objects lay on the floor, evidence that the table was swept clean in a rush.

Cyrus, who had thankfully donned pants of his own, was leaning over the table and the eerily-still wolf that lay on top of it.

On the other end of the table Soriah was working quickly, shooting off orders to Del who was at her side with an arm full of various first aid equipment. Tirelessly, the women worked as Syve slid to the floor, leaning against the door frame, unblinking as she observed.

Sometime later, exactly how long she had no idea, Soriah sank into a chair, head tipped back as she heaved a deep breath. "*Osito*, can you get him to bed without jostling him too much?"

Cy nodded sharply, grunted in Del's direction, which must have translated to something about the bandages because the girl dove in, laying a hand gingerly over the gauze that wrapped around Bastien's body.

Syve stood, helping Soriah from her chair when the older woman flagged her over, and together they ascended the stairs.

"The bleeding has stopped. It was through and through, thank God. If it wasn't for the shifter healing, I doubt he would have made it home. Now all we can do is wait," Soriah said, voice barely above a whisper.

They were circled around the massive bed, Bastien still in wolf form laying in the middle looking every bit out of place.

"Why is he still...why didn't he change?" Syve questioned, her words were stiff, her mouth dry and her body drained from exertion.

"It's a conscious act, shifting. If you go to sleep, lose consciousness or..." Cyrus audibly swallowed. "You stay as you were. It wouldn't be a good idea for him to shift right now even if he were awake, we don't know if it would interrupt the healing—it could make it worse for all we know."

Syve thought back to Bastien's brother, a light bulb flickering to life in the back of her mind. Bastien had mentioned they had never been able to recover Dez' body, and she initially thought that meant the carrion had gotten to it before they could return but no. Now she understood it was more likely he was taken as a trophy. She wanted to vomit.

"What happened out there?" It was Del who finally asked.

"We went for a run. We were...sitting by the lake when he mentioned a smell—tobacco? He got angry. I've never seen him angry. He shifted, tore off into the woods...I barely managed to catch up before..." She trailed off, swallowing hard.

"By the time I got there they were already fighting. I think...I think he recognized the smell. I think it was the same man. The poacher..."

She did not finish the thought. She didn't have to.

Yelling, Cyrus turned, kicking the dresser hard enough for everything on top to rattle before stomping to the door.

"*Osito*, don't be reckless," Soriah warned.

"Stay with him, Mama," he answered without turning back. Then he was gone, the back door slamming a few seconds later.

"I'm sorry. He was gone, the man, when Cyrus and I got back. I should have checked; I was just so...I panicked, I couldn't carry him, I thought..." Syve stammered, stopping only when Soriah placed a warm palm to her cheek, shushing her.

"Sweet girl, you saved my son. Thank you." She patted Syve's cheek a few times then beckoned Del to follow her. "I'm going to get you some water, and something warm to drink."

Silence crashed into her as the door snicked shut and she sank onto the edge of the bed, careful not to jostle the wolf-man resting there. She reached out, fingers threading through the thick fur of Bastien's back leg. Beneath her hand she felt his muscles twitch, and with a soft whine he began to stir. Syve jumped up, moving closer to his head with only a fleeting worry for approaching the sharp teeth of a wounded animal. She slid a hand along his muzzle, over his head and down to the side of his neck where she burrowed her fingers through the hairs to his skin, shushing him as she went.

"I'm here, it's alright. I'm here," she cooed.

At the sound of her voice Bastien's eyelids fluttered a few times. Suddenly, soft vibrations rippled up through Syve's hand.

"No, no, no! Bastien, don't do that!" She panicked when she realized what was happening, but it was too late—he was barely conscious anyway.

"Shit, dammit, okay." She scrambled to the foot of the bed, snatched up the blanket that had been folded there and haphazardly threw it over the bottom half of Bas' now very naked human body.

"Syve." Her name fell from his lips so quietly she almost missed it.

"Here, I'm here."

His eyes were still closed; brows furrowed in pain.

Gently she reached out and smoothed the sweat slicked hair from his forehead. He visibly relaxed under her touch, so she left her cool hand on his warm skin while reaching with the opposite to check his bandages. Blood had seeped through the now loose and ill placed bandages, informing her that his shift had done exactly as Cyrus predicted—agitated the wound.

Copying Soriah's actions, as best she could, Syve re-placed the wrapping with fresh bandages, taking advantage of the hairless patient and taping everything down so she would not have to roll him. That would have to do for now, she would have Soriah double check it when she came back—leaving his side for even a breath was not an option.

"I swear, as soon as you're healed, I'm gonna beat your ass. You're in the doghouse for the rest of the century for scaring me like that."

She sat back on the edge of the bed, holding his hand as she gave him a watery scolding. Bastien remained unconscious, panting softly in his sleep.

"Please be okay," she whispered to the quiet room. "I love you."

By the time Soriah returned, Syve was asleep—curled on the bed, facing Bastien, his hand tucked between both of hers beneath her tear-stained cheek. Soriah set a glass of water on the nightstand, checked her son's bandages, then gently tugged his blanket over Syve as well.

SYVE

BASTIEN SLEPT FOR FOUR days.

It took Cyrus threatening to physically remove her from the room and bathe her himself for her to leave Bas' side. The steaming hot water had felt transcendent—though she was loath to admit that to Cyrus. When she stepped back into the room fifteen minutes later, it was one of those rare moments he was actually there.

After helping Bastien to bed and storming out of the house, he had been scarce, gone for *hours* at a time. He would show up, grim faced, demanding an update and then he would be gone again. Multiple times Soriah had to corner the man to force food in his face and twice she backed him into the bathroom for a shower. Ironic that he was the one to finally get Syve to bathe.

Someone, likely Del, had recovered Syve's clothes from the yard and washed them for her. It felt nice to be in her own clothes again, minus the underwear she had shredded while teasing Bas, and her phone had been in her shorts.

Sending Aimi into another panic on top of everything else would have been *fantastic*. Syve had barely spoken five words when she called her friend, but it was enough. Aimi showed up to the Yerovi house thirty minutes later with hot coffee, a box of mac'n'cheese from Thyme to Eat and a duffel bag full of Syve's clothes.

The clean clothes and feel-good food were a boon, the coffee being the cherry on top. The next morning, and every morning since, she had shown up with coffee for the whole house—Cyrus included, to Syve's surprise.

On the fifth day, Syve woke up to a hand stroking her hair. "Good morning, Bambi."

She blinked up at Bas, her nose a breath away from his chin. Eyes wide, she looked down to see she had clearly burrowed into him, again, while she slept—her fingers still threaded into his chest hair and one leg thrown over his hip.

An inhuman sound escaped her throat as she quickly removed her leg and rolled onto her back, fire engulfing her face and chest. Just as abruptly as she had rolled away, she was back again, this time fussing over the dressings across his torso.

"I didn't hurt you, did I? That's not what—I didn't wake you did I? Thank God, it's not bleeding again—what an idiot. I'm so sorry Bas—"

Fingers on her chin stole the rest of the words from her mouth.

"I'm fine, Bambi." He tilted her head up, forcing her to meet his eyes. "And I won't lie, waking up next to you would be worth reopening the wound." The corner of his mouth quirked up for a second and then immediately melted away, replaced with a worried frown. "Bambi, what's wrong?" He searched her eyes as he wiped tears from her cheeks with his thumb.

She hadn't noticed she was crying, though she did know *why*.

Her lip quivered as she glared at him. "If you *ever* do that to me again—" The threat died on her tongue, swallowed by the sob building in her throat. Bastien shushed her sweetly, tucking her head beneath his chin and stroking her back. "I am so sorry, Syve. I just..."

"I know," she whimpered, and she did know.

Without a doubt she knew that if there had been any opportunity for revenge against the loss of her family, she would take it—she could not fault him for that.

"How long was I out?" His throat vibrated against her forehead, the breath of his words tickling her scalp as it passed through her hair.

She opened her mouth to reply when a voice cut in.

"Four months. Really thought you were going to miss Christmas. Nice of you to wake up in time to open presents but not buy any."

Begrudgingly, she pulled away and turned to scowl at Cyrus. "Don't be a shithead, shithead."

As he howled with laughter, she turned back to Bas and added softly, "It's only been four days. Ignore him."

Bastien's furrowed brows melted leaving one raised a fraction as he mumbled conspiratorially, "I usually do." He winked and she snorted, giggling into her hand.

"Hey! That was rude." Even without looking Syve could tell Cyrus was pouting. "All that after I came up here to stand guard so you could finally go home."

Syve tensed at his words.

Bastien's brows dipped in confusion which Cyrus took as a sign to explain, much to her distaste.

"Oh yeah, I had to threaten her—metaphorically. Don't look at me like that! She wouldn't leave your side! I made her go take a shower, that's all! Mama is the one that got her to promise she would go home for a day once you woke up. I'll bet there's work to catch up on, or something. It would be good to get some fresh air if nothing else—it's been a week."

Now it was Syve's turn to pout, she knew she should not have agreed to that.

"Bambi, I really can't believe I'm about to say this, but he's right. I'm okay—You should go home, check on the shop—"

She opened her mouth to object, only to snap it shut when he cut her off with a quick, "Nope. Non-negotiable."

"I swear I won't leave this room until you get back, scouts honor."

Syve turned her head to see Cyrus holding one hand over his heart and the other in the air.

"Hell, I'll even crawl in bed and snuggle him too, if you want." He waggled his eyebrows and winked, ducking when she launched a pillow in his direction.

That was what led to her standing forlorn in the center of her shop, one chaste kiss and a half hour later. Dragging her feet, she trudged over to the counter, booting up her tablet so she could check her email. She was just about to press the play button on the answering machine when the door swung open as none other than Gunther came stomping in.

"Syve, Lord, there you are! I've only called about a hundred times!" He sighed dramatically while she glanced at the number on the phone receiver. Seventy-three. Silently she contemplated clearing the messages unheard—it would be worth missing one or two genuine calls to not be forced to listen to seventy voicemails from Gunther.

"Are you listening to me? Where have you been?"

"Well, good to see you too. I'm fine, thanks for asking," Syve deadpanned, crossing her arms. "What do you need, Gunny?"

Wrinkling his nose in disgust, he walked to the counter, clearly favoring his right leg. She hadn't noticed before that he was holding anything, until he slapped a pile of fabric in front of her.

"Gunny? I'd rather you called me 'Stud' or even 'Hot shot'," he mocked. "Unfortunately, Doll, I'm here on business. I'm embarrassed to admit it, but I slipped on a wet rock crossing a creek last weekend. Twisted my ankle and caught my sleeve on a branch just right—ripped a hole right through it. I need you to doctor it up for me."

"I can take a look at it, but I can't make any prom—" A loud ringing interrupted her. Gunther held up one finger, digging his phone from his pocket with the other.

"Go for Gun," he said with the phone to his ear, covering the speaker for a beat to whisper to her. "Thanks, Doll. Just drop it by my place when you're done, yeah?"

Leaving no time for her to answer, he smacked the counter once, shot her a finger-gun salute and was out the door.

Blinking a few times and shaking her head at the menace that was Gunther, she turned back to her tablet, choosing to ignore the answering machine all together for the time being.

Syve opened the email app, and her stomach instantly fell to her toes. The first email in her inbox read, "Montana State Women owned business grant: Final submission deadline is today by 5:00pm MST."

The email was two days old.

It had been years since she'd been to Gunther's home. Erhard had taken her once before Noah was born and then they'd never gone back. One step in and she remembered why.

The front door was wide open when she walked up.

"Hello? It's me, Syve—doors open so I'm coming in!" she hollered as she stepped inside.

Deep in self-pity for having missed her deadline, she had buried herself in her work and Gunther's camo had proven quick and simple to repair. As much as she wanted to refuse his 'request' to drop it by his house, it was on the way to Bastien's and it meant she would not have to dread the man showing up to her shop any time soon.

So, she texted him, asking when he would be off work, then spent the rest of the day finishing the final touches on the remaining piece from her submission—though she asked herself why she was bothering at least a dozen times.

"Be out in a minute, Doll." Gunther yelled from somewhere deep in the house.

A plethora of taxidermied heads greeted her as she turned from the entry hall into the living room, causing her stomach to sour. She spun in a slow circle, searching for anything to look at that hadn't once held a beating heart—and found a wall of photographs at the back of the room.

Carefully stepping around fur rugs, she made her way over, hoping to find family pictures or even pictures of fish. Instead, she found shot after shot of Gunther posing over his trophies.

Disgusted, she was about to turn away when one photo in particular caught her eye. In a simple black, five by seven frame, was Gunther kneeling with a rifle in one hand, the other pointing a cigar at the camera, or likely the person holding it, grinning like the cat that caught the canary. But that wasn't what had gained her attention, no, it was the body lying before him.

Awkwardly bent, with blood oozing from its slack jaw, was a majestic wolf with coal black fur. Its beautiful copper eyes almost appearing gray from the fog of death.

She stumbled back, hand over her mouth, until she bumped into a piece of furniture, her hand reflexively reaching back to catch herself. Thick fur slid between her fingers like a memory, soft and familiar. Hesitantly, she looked down at the pelt, carelessly tossed over the back of the sofa. Chills skittered across her skin and bile rose in her throat.

Syve whipped around, the room spinning more than it should, and stared in abject horror at the black wolf, preserved in its entirety save for its eyes—so clearly just yellow marbles. Her knees buckled beneath her but before she could meet the floor a strong arm slipped around her waist and spun her into a broad chest.

"Shit, Doll, you don't have to get all swoony for me," Gunther teased, his breath on her ear sending unpleasant shivers down her spine.

Careful to school her grimace, she pushed him away, leaving him to grab at his repaired coat as she stepped back and let go of it.

"This," she whispered, pointing to the pelt on the couch back, "is yours?"

"It's in my house, isn't it? Who the hell else would it belong to? Though my offer still stands—the other half of my bed is still yours when you're ready to take it." He stepped behind her, tapping a finger against the picture. "Shot this mutt myself three years ago—biggest damn wolf I've ever seen. Well, aside from the ghost that was with him, I'm still mad as hell I didn't see that one first."

Mind spinning and gut roiling, she stared at him. Unable to believe the words coming from his mouth.

Gunther, seeming to recall the jacket he held pressed to his chest, shook the article out, holding it up to inspect.

"Not bad, I guess. It'll do until I can find a replacement," he hummed, discarding the coat to the floor behind him. "You know, I can't get the wet dog smell off that damned thing. If you like it, I'll let you take it."

Syve glanced at the couch, then turned to find he had moved closer.

With a devilish grin, he snapped a hand out, catching her by the back of the neck. "On one condition." His mouth slammed down to hers.

She reeled back, fighting his hold, and slapped him across the face. "Don't *ever* do that again." She snarled between clenched teeth.

With a mocking laugh, Gunther growled, "We'll see, Doll."

She made a show of wiping her mouth with the back of her hand, then collected the pelt and bolted from the house.

Bastien

Consciousness returned to Bastien the same way sunlight returned with the dawn. Slowly he became aware of a dull ache in his side, triggering memories that steamrolled through his mind—a film he couldn't pause and leave unfinished.

A gentle weight bore down on him; one he could not place. Puzzled, he opened his eyes, blinking until her face came into focus.

Syve.

She was asleep, the weight he felt was nothing more than her leg stretching over him, her fingers twitching against his chest while she dozed. The door opened, only the sound of the wood dragging across the carpet giving the action away at all.

Tears welled in her eyes when his mother noticed he was watching her, awake at last. Bastien quickly placed a finger to his lips, glancing down toward the woman nestled against him. Soriah smiled softly and whispered something about food before ducking back out into the hall.

Bastien replaced his attention to Syve. The skin around her eyes was dark, her brows creased, even though she was snoring softly. She looked as though sleep took her, not by choice, but necessity.

Unable to refrain, he reached out to smooth the tangled mess of auburn hair haloed about her. Hazel eyes blinked open before he even reached her neck.

Just as he had sworn, Cyrus had not left Bas' side for even a second after Syve left. Not even after helping Bastien out of the bed and to the bathroom to relieve himself.

"Cy, goddammit, I can piss on my own!"

"I am nothing, if not a man of my word, Pup. By your side means by your side," Cyrus said to the door. He shrugged, throwing his hands in the air. "Keep bitching and I'll turn back around. At least I'm not offering to hold it for you."

Soriah had brought up enough food to feed five grown men, which turned out to be a good call. Being shot and then sleeping for four days did a number on his appetite—that and Cyrus kept stealing bites.

Mid chew, Bastien froze, his eyes tripling in size before he groaned. "Fuck! Hal probably thinks I died! Where's my phone? I need to call and grovel—"

Cyrus cut him off, "Whoa, whoa! Hal is fine, and no one thinks you're dead. Syve called him Monday morning. You do have some God-awful case of pneumonia though." He pointed at Bas with a spoon, *his* spoon.

"Gimme that, you hog!" Bas snatched the spoon back but was too slow to stop Cyrus from picking up the bowl instead, drinking the soup from it like a cup.

"Hope I'm not interrupting anything?" Both men turned to see Aimi standing in the doorway, looking every bit like an angel with the drink carrier in her hands.

"You're always welcome to join, Daisy," Cy crooned.

"If one of those is for me, I swear I'll love you forever," Bas practically begged, mouth watering.

"Butcher Boy, you'd better already love me forever. Syve and I are a package deal—not that kind of package you idiot," she scolded a giggling Cy, kicking him in the shin as she walked past to hand Bas one of the cups.

Surprisingly, she didn't bat an eye when Cy reached out and pulled a drink from the carrier for himself.

"Thank you, Aimi," Bas said reverently. "Syve left a little bit ago—not that I'm not glad you came by—"

"I know, she called me on her way home. I came to see you. Well, to yell at you, actually. Syve said you were finally awake, so I came to tell you how much of a dipshit I think you are. You think out of everyone on this planet *she* of all people needs to worry about someone almost dying because they're being stupid?" she admonished, wildly gesturing with her arms all the while. "But...I'm glad you're okay."

A melodious trill emanated from Aimi's bag, catching all three of their attentions. She quickly dug her phone from her tiny plastic, neon yellow backpack. After a double take at the screen, her shoulders slumped and her playful smile disappeared.

"What's wrong?" Both men asked simultaneously.

Aimi looked up from her phone, misery painted across her features. "It's Syve."

Bastien's heart thumped wildly in his chest.

"She missed the deadline for the grant submission. She needed to submit everything on Monday..."

Nausea overwhelmed him. Though Aimi's tone showed no sign of accusation, Bas could not help but feel heavy with guilt.

Aimi must have noticed the change in his demeanor, because she added, "If you blame yourself, it will only make her feel worse. So don't do that. Seriously. Don't."

Cyrus asked her something; the two of them argued while Bastien spiraled.

Don't blame yourself. That was easier said than done.

"Will you tell me?" he blurted. Aimi and Cy both turned to look at him, confused. "If there's something we can do—something I can do? I know she really needed that grant...maybe there's another one?"

Aimi held up a hand silencing him.

"Just let her process this—don't tell her I told you either! Let her tell you on her own." She raised her eyebrows, silently demanding secrecy from each of them before softening. "But, yes. If there is anything you can do—not you, put your wallet away!" She pointed a finger in Cyrus' face. "I will let *you* know if you can do anything," she said to Bastien.

Cyrus scoffed and rolled his eyes.

"Butcher boy," Aimi added softly. "I really am glad you're okay, not just for her sake. And if Cam says anything, I don't *really* think you smell like a wet dog."

Before he could respond, she was gone, Cyrus trailing after her.

Bastien turned his head to sniff his shoulder—he actually *did* smell like a wet dog. *Time for a shower and some clean sheets.*

At least three, maybe five, hours had passed since Aimi left and aside from the ten minutes he spent showering—he had spent every single second digging and *digging* for any kind of loophole that could be used to help Syve. He wished Dez was there. If anyone could find a solution, it would be him.

Dez. It was the twentieth of August. That meant he had gone and gotten himself shot on the anniversary of his brother's death.

Groaning in frustration he dropped his phone in his lap and buried his face in his hands.

"Well, I guess that answers my first question."

Bas peeked between his fingers to see Cam unloading a large plastic container onto the TV tray by his bed. "How are you? Just peachy, thanks for asking. You're very welcome, Bastien." She acted out their conversation and Bas could not keep from laughing when she dramatically lowered her voice to imitate him.

"I do *not* sound like that!" he complained, adding incredulously, "I don't!"

When she raised an eyebrow, he asked, "What is all this?"

Cam sighed, dropping into the corner chair Cyrus usually occupied.

"Well, I made the mistake of having Aimi on speaker phone when she called to tell me you were sick. Kayla overheard and she has been all over me to make her Uncle Bas soup." She huffed a laugh with a palm to her forehead. "I told her you wouldn't want any while you were sleeping, but she wasn't having it. The second Syve messaged the group chat saying you were awake and probably not contagious anymore, I dove right into the kitchen." She cracked open the lid to the bowl, giving a Vanna White wave as she did.

"I present my great-aunt Aggie's famous homemade chicken noodle soup!"

"Uncle Bas? Does that mean I have Kayla's approval to stick around?" He laughed. "But seriously, thank you. This looks amazing."

"Actually, we all approve of you, so you better plan on sticking around. Syve...she's been acting more like *Syve* since you two started hanging out. I'm not saying she needs to be fixed, but she's definitely a little broken. I'm just glad to see she's ready to glue the pieces together, instead of throwing them away."

Bas hung his head. Sure, she said that now, but would she still think the same when she learned that he had cost Syve her shop?

"Let's hear it."

"Hear it?" he asked, raising his head to look at her, confusion written all over his face.

"You look like someone kicked your dog."

Bastien winced at her chosen phrase.

"I'm guessing from all the praise you haven't heard about the grant yet," he sighed.

"I've heard. You don't seriously think we're going to blame you for it, do you?"

The sheepish look on his face must have said enough because Cam started to laugh.

"You're a dumbass."

"Hey! Because she was here with me, she missed the deadline—I've spent all day looking for other grants, or a way for her to get away with submitting late and nothing."

"Did you try calling? Telling them why she missed it? That it was your fault because she was nursing you back to health?" She crossed her arms giving him a look that said she already knew the answer.

"I'm a dumbass," he confirmed, slapping his hand over his phone and slumping against the headboard.

Cam nodded in agreement as she stood from the chair. "Well, sounds like you have some work to do. I'll be sure to tell Kayla that you're doing better. Try to stay off your deathbed from now on, yeah?" She shot him a two-finger salute then walked out of the room.

He had his phone up to his ear before her blonde head had even disappeared around the corner.

SYVE

THE DRIVE TO THE Yerovi house felt years longer than it should have. Her eyes lingered on the bed of the truck in the rear-view mirror more than the road ahead of her. By the time she pulled into the driveway, she was a trembling mess with tears streaking down her face.

On wobbly legs, she walked to the door—only for it to swing open before she could even raise her hand to knock.

Bastien's welcoming smile fell when he saw her face. Without hesitation he slung his arms around her, pulling her in tight to his good side.

"What happened?" he demanded, already on the offense, even though he couldn't have been out of bed for very long.

"I-I need Cyrus," she stammered, burrowing her face into his neck.

She wished she could spare him the pain he was about to endure.

Bastien barked Cyrus' name without question. When heavy footsteps pounded down the stairs, she backed away, leading Bas by the hand down the driveway.

Cyrus stepped up beside Bastien just as they reached the truck bed. Neither man moved—Syve wasn't even sure they breathed for a long, heavy minute.

Cyrus was the first to break the silence, reaching in to place a hand on the pelt that she'd hastily thrown in the truck while she made her escape. A choked sound came from the usually jovial man who then delicately lifted the pelt from the metal bed.

After sharing a quick look, Bastien jerked his head in a quick nod, answering some silent question. Syve watched as Cyrus carried what remained of his best friend along the side of the house and through the back gate.

"We should go get Mama," Syve whispered, tightening her hold on Bastien's hand and getting another small nod in response. She led the way into the house, aiming for the kitchen when Del came skipping down the stairs.

"Syve! Wait, what's wrong?"

"Del, can you get Mama and bring her out back please? I need to get your brother to sit down."

Del hesitated, clearly brimming with questions, but not asking them. She agreed with a whisper before dashing down the hall.

A makeshift pyre, born of left-over wooden pallets, was set in the center of the fire pit. Syve could not ignore how fortuitous it was that the pit even existed at all.

Soriah's wail was mixed with both grief and relief upon seeing her lost son—the sound cleaving its way through Syve's very soul.

Del had taken one step onto the porch before she stopped short, eyes widening when she noticed the wolf skin draped over the wooden slats. She promptly spun on her heel and vanished back into the house.

Sighing, Bastien looked away from the empty doorway where his sister had disappeared, attention landing hard on Syve when he finally spoke.

"I...how? Where was he?" he whispered. The unspoken 'who?' hung heavy in the air.

"I'm going to tell you, but I need you to swear to me you won't run off half-cocked and do something stupid—I'm serious!" she hissed her warning when she noticed a glint of malice in his eyes.

"You're still healing, first of all, and this man has already almost killed you *twice*! I know you want to be and I know it will be hard not to, but don't be selfish. Think about Mama and Del! Even Cyrus and..." She looked away from him, inhaling deeply before continuing.

"Think about me. *Please.*" She begged. "You have to swear you won't go on another murderous rampage. Let me help you. We'll figure out what to do about him together. He won't get away with this—just *please.*"

Resignation was painted all over his face when she turned back.

"This fucker *tore my soul apart*. I have wanted nothing more than to personally rip his throat from his neck—but you, Syve, you have stitched my tattered edges back together. I love you more than I hate him. For you, I swear I won't go after him myself."

Tears welled on her lashes as her hand slid into his. She would tell him again what she already admitted while he slept—once this was all over.

She quickly recapped her morning—the jacket mending and drop-off, how she'd stumbled across Dez. Mercifully, she kept the finer details to herself. He would not gain anything by knowing about the picture on the wall, how the fur was used as furniture decor—the kiss.

Her short story ended as she whispered, "It was Gunther."

BASTIEN

EXPLODING FROM HIS CHAIR, the force toppled it backward. Bastien growled, "I knew that fucker was a piece of shit!" He pulled at his hair, pacing short lines in front of her.

"Please! You promised you wouldn't do anything!" she begged.

"I'm *not* doing anything—I just can't believe it. I've had conversations with him—stood right in front of him! I've looked him in the eye and I didn't know?!" He stopped, tipping his head back with a frustrated yell. "How could I not know?"

A finger hooked in the waistband of his shorts, tugging him back until he sank into the chair Syve must have righted.

The sound of liquid dousing the pyre interrupted them. They both sat transfixed as Cyrus emptied a bottle of lighter fluid onto the fire, then threw it into the pit.

In one fluid motion, he pulled a lighter from his pocket, spun the wheel to spark a flame, then tossed it.

Within seconds, flames claimed the wood and fur, the smell of burning hair wafting on the wind—a smell Bas would never forget.

As his gaze followed the orange and yellow tongues licking the air, he found Cyrus staring back from the opposite side of the fire. A strange look creased his features as he stepped back, then another, then melted into the shadows.

How much had he heard?

Long after the coals had grown cold and Syve had helped his mother scoop the ashes into a decorative vase, Bas finally stood. He found Syve in the kitchen, wiping down the counters while Soriah sat at the table with her arm slung around the ceramic vessel.

Mama nodded off for a second before jolting awake to ask, not for the first time, if he had to wager, if Syve was sure she did not want any help.

"Mama, if you get up from that table again, I'll hide your apron and padlock your oven shut!"

Soriah tisked in return but made no move to get up. De-lanira's absence concerned him, she still had yet to make a reappearance since before the pyre was lit.

"I'm just about done here," Syve murmured over her shoulder when Bas slipped up behind her, wrapping his arms around her waist. "Tea for Mama and Del, then I'm getting you up to bed—have you seen Cyrus?"

"Don't worry about him...Can I teach you how to make Mama's cocoa?"

Her eyes lit up, darting to Soriah, who was fully asleep in her chair now.

"Is that allowed?" she whispered.

"Bambi, I'm not sure if you've noticed, Mama seems to like you more than she likes me. It'll be fine."

Syve listened intently as Bastien walked her through the process: break up the dark chocolate while heating the milk, sugar, salt and cornstarch in a small pan. He added the chocolate chunks to the gently boiling mixture, stirring until it all melted.

After pouring the cocoa into four mugs, he sprinkled a pinch of cayenne pepper over three of them, whispering to Syve that Del couldn't stand the spice.

Ten minutes later, Soriah was settled into her bed, her favorite book in one hand and cocoa in the other, the vase safely settled onto her dresser.

Del had already fallen asleep when they stopped by her room, so Syve set her cocoa on her nightstand, pulled the blankets up a little tighter around the girl's chin, and pressed a quick kiss to her hair. Bastien's heart swelled every time he saw Syve dote on his family like that.

Back in his room, he settled onto the bed, handing her mug over before curling around his own. She snuggled in beside him, both leaning on the headboard, silently sipping from their steaming mugs.

"Stay tonight," he said quietly. "Just to sleep. Stay with me."

"I already promised Mama I would." She chuffed at his surprised look. "I do have to get some work done in the morning...Hal isn't expecting you back until next week. Do—would you want to come to the shop? The sofa is all yours, if you want."

"Only if there's coffee involved," he teased with a wink.

"Deal," she whispered, placing a soft kiss to the corner of his mouth.

It was not long before Syve's empty cup rolled from her sleeping hand. Bas carefully placed both mugs on the side table, then slipped down into the pillows and coaxed her to follow. Thanks to his shifter healing, he was practically good as new—minus the lingering tenderness and slight muscle weakness—which was good because Syve had turned over and was clinging to him like a little barnacle.

As she softly snored against his chest, he remained awake, contemplating—unable to close his eyes no matter how hard he tried.

SYVE

AIMI'S BLACK AND BLONDE space buns bounced around behind the counter as she and Toni tackled the morning rush.

Legs tucked under herself, Syve waited from her spot on the little green sofa for her friend to return. She had just finished telling Aimi about everything that had transpired the night prior when dozens of patrons poured in for their daily AM brew.

Before walking down to The Glass, Syve and Bas had parked her old truck and his Jeep behind the loft. She had led him inside and given him the option to watch TV upstairs instead of freezing in the shop, then warned him it would likely be a half hour or more before she returned.

Bas said he already assumed 'a quick coffee run' between Syve and Aimi would take at least that long, if not more—especially with the news Syve would be sharing.

They agreed during that morning's pillow talk that Aimi would be allowed to know, mostly because Syve refused to keep a secret from her best friend, but also because her brother was a lawyer and that meant she had insider knowledge of ways they could legally take Gunther down. The last reason was because Cyrus was missing and of everyone in town, Aimi was the most likely to see him.

"Bitch, you need at least twelve extra shots, but I don't want you to have a heart attack," Aimi said, presenting Syve with one of her signature extra-large to-go mugs, steam spilling from the top. "So, I put in three."

She plopped onto the sofa, careful not to spill her own drink. Syve huffed, amused and wrapped her hands around her coveted coffee.

"So, any ideas?" Syve asked.

Aimi opened her mouth but Syve quickly added, "*legal* ideas."

Aimi snapped her jaw shut with a frown.

The women sat back-to-back on the couch for a few minutes, each scouring the internet on their phones for anything useful. Syve learned that even with evidence of poaching in Montana, the defendant would, at worst, only receive six months of jail time, possible seizure of their firearms and a lifetime revocation of their hunting rights. When she shared that news over her shoulder she had been met with a string of very creative expletives.

"I'm not going to lie to you right now. It's a real shame Butcher boy wasn't able to—you know. I wouldn't feel bad or miss the guy, personally. In fact, after hearing what he did to you, I *dare* him to walk in here so I can finish the job myself—the *audacity!* To put his nasty ass mouth on yours—makes me want to gargle bleach."

Her animated rant had her shaking the entire couch as she carried on, arms waving chaotically.

A ringing phone cut Aimi off and she shifted to put her chin on Syve's shoulder. The two looked at the phone, still ringing in Syve's hand.

"Who is it?"

"Dunno, I don't recognize the number. It's a 406...so, local? I should probably—Hello?"

She answered before Aimi could convince her not to. On the other end, a lady by the name of Eva spoke quickly, as if she had somewhere far more important to be. Syve froze at her words, convinced she was hearing them wrong.

"Tomorrow morning, 9:30 a.m., yes, I can be there. Thank you!" She ended the call and blinked.

The curiosity and anticipation rolling off of Aimi was palpable.

"Well?" Aimi prodded.

"It was the assistant in charge of scheduling applicants for the grant. Apparently, even though I wasn't able to submit my final proposal, they still want me to come in and present."

"Syve! That's incredible! Did they say why? Actually, who cares why, you have to go, right now! Get everything together, you have to be up early! Do you have something to wear? That's a silly question, you'll wear one of your pieces, naturally."

Aimi tugged Syve off the couch, leaving her own coffee on the table in favor of pushing her friend toward the door.

"Don't forget your lucky pigtails and if you don't call me the second you walk out of that meeting, I swear on my Chuck's, Syve—"

Toni leaned over the counter as they passed, handing over a new cup, an Americano for Bastien. Before she knew it, Syve was standing on the sidewalk, a cup in each hand and the door clicking shut behind her.

Once back at her shop, Syve dug out her keys to let herself in the front door, deciding against the longer walk around to the alley. After a few seconds of fumbling—trying to slip the key into the lock while juggling two coffees—a soft click sounded, and the door swung open to reveal Bastien shirtless and wearing a goddamn tool belt.

"Hey! So, the lock—it wasn't lined up right, so I replaced it. Your new key is on the counter, plus one for Aimi, cuz I know she has one. Then I replaced the spring, so the door will close slowly again—shouldn't slam on you anymore. Oh! I hope you don't mind, I heard how your truck was running on the way here, so I also took a look at it. I ordered a few parts and can have it running like new in about a week..." Bas pulled his shirt from his back pocket to wipe at his face.

Syve stared at him, "You didn't have to do all of that, Bastien, but thank you, really—and I'm sorry I was gone so long." The startled look on his face made her realize she was on the verge of tears. He smiled down at her, dropping his shirt to the floor to pull her in for a crushing hug. Chest hair tickled her nose as she nuzzled into his chest.

"Oh, here's your coffee—before I spill it all over. Where did you get the belt?" she asked, as he opened his arms, allowing her to step back, and accepted his drink.

"It was in the Jeep. I dug it out of the garage when I started the cars this morning." His eyes twinkled mischievously.

"You sneak! I have to say though," she paused to make a show of looking him up and down, "This look works for you." With a flirty smile, she brushed past him to the counter, yipping when he smacked her ass.

"You like a man who's good with his hands, huh?" He smirked, backing her up to the counter, and caging her in with his arms.

Those were not butterflies in her stomach, those were full ass pterodactyls. A shudder ran through her when he leaned down, running his nose along her hairline until he could whisper in her ear.

"I can be *really* handy." The nip at her ear made her gasp.

"Wait, wait!" She placed her hands on Bastien's warm body, but lacked the power to push him away. "Wait." She exhaled the words, not sure if she was telling him or herself at this point.

"What's wrong, Bambi?" he asked, pulling back immediately to look at her, worry creasing his brows.

"Nothing. Nothing is wrong. I have some news—but it means I really don't have time for," she gestured between them, "this right now."

He straightened even more, hands dropping from the counter to her hips.

"News?"

"Not about *that*, unfortunately. You probably don't even want to know the lack of progress I made on that. No, this is different."

He tried to hide it, but she could see him deflate a fraction.

"It's good news, though! I got a call...about the grant. They're going to make an exception and let me submit late. I have to get the paperwork in before five tonight and then

I'm driving to Bozeman first thing tomorrow to give my presentation. They said I should know if I got it or not before I leave."

It was so unexpected when he scooped her up to spin her that she squealed like a little girl, giggling until she remembered his injury.

"Put me down before you hurt yourself and I have to tell your mother!"

Bastien scoffed, "Did you just threaten to tell my mother on me?" He let her body slide down his until her feet touched the ground.

"I'll do it, too!"

He shook his head, smiling warmly at her while she chided him with eyebrows raised.

"Wait!" she said again, an edge of panic seeping into her voice. "This is insane—I got so swept up when they called, I didn't think—I'll cancel. I promised I'd help figure out what to do about my stupid cousin-in-law. I can't just run off for an entire day—two—two entire days. How selfish of me! I'm so sorry, Bas." Mortification nearly knocked her off her feet. Her stomach twisted, unsure if it wanted to crash into the earth's core or rocket through the ceiling and launch itself into the sun.

BASTIEN

THE SPEED IN WHICH the happiness melted from her face in favor of shame was sickening, and all he wanted to do was make it change back.

"Bambi, I'm fairly certain I've told you before not to apologize for being excited about something that means a lot to you." He sighed, crossing his arms and tilting his head to the side. "I need you to take this win, if not for yourself, then for me. You said yourself you haven't found a solution to the *other* problem—neither have I. That means there's nothing we can do right now anyway, so you really might as well work on getting this grant."

When she went to argue he silenced her with a searing kiss, doing his best to imprint the feel of her lips on his so he could feel her touch linger long after he walked away. When he forced himself to back away his entire body protested, pulsing with the need to crash back into her.

"Okay," she squeaked, swaying slightly on her feet with her eyes still closed.

"God, I love it when you look like this."

"This?" She blinked her eyes open, confused.

"Like you're intoxicated when all we did was kiss."

The blush that crept across her face and chest mixed with all the words and emotions they had shared over the last week, emboldening him.

"One day I'm going to see exactly what you look like when you've been fucked silly."

Syve's eyes widened a comical amount. She must have blinked a dozen times while he reached to pick up the coffee he'd set on the counter.

"Until then, this is how I'll picture you when I come in my hand later tonight."

Her jaw hit the floor and Bas chuckled, leaning in to place a kiss on her cheek. "Call me after, so you can tell me you got it." He left her there, dumbfounded, jogging up the stairs to get his keys and leaving through the loft.

The smell of grilled meat and onions met him at the door when he got home making him realize just how hungry he was. He chugged his coffee on the drive home, but aside from that he hadn't eaten all morning.

Kicking his shoes off, mostly out of the way of the door, he padded to the kitchen. Del was leaning against the counter, scrolling on her phone with one hand, the other holding a wooden spoon idly over a pan of rice.

"Where's Mama?"

"Porch," Del replied flatly, not bothering to look up from her phone.

"Okay," he drew the word out, expecting more to her answer.

When it became obvious she wasn't intending on speaking again he asked, "Are you mad at me? You've hardly said two words to me since—"

"What? Since you went and got yourself *shot*?" she snapped, lowering her phone and cutting him with a sharp glare.

"Bug—"

She cut him off again, "No. Don't 'Bug' me. Papa is *gone*. Dez is *gone*." She pointed the spoon at him, voice rising with each sentence. "And *you* intentionally put yourself in danger! Yes! I'm mad at you!" She slammed the spoon onto the counter then crossed her arms over her chest. "Honestly, it baffles me that I'm the only one. You almost *died*, Bas. You weren't thinking about anyone other than yourself and you went out and almost got yourself *killed*."

"I know, Del, I'm sorry. I wasn't thinking—"

"Obviously! If you were *thinking* you would have considered that if you were dead Mama would have to go back to work—"

"That's not true, she would get the money Dez left—"

"That is *so* not helping. So, she would have had money for a few years—eventually it would run out and she would have to go back to work. I would have to stay in Timberfall to help her, or she would have to move with me to whatever college I pick. Oh, yeah, and *you would be dead*!"

Shame began slithering across his body. She was right, he hadn't been thinking and honestly, he still hadn't thought of any of this, even after the fact.

Hanging his head, he remained quiet.

"Worst of all?" she whimpered quietly, and he snapped his head back up to see her lip quivering, tears streaming down her cheeks. "You would have broken your promise."

His promise.

The promise he made the night he came home and was forced to tell her what happened to their brother. He promised to never leave her alone on this earth—to fight anything that would ever try to take them away from one another. In a blink he crossed the kitchen and wrapped her in a hug.

"You're right, and I am so, so sorry." He rubbed circles on her back as she sobbed into his shoulder. "May my shoes never be tied the same tightness, and my water always be lukewarm." The vow pulled a laugh from her and she pulled back to look at him, wiping her face with her hands.

"You're so dumb."

"I am. I truly am sorry. You would think after the reprimand I got from Syve, I would have learned something and come to apologize to you sooner."

"She yelled at you?" Del smiled, clearly impressed.

"Well, she never raised her voice, but just like Mama, she didn't need to."

Del laughed again.

"I'm glad she's keeping you in line."

"Oh, yeah. She made me promise no more dumb shit, too. So, between the two of you, I'll be spending the rest of my life as a saint." He held his hands up like he was praying, blinking innocently.

Del's phone pinged, and she rolled her eyes at her brother as she raised it. "Yeah, whatever." But before she could unlock it, her phone buzzed three more times in rapid succession. "Oh my God, did somebody die? What is going—" She stopped short with a cringe, then her eyes widened and her gaze darted to his.

"What is it?"

"You were with Syve this morning, right? And you saw Aimi too?"

"Yes, Del, why? What's going on?"

"Did you see Cyrus this morning? He never came home last night, did he? He hasn't been around all day either." Del's voice was fast, tinged with panic.

"Delanira! What happened?" Bastien's voice rose as he grasped her shoulders, trying to steady her focus.

Instead of answering, she sucked her lips into her mouth and turned her phone around so he could see the screen. One of her friends had sent her a screenshot—a social media post by the local police department.

A body had been found in the woods.

Syve

THREE HOURS OF SLEEP—THAT was all Syve had managed after pushing to finish preparing everything for her presentation, then waking early to make sure she looked, well, presentable. Aimi had brought her coffee—one cup for now, one for later—she had said when she pushed one cup into Syve's hand and set the other in the truck's cup holder.

Her best friend had helped her load her suitcase full of freshly pressed clothes into the passenger seat, as well as two dress forms and a small hanging rack into the bed of the truck.

"You've got caffeine, clothes, and creepy ass mannequins. Drive safe, don't let them tell you no, and call me as soon as you walk out! I want you to tell me about all the tears they shed over your beautiful work," Aimi said, slapping Syve on the ass, then giving her a quick kiss on the cheek.

"Go now, so you're not late!" She pushed her friend into the driver seat and closed the truck door with a slam.

Eighty-five miles later, Syve was putting the truck in park outside of an old brick building in downtown Bozeman. Unlocking her phone, she sent a quick text to Aimi letting her know that her brain thanked her for the second coffee, but her bladder would be sending a hospital bill for repairs after rupturing around mile sixty. Then she sent Bastien a GIF of Sheldon breathing into a paper bag, letting him know she'd arrived.

It took fifteen minutes—and three trips—to haul all her things inside, plus a pit stop to the bathroom, before she found herself standing in the middle of a conference room. A table of serious-looking people in suits all fixed their eyes on her. The little gray poncho that Cam had broken the sound barrier over, hung on the rack alongside a child's shirt, the children's pants with reinforced knees, and a pair of men's pants. On the dress forms were a men's shirt, with mesh panels hidden along the back and under the arms for air flow, and a unisex jacket that had an obscene number of pockets and a removable top layer that could be worn separately as a raincoat. She'd laid out the flowy skirt—with hidden pockets and button details to pick up the length—across the table for close inspection.

On herself, Syve wore a loose-fitting shirt, fitted cargo pants with deep pockets and an adjustable waistband, and held a hanger bearing a tiny dress—complete with coverall straps and shorts hidden beneath the skirt.

"Alright, Mrs. Gehring, show us what you've got."

Aimi picked up on the first ring.

"It has been two hours! I was worried you got *lost*! Girl, you'd better start screaming!"

Syve's voice was barely above a whisper, breathless and full of disbelief. "I got it."

"Bitch! Yeah, you did!" Aimi hollered, followed by a muffled apology. "Shit, I got too excited and upset Mr. Halsen. Toni! I'm taking five. No, better make that fifteen...or thirty—can you just cover the counter till I get back? Cool, just holler if you need me. Okay, start talking. I want everything—don't even leave out if one of them breathed weirdly!"

Syve told her everything—how the panel was impressed by the numbers she'd run for cost, to the data she'd collected across various social media sites, including real poll results from actual people about whether they would buy the items she designed, and at what price.

One of the ladies, who seemed especially curious from the very beginning, made a comment about wearing the same size as the skirt on the table and asked to try it on. Syve laughed as she explained the skirt was no longer in her possession—but that she did have thirty dollars cash in her pocket after the woman had begged to buy it so she never had to take it off.

Two other pieces had not made it back to her truck either—the poncho and the little dress went home with one of the men, who excitedly mentioned they'd likely fit his daughter by her birthday next spring.

"He offered to personally help me set up a website for Sew It Seams, since I still don't have one. If this really goes the way I hope, I'm going to need a webpage for online sales."

"Imagine selling a man a dress for his kid and getting paid with a 'www dot,'" Aimi cackled. "I'm so proud of you! So, you get the dough? How does that work?"

"I do. I'll be getting the money, and it's more than I expected. I can use it for expenses, like the mortgage and utilities, and also fabric and stuff to start making more pieces. I now have the option now to hire someone to help—basically as an assistant. Maybe a student or something, just to handle the simple mending while I focus on the big pieces, or even just to cut things out, I'm also getting full support for the entire release of the line. They've given me contact info for a few people I can talk to about financial planning and other logistics, so I'm not running in blind and doing this all solo."

"I'm calling it now. I give it three years tops and your name will be on billboards along the coast."

Syve could hear Toni in the background grumbling something about a high school half-day.

"Go, go. Handle the teenagers, I still need to call Bastien anyway."

"Pray for me. I'm so proud of you! Love you!"

"Love you, good luck."

The call ended and she quickly tapped Bastien's contact, giggling again at Hattie's ducklings when they popped up on the screen.

"Bambi, when can I expect to see your clothes in magazines?"

"Awfully presumptuous, aren't we? You don't even know if I got it or not yet."

"Of course I do. They would have to be insane to tell you no. Are you home yet? We should celebrate."

"I just pulled into town, actually."

"Perfect, I'll head over—see you in a few."

Syve had just backed the old truck into a spot in front of the shop to unload when a silver Tahoe pulled in next to her.

"Sheriff, long time no see. Need help with anything?" she asked as the gray-haired man stepped out.

"I should be asking you, can I carry something? I was hoping to chat a minute, but I might as well get you all inside first."

Her stomach turned as they hauled her things in.

No one ever made you wait for good news.

"I appreciate the extra hand. Would you like anything to drink?" she asked warily once the truck bed was empty.

"I'm fine, thank you. Listen, I'm sure you heard about the body?"

Syve nodded, she recalled seeing it mentioned in the group chat with Aimi and Cameron during one of the few breaks she had taken the night before.

"Well, we haven't released this to the public yet, but we're fairly certain it was an animal attack. It took us a bit to be able to identify the victim—maybe you should sit down."

"Why are you telling me this? Who was it?"

Everyone she was close to she had talked to or heard from since the body was recovered. Well, almost everyone.

Shivers zipped across her limbs and she did exactly as the sheriff suggested—stepping back and sinking down onto the sofa. There was one person she hadn't heard from in two days now. A cold sweat swept over her and she shivered; regretting having changed into shorts before the drive home.

"We had to use dental records. I'm sorry, but we're positive it's Gunther."

Gunther. It was Gunther.

Gunther was dead.

She waited for the pain, guilt, anything—but the only emotion that came to her was *relief*.

"Syve?" She heard Bastien's voice, but the flood of conflicting emotions kept her from responding right away. The two men spoke for a moment by the door, then the sheriff called out to her as he walked out the door, letting her know he would be in touch.

"It's not Cy," she finally mumbled when Bastien took a seat next to her. "I think I'm supposed to be upset that Gunther is dead, because he was technically family, but I'm not. I'm *relieved*, and I feel bad because *I don't feel bad*. That makes me such an awful person, doesn't it? God, Bas, for a minute I thought he was going to tell me it was Cyrus, because we haven't seen him in days—I was more worried about Cy than anyone else. What if he was involved? What if they just haven't found him yet? What if Cy is out there hurt—"

"Cyrus is okay, Bambi. Mama called me when I was on my way over. He showed up just after I left the house; I had to have just missed him."

Syve let out a tense breath.

"Bambi. I think you and I both know what side of an animal attack Cyrus is more likely to be on."

The way he said it made her pause, she turned to him, wide eyed.

"Did he know? Did you tell him?" she whispered.

"I think he overheard us, by the fire. I also think it's probably best if we don't talk about it again either—unless you have a problem with that?"

"No, you're right. We shouldn't talk about it after this. Probably ever." She took a deep breath. "Are you okay though? Do you feel...I don't know...how do you feel about this?"

"It's the ending I was aiming for originally, so I can't say I'm mad about it. I feel better knowing the son of a bitch isn't a threat anymore, but...I just wish there had been a conversation about it first, you know? It would have been nice if we had been included in the decision, or at least informed of it. I shouldn't be surprised that Cyrus *took care of it*. That's kind of his thing, he's a fixer." He slid from the couch, landing to kneel between her legs. "I don't want to talk about that anymore right now. I came here to celebrate you and that's exactly what I'm going to do."

BASTIEN

EYEBROWS RAISED, SYVE STARED down at him.

"Celebrate?"

"You got the grant, Bambi. That deserves a little bit of a celebration. Or a reward—call it what you will."

His hands found her ankles and he felt her skin prickle at his touch. With a fox-like grin, he slid his fingers slowly up the outsides of her legs, past her thighs until he had a firm grasp on her ass.

She hummed, pupils blown wide. "I like rewards. I'm *very* responsive to positive reinforcement."

"I'm so proud of you, Bambi," he spoke the words into her skin, kissing his way up her thigh from her knee, only to stop at the hem of her shorts and start again on her other leg. "You worked so hard for this, you deserve every single piece of it." He enunciated the last few words with little nips, catching the skin of her inner thigh between his teeth, just enough to make her squirm.

"Bastien."

The way she moaned his name as her fingers thread through his hair was intoxicating. With a grumble emanating from deep in his chest, he slid his hands higher until he could slip his fingers around her waist band and pull.

Syve's thighs flexed against his arms as she raised her hips just a fraction, allowing him to slip her bottoms off. When she dropped back onto the couch she raised one leg, dropping her sandal to the floor as Bastien slipped her shorts over one foot. He didn't even bother with the other, instead leaving the denim pooled around her ankle.

"I have dreamt of tasting you, Bambi," he crooned, shamelessly staring at her exposed body.

Soft pants fell from her lips as his hands rested upon her knees. A sharp gasp followed, when those same hands dropped under her knees so he could flip her legs up over his shoulders, pulling her hips to the edge of the couch. He didn't leave her anytime to react before he descended, devouring her slowly, methodically, savoring every second. Relentlessly, he pressed on until she broke apart, molten under his touch and gasping his name.

"Bastien!"

"How's that for a reward, my love?" he asked, a single brow raising when her glazed eyes finally met his. The argument could stand, however, that he was the one who had actually been given the prize.

"That's it?" she breathed. "What if I feel like I deserve a *bigger* reward?" Coyly, her gaze shot to his painfully bulging pants.

"Syve, whatever I have is yours. Anything you could ever long for, I will deliver without question. You never even need to ask—if you want it, *take it*. Demand it from me, and I will give it freely." Her mouth was on his, feral and needy while she coaxed him off the floor, slowly backing him across the room.

"Door—" she began when they separated a split second to tear his shirt over his head.

"Already locked," he spoke the words into her mouth, refusing to allow any more space between them.

She kept pushing him back until his thighs bumped into something solid. The island. Bastien's brows shot into his hairline just as Syve two-hand shoved him, pushing him to his back on the countertop and leaving his lower legs dangling.

"You look good as the predator," he growled low as she dragged her nails down through the hair on his chest to his jeans, quickly flicking open the button and dropping the zipper.

"You know what would look good on *you*?" she asked, peeling his pants and boxers both down to his knees, a groan slipping through his teeth at the immediate relief.

He raised his arm, slipping it under his head to prop himself up so he could look down his body and see her. The animalistic hunger in her eyes almost made him blow his load right then and there.

"If the answer to that question isn't you, I'm going to be a little disappointed," he teased.

She grinned deviously, raising a brow at him.

"I guess we're about to find out."

She crawled onto him, straddling his hips, her warm center hovering above him. He watched her reverently as she unbuttoned her shirt, letting it fall down her shoulders, leaving her in nothing save a simple gray bra.

"God, Bambi. You're a fucking work of art," he praised, sliding his free hand up her thigh to grasp her hip.

With a breathy laugh, she popped the clasp of the bra and flung it to the side.

"Bastien."

With no small amount of effort, he dragged his gaze from her perfect tits to her face.

"I love you."

A shudder wracked his body and he wasn't sure if it was from her words, or the firm grasp she now had on his cock.

Words threatened to fail him as she aligned herself with him.

"Bambi, wait."

"IUD. It's been two years, and I'm clean. Please don't make me wait any longer. I want you. I *need* you."

Rapidly nodding, he croaked out, "Okay."

And down she sank.

Her head fell back as her hips slammed flush with his, lolling to the side so she could meet his hooded stare.

Self-restraint left him and he bucked his hips, smirking when she moaned in return.

She leaned down, nipping at his lip before scolding him. "Uh-uh, I'm in charge right now, not you. So be a good boy, and let me use you."

"Fuck, Syve. Keep talking like *that* and feeling like *this* and I won't last much longer," he warned, very quickly realizing that was the wrong thing to say.

The devious glint in her eyes screamed *challenge accepted* and he knew he was screwed. *Literally.*

"You can make it up to me later." She sat back up. "Again, and again and *again*." Each word emphasized with a strong roll of her hips. Syve continued to rock against him, granting him mercy when she took him by the wrist, guiding his hand to her breast.

He took the invitation greedily, removing his arm from under his head so as not to leave a nipple neglected.

"Syve," he begged as she sped up, fingers sliding through his chest hair, nails digging into his muscular chest. "Syve!"

"Come with me, Bas," she demanded.

He required no further instruction, as he felt her shutter and clench around him, tipping him instantly over the edge. He came so hard his ears rang and his jaw ached from praying her name through clenched teeth.

She slumped forward, rolling to his uninjured side.

With a kiss on her forehead, he wrapped his arm around her and pulled her close, her nails drawing lazy circles on his skin.

"I love you, Bambi."

With a satisfied hum, she nuzzled into him. He reached up, fingers sliding over hers until he reached her tattooed ring.

"Does it bother you?" she whispered.

"No," he replied without hesitation. "Neither do the pictures. I would never ask you to put them away, or to get rid of this," he tapped her finger, "you love him, and I would never ask you to stop."

"I love *you,*" her voice warbled.

"And I know that you can love us both. I'm grateful for all the time you had together, all the years he kept you happy and safe. I am forever sorry that he was taken from you, but I'm not sorry that it means, I'm yours now."

"Mine?"

"Yours," he confirmed with a kiss to the tip of her nose before rolling up and off the island, staggering a step because of the pants still around his knees.

Syve giggled and Bas glared playfully at her as he kicked free of his jeans, then he grabbed her by the ankles, dragging her to the edge of the table. He tossed her over his shoulder, nibbling her ass cheek as he dashed up the stairs, her squeals echoing off the walls the entire way.

"You have your phone? And you have our numbers written down in case you lose your phone? Who did you list as an emergency contact—you did list an emergency contact, right?"

"Mama, I have everything. I've had your numbers memorized for years, and I listed four emergency contacts. You, Bastien, Cyrus and Syve." Del turned to where Bas stood with Syve, a giant smile plastered on her face.

Eyes shining, Syve smiled back at his little sister.

Cyrus slammed the hood shut on the white Range Rover and wiped his hands on a rag as he walked over to where Del was hugging their mother.

"Alright, Princess." He pulled a key ring from his pocket, holding it up in front of her. "She's all yours. Congrats on getting into college. Go show all those snotty rich kids you're smarter than all of them."

Eyes bugging out of her skull, Del squeaked, "What? But that's your car!"

"Not as of five minutes from now. You just have to sign the title and Syve can notarize it. I've sold it to you for one whole dollar."

It was Bastien's turn to balk, he glanced between Cyrus and Syve to see the latter pulling a pen and a stamp out of her back pocket.

"Sneaky," he whispered, and she winked in return.

"But my stuff—"

"I brought down to load up for you. In your car," Cy finished.

Completely sobbing by this point, Del jumped up to hug him, blubbering her thanks into his neck. When she finally released the poor man, she moved down the line to say good-bye to everyone else.

Syve hugged her tightly, both women whispering to each other through their tears.

Bastian was next.

"Brother."

"Bug." He pulled her in, squeezing her as much as he could without hurting her. "I am so proud of you, Delanira. I love you."

"I love you too, Bastien. Take care of Mama for me, and be good to Syve. I'll be home for Christmas."

Then she was in the car, driving down the road while they stood waving in the driveway, Syve squeezing his hand.

Be good to her?

That would be easy.

SYVE

SEVEN MONTHS LATER

"I SWEAR TO JESUS and Carlisle, if you don't put that lighter down—" Aimi's threats from the backyard carried to the front of the house, where Bastien was currently helping Syve unload the last of the boxes from her truck.

"I'm surprised she hasn't given up on him yet," Bastien scoffed.

"To be fair, he hasn't really given her the option." Syve laughed.

It was true, Cyrus continued to spend every ounce of his free time at The Glass. On top of that, Cyrus decided to stay in Timberfall on a more permanent basis and moved into his own place. That place just happened to share a wall with Aimi.

Bas laughed, agreeing with her as he hefted a box into his arms and they strode into the house.

Since getting the grant, Syve managed to launch her clothing line—even expanding on it with all the other ideas sketched out in her notebook. She hired Elijah in November. He was interested in getting into the fashion industry and had begged her to teach him everything she knew. He was the best assistant she could ask for. Currently she was looking for a larger office space, to expand Sew It Seams, so she had put her shop and the loft up for sale.

When she mentioned apartment hunting, Bastien made the suggestion that she just live with him, since they had been spending almost every night together anyway. He immediately back pedaled, asking her if she thought it would be weird to live with his mother. Syve silenced his stuttering with a kiss, telling him she would move in and that living in the same house as his mother meant she could eat Mama's cooking every day.

When they told Soriah, she cried for twenty minutes, made cocoa, then dug out a handful of vegetarian cookbooks saying she promised to get really good at cooking with meat alternatives.

Bastien finalized the sale with Hal and was now the sole owner of the butcher shop. On the day Hal handed over the keys, a delivery truck arrived, unloading a crate with a brand-new motor for the cooler rail system. Bas laughed until he cried.

So, there she was, standing in the middle of her new living room, holding her mother's chest of journals and looking at pictures of Desiderio, Erhard and Noah all hanging side by side on the wall. Soriah and Del—home for spring break—were making vegetarian paella while Aimi supervised Cyrus and his fire in the backyard.

"Coming?" Bastien called from halfway up the stairs and Syve smiled.

"Yeah, I'm coming."

Time does not heal all wounds, but it does make them easier to bear—and she did not have to bear them alone.

A MESSAGE FROM SYVE

Syve's story is fictional, but Carbon Monoxide (truly called the silent or invisible killer) is real. It's recommended to have at least one CO detector for each floor of your home (basements count) and one within ten feet of each sleeping space. Be sure to test the batteries every month!

Here are some resources for you to learn more about carbon monoxide and safety precautions you can take.

National Fire Protection Association (NFPA): https://www.nfpa.org/education-and-research/home-fire-safety/carbon-monoxide

Carbon Monoxide Laws (provided by Kiddie): https://www.kidde.com/safety-hub/smoke-and-co-detection/carbon-monoxide-laws

Recipe: Mama's Cocoa

OCCASION:
every occasion

PREP TIME:
5 minutes

COOK TIME:
5 minutes

ingredients:

- [ ] 4 ounces dark chocolate
- [ ] 2 ¼ cups whole milk
- [ ] 2 teaspoons sugar (to taste)
- [ ] 1 pinch of salt
- [ ] 1/2 teaspoon cornstarch
- [ ] cayenne pepper to garnish

directions:

1 – break up the chocolate

2 – add milk, sugar, salt and cornstarch to a sauce pan and whisk like you mean it

3 – place over medium/medium high-heat, stir until the milk starts to simmer

4 – remove from heat, quickly whisk in chocolate until completely melted

5 – serve immediately with cayenne on top

ACKNOWLEDGEMENTS

This story has been stuck in my head for twelve years. Thank you, B (aka, milesonpaper_) for convincing me (see: coercing me) to actually believe in myself and to just sit down and write the damn thing. You have always been my biggest Stan, no questions asked. If it wasn't for you and MOP (my found family) I can honestly say I never would have finished this book and Syve and Bas deserved to have their story out of my head and into everyone else's.

Kier, I can't even begin to list the ways you have helped me on this adventure—we would literally be here for another thirty pages. Thank you for being next to me every single step of the way. *Now the day bleeds into nightfall and you're* ALWAYS *here to get me through it all.*

Huge, HUGE, thank you to Mak and Jaz for following me along that first full draft. Your unhinged comments really pushed me to keep writing! Any time I have ever needed a second set of eyes or hands, you both have been right there, zero hesitation, and I am eternally grateful.

Mirai, thank you for being the owl to my donkey!

These beautiful chapter headers and page breaks are all thanks to Morgan—You took "Uh...I don't know, I guess something cool?" and turned it into perfection.

THANK YOU to my incredible beta squad: Kier, Steven, Lys, Ribbet, Cassie, Sanikki, Lala, Laura, Allyson, Lina S, and Espi. The love, hate (looking at the Gunther Anti-Fan Club), and brilliant feedback you all had is more than I could have dreamt of.

I have a love/hate relationship with punctuation. I either use too much, or none at all—so massive shout out to Sarah Emmer for teaching me (or trying to) how it all works *correctly*. I promise, I probably won't have as many spaces to delete in the next book...maybe...

Five head-pats, a plate full of frickles and a forehead kiss to every member of The Forget Me Naughties, and the Indie Babe Circle Jerk. I can't imagine a better group of heathens to surround myself with and I love you all!

To my ARC team and you, my readers: telling a story is so much more fun when there is someone to listen. Thank you for taking a chance on me and Forget Me Not.

Last but not least, thank you to my husband for listening to me yap for hours about fictional chest hair and never shaving yours. It was so easy to write this walking-green-flag of a man with you out here as inspiration. To the moon and back~

THANK YOU FOR READING!

To stay up to date with all the things happening in Timberfall, check out Alexandria's website and follow her on Instagram!

*Scan Me for
Alex's Website!*

Plan your return visit to Timberfall, The Glass is Half Empty and the effects could prove grizzly...